NICOLE A. SCHROEDER

TWISTED FATE

PLAYBACK'S STORY

LOST LIBRARY
P R E S S

To Mom and Dad, who taught me how to make a difference.

CHAPTER ONE

I F I DIDN'T DO something soon, we were going to die.

Come on. Stay calm.

I took a shaky breath, trying to steady myself. I couldn't panic now. I had to think. But I couldn't seem to make sense of anything. My brain felt fuzzy. Unfocused. My thoughts muddled together.

I squinted in the dim light, taking stock of my surroundings. The world listed at an odd angle, and my legs ached from trying to free them. My ankle throbbed. And the rest of me . . . I could still feel that icy, searing pain, as if I were on fire, as if my bloodstream had become an electric current, ripping me apart from the inside. The remnants of it danced like static across my fingertips.

I shuddered and closed my eyes.

No, I decided. *We are not going to die.*

I was going to get us out of here.

Hours earlier, I hurried my footsteps as if the early October chill were chasing me across the street. I blew on my fingertips as I went to keep them warm. I really needed to find a decent pair of gloves. The trees that arched above me over the path shivered in commiseration, their crunchy leaves rattling on the branches or skittering across the cement. Fall break at Everett University only lasted a few days, but it had been aptly named. The trees had been bright green when I'd left last Tuesday; now they almost glowed with golds and ambers as the morning sunlight peeked out from behind the buildings on campus.

Thankfully, it was a short walk. I rounded one last corner, and the red brick building I was heading for loomed behind a small courtyard of tables and benches. The smell of breakfast sandwiches and warmly spiced espresso drinks wafted toward me, and their scent scared the last bit of cold from my bones as I descended the couple of steps at the entrance. I ordered and grabbed our usual table by the elevators, then let my eyes wander as I waited for our food. And for Andrew. He'd texted me early this morning to ask if I'd be up for grabbing breakfast with him before my first class. The message was more of a formality—at this point in the semester, our Monday morning coffee dates at the library's added-on café were pretty much a tradition, one that I was more than happy to keep.

The elevator's *ding* and the sound of the doors opening brought my attention back to the present, and I smiled as Andrew rounded the corner. I waved him over, moving my backpack to the other side of my chair so he could park his wheelchair closer.

"You look like you're enjoying the weather outside today," I joked as he got settled. His cheeks and nose were rosy, and the corners of his thin, wire-frame glasses were still foggy from the temperature change.

"Oh, of course," he said, waving a hand dismissively. "I love hiking all the way over to the physics building in the mornings."

"Frost on the ground, still dark outside . . ."

He nodded. "Helps you wake up, you know? Who needs caffeine for an 8 a.m.?"

I rolled my eyes. "You, evidently, if you're making jokes like this."

He just smiled, his lips pressed tight around whatever secret he was keeping.

I smiled back in confusion. "What is it?"

"Maybe I just love getting to hang out with you after I get out of class."

I made a fake noise of disgust in the back of my throat. "Sorry, I didn't order all this cheese with my breakfast. Next."

"Fair enough." He laughed. "Then maybe I finally spoke to my professor and convinced him to let me work in the lab in the afternoons."

"Wait, are you serious? As a freshman? That's amazing!" I opened my mouth to say more, but the barista at the checkout counter interrupted before I could.

"Cassidy?"

She called my name as a question, and I held up one finger to Andrew in a silent "hold that thought" gesture. He was still beaming by the time I got back to the table with our food.

"Okay," I said. "Now you can spill—just not that, preferably." I gestured to his coffee cup as I passed it to him.

"Well, it's just paperwork and errands and stuff for right now, so don't get too excited. I'm not going to be part of any big projects or anything like that yet." He sounded like he was cautioning himself as much as me. "But I'm getting a foot in the door at least."

"Exactly. So I'm still going to get excited. We definitely need to celebrate."

"What's tonight look like?" he asked with a smirk.

I gave a small frown. "I can't tonight. We're going out for my dad's birthday dinner since I've got midterms next week."

He hit his palm against his forehead. "That's right; I knew that. Well, later this week then."

"Absolutely."

We sat for a little while longer, chatting in between bites of the sandwiches I'd bought us. After a few minutes, I glanced at my watch, then leaned over and gave him a peck on the cheek. "I've got to head out so I can print my paper before class. Text me later though, okay?"

"Sure thing. And tell your dad 'happy birthday' for me." He blew me a kiss as I headed for the door, the gesture as sarcastic as his earlier gushiness had been, and I rolled my eyes and laughed.

Andrew and I had been together for about two years. We'd met when he'd joined our high school study group, where he'd started simultaneously flirting with me and scoring leagues ahead of all of us in every science and math exam. It hadn't been a complete surprise that we'd both decided to go to Everett University. After all, the campus was only a thirty-minute drive from where we'd grown up, and it was the place where my dad had worked and taught for close to twenty years. Between scholarships and my discounted tuition, it was easily the most affordable place we could've gone—well, "affordable" in the way most colleges were these days. But it especially made sense for Andrew: a renowned physics program, a wheelchair basketball team, a big campus with plenty of ways to get involved. To make friends.

That had never been me. Not that I didn't get along with others; I had plenty of people who waved hi to me in the halls, offered to work with me on group projects, made polite small talk when they passed me in the grocery store. People had always been friendly with me, but I'd never been the kind of girl to have many true friends. I didn't necessarily mind it. I could keep my nose in my books as much as I liked, and no one's expectations of me were ever any higher than the expectations I had for myself. For now, Andrew's popularity and charisma were enough for the both of us, and I was perfectly happy sharing the limelight.

The line to use the library's printer wasn't as long as I'd expected it to be, so I made it to my lecture hall with time to spare. I turned in my paper in the basket by the door and found an open seat toward the back of the room, then pulled out my laptop. I was an anthropology major—or at least, I would be once I finished all my prerequisite classes—but of course I'd lucked out schedule-wise and had my most difficult class first thing in the mornings. Professor Wasserman's was the kind of history class everyone had taught us in high school to fear: plenty of hard-and-fast deadlines, an unforgiving grading scale, and a strict attendance policy. "I want you all to be as knowledgeable about the culture of the world today as the one yesterday," she'd told us all during our first lecture, her heeled shoes clicking back and forth behind her lectern. It meant that even though it was a history class, our attendance question always had to do with some big news event from that week. Usually not one I recognized.

Today, though, I was pleasantly surprised. I actually knew this one. As the class web page finished loading on my screen, I pulled out my phone and took a quick glance at my newsfeed, just to be sure. "Which public figure from Everett was recognized as a 'dedicated changemaker' in this weekend's edition of the *Santina Enquirer*?"

My cursor blinked only once before I typed in my response: "Phase."

That was the one corner of the news I actually *did* pay attention to, and not just because Wasserman's class required it. People had accepted the existence of superheroes for a while now, at least in theory, but they almost all lived in big cities, or they kept such a low profile that their identities—even while wearing the mask—were hard to separate from myth and rumor. But Phase was different. She still kept her real name a secret, always hid her face behind the same sleek black motorcycle helmet that matched the leather jacket she'd detailed with fire-engine red piping that faded to a baby blue along the sleeves. But unlike the others, she lived here in Everett, a Midwestern town with a population that could only be considered impressive when the university students were in town. She'd shown up out of nowhere a year and a half ago, and she was still here, cropping up in the news every so often or in blurry photos on social media. And her ability to manipulate phases of matter? It could keep Andrew and my dad talking for hours, sure, but it was flashy enough that even I would've been a bit awestruck to see it in action.

As I'd expected, the answer I'd submitted turned into a green checkmark on my screen. I smiled, then swiped over to a blank notes page just as the last of the students trickled into the auditorium and Professor Wasserman cleared her throat to begin class.

The rest of the day passed rather uneventfully, and much faster than I'd expected, I was back in my dorm room, with nothing much to do but work on homework before dinner that night. I'd opted to take a nap instead and startled awake only when my phone's alarm had buzzed for me to get ready. Now, I stood in the doorway to my dorm and hugged my jacket around myself to keep out the cold, checking the clock on my phone every few minutes. Dad had told me he'd be picking me up by 7:30, so he still had fifteen minutes before I felt obligated to call and see if he'd gotten lost somewhere in the university parking lot. As silly as it sounded, I was excited to see him again. Even though Andrew and I had gone home over fall break, I hadn't felt like I had near enough time to spend with either of my parents. Hopefully having dinner tonight with just the three of us would make up for it. At the very least, any excuse to give myself a chance to eat somewhere other than a dining hall was a good one in my book.

After drumming my fingers for a few more minutes, I checked my phone again. 7:23. I grumbled a little at my own impatience and clicked into my phone. Just as I started scrolling for my dad's name, though, the shine of headlights pulled my attention. I grinned and headed outside.

The passenger side window rolled down as I approached. "What, no phone call?" Dad asked as I got in. "Could it be that you finally mellowed out?"

"Ha!" I climbed in and buckled my seat belt. "Says the man who acts like he hasn't driven us into the wrong state during a family road trip. Twice. Nah, you just lucked out this time."

He clucked his tongue. "My own daughter doesn't trust my navigation skills."

I snickered and shook my head, then glanced into the back seat. Before I could say anything, he answered my silent question. "Your mom had to work late at the office, so she said she's going to meet us at the restaurant," he said. "It's just the two of us for the drive."

"Hey, I'm okay with that," I said. I turned toward the window to watch the familiar campus scenery melt away, then felt my phone buzz. I glanced at it and let out a snort.

"Andrew?" Dad guessed.

"Yeah. He says he still can't believe I chose hanging out with you over him tonight." He'd added a winky emoji, so I knew he was kidding. Still, I shot back a quick text of my own:

Consider it a rain check. ;)

I turned back to Dad. "He actually got some exciting news today. They're going to let him start working in the physics lab this year."

"That's wonderful!" His eyes crinkled in the corners when he spoke, the way they always did when he was especially excited about something. "You'll have to let me know who he's working with. I think Jeff Scanlon is there part time again, and I'm sure there are a couple other guys I used to work with who are still around."

I smiled. Dad had been retired for probably close to two years now, but he still got giddy when he talked about the work he used to do at Everett. I, on the other hand, wasn't even sure I understood what he'd studied, much less had the ability to talk about it. The most I'd ever managed to explain to anyone was that it had something to do with how subatomic particles moved through time.

"He says he's going to just be doing menial stuff to start, but hopefully they'll let him move on to bigger stuff before long."

"And what about you? How are classes?"

"You mean for the couple of days I've been back since fall break?" I joked. "They're okay. Still nothing too interesting—but you would've loved the attendance question in our history class this morning." I recited it to him, and he gave half a smirk.

"Was the answer Phase?"

"Of course."

He smiled for a moment, but then his face fell into a concerned frown. "Sweetheart, you are careful when you go downtown at night, right? You travel with someone else? You keep your phone on you?"

"Dad, you know I do." I frowned. "What is this about?"

"I know, I know, but it's my job." He drummed his fingers for a moment on the steering wheel. "I read something in the news the other day about a superhero in Lakewood, and it just got me thinking." He sighed, slowing the car to a stop at the red light in front of us. He turned to face me. "Phase being here to protect this city is great, but it also means it needs protecting. Whether one of them invites the other or vice versa, a town with heroes is also going to have . . ." He trailed off, leaning in his seat to squint at something over my shoulder. "Cassidy, do you see that?"

I shifted in my seat, turning my attention in the direction he pointed. All I could make out was a dark field. "What are you looking—"

Before I could finish my question, a blinding white flash filled my vision. It was as if a bolt of lightning had struck the ground right in front of us, rattling my teeth in my jaw and filling my vision with light. I couldn't see anything, but I could feel my limbs flinging about like a rag doll's as the car spun out of control. A searing pain started on the top of my head, spreading in icy hot tendrils down my spine and into my fingertips and toes. It was as if I were being ripped apart. I jolted with our impact against something solid, and the sound of crunching and grinding metal screamed in my ears.

I came back into myself after just a fraction of a moment, enough to notice the world had stopped spinning. My vision was hazy and filled with spots of color, as if I were pressing on my eyelids with the heels of my palms. Still, I could make out my dad, draped across the steering wheel. He was bleeding from a cut on his head. I tried to reach out for him, but my body was pinned somehow. A fiery pain twinged up through my ankle, and I hissed out a curse.

"Dad?" I whimpered, turning to him. He didn't move. I tried again. "Dad, please! Wake up!"

I turned back around and managed to unbuckle my seat belt, but the dashboard had come toward me in the impact, pressing against the tops of my thighs. I tried to wriggle my left leg—the one that wasn't throbbing—free, but it wouldn't budge.

My lungs ached. My heart stammered in my chest. If I didn't do something soon, we were going to die.

Come on. Stay calm.

I took a shaky breath, trying to steady myself. I couldn't panic now. I had to think. But I couldn't seem to make sense of anything. My brain felt fuzzy. Unfocused. My thoughts muddled together.

I squinted in the dim light, taking stock of my surroundings. The world listed at an odd angle, and my legs ached from trying to free them. My ankle throbbed. And the rest of me . . .

I shuddered and closed my eyes.

No, I decided. *We are not going to die.*

I was going to get us out of here.

I patted around on my seat for my phone, but it wasn't there. A rock settled in my stomach as I realized it must've slid down by my feet. My breath hitched.

Stay calm. The words repeated themselves over and over in my mind. With my good foot, I felt around on the floor for the small device, and after a few seconds, the toe of my shoe landed on its corner. I slid it back toward my seat, then leaned forward. The movement sent a sudden wave of dizziness through me, and I fought to keep the world from spinning. There was a thin gap between the edge of my seat and the dashboard. If I could just move my seat enough, maybe I could reach my arm down and grab it . . .

Using my heel, I felt around for the bar underneath me that adjusted my seat. After a few tries, I disengaged the lock, grimacing a little at the angle it required of my good leg. I placed my hands on the dash in front of me and took a steadying breath. Then, I pushed.

In an instant, my nerves were electric. The dizziness and nausea I'd felt a moment ago returned, and this time I wasn't able to keep the ground from pitching beneath me as my eyes drifted closed.

Chapter Two

I awoke to a dim fluorescent light shining from another room and a machine incessantly beeping and whirring in the corner. I blinked a few times and squinted as my eyes adjusted, trying to figure out where I was. The scratchy blankets against my arms. My clothes replaced by a gown that swallowed me. Something blowing air into my nose, and other tubes draped across my arm. A hospital?

I turned my head to the side and spotted someone curled up in an armchair in the corner. It was my mother, deep asleep. She wasn't wearing any makeup, and her clothes were wrinkled.

"Mom?"

I said the word quietly, but it was enough to wake her up. Her eyelids fluttered open, and when she saw me, tears welled up and threatened to spill onto her cheeks. "Oh, honey," she said, coming closer to kneel next to my bedside. She grabbed my hand and squeezed it with both of her own. "You're awake. How are you feeling?"

"I'm . . ." I trailed off. I was still too groggy to really be sure how to answer her. "How long have I been asleep?"

"It's been a little more than a day. The doctors were concerned about your head and your spine, so they kept you pretty heavily sedated. It's technically Wednesday morning now—I sent Andrew back home a couple hours ago so he could try to get some rest and eat something. He refused to leave your side all of yesterday."

I studied the room around me a bit more. There was a large window behind Mom with the curtains drawn up, but from a small gap in the fabric, I could tell it was early enough that it was still dark outside. A small collection of cards and a teddy bear holding a toy-sized "get well soon" balloon were set up in the windowsill. On the wall across from me, a white board had something scrawled on it in illegible script. Or maybe I was still just squinting too much to read it. I furrowed my brow, trying to work past the fog that filled my brain. "What happened?" I asked, turning back to Mom. Concern suddenly shadowed her features.

"Honey, do you not remember? You were in the car with your father, and you two were driving to the restaurant—"

I sucked in a breath, the wreck suddenly replaying itself in brief flashes in my head. That blaze of light, the sound, the feeling of being pinned in my seat. My eyes widened, and my voice wavered. "Dad? Is he . . . ?"

She lowered her gaze. "He, um . . ." She paused to collect herself. "He's in a coma. The neurologist says he's showing signs of coming out of it, but with the severity of his brain injury, they're just not sure—" Her voice cracked, and she met my gaze again, her eyes misted over. "They're just not sure when he'll wake up."

I took a deep breath, trying to stop the panic suddenly clawing at my chest. The realization of what she'd said took a moment to settle in. *No. Please, no.* The air evaporated from my lungs faster than I could breathe it in. Tears spilled onto my cheeks, and Mom squeezed my hand, wearing her own pain and understanding plainly on her face.

I wasn't sure how much time passed before I could finally settle myself. As my tears ran out, I felt the warmth of Mom's hands on mine, tasted the saltwater that had caught on my lips. Eventually, I heard the beeping of the machine behind me slow until it was back to the same steady rhythm as before. Mom wiped at her eyes with a tissue and blew her nose delicately, and I watched her body language shift as she tucked her emotions under the surface once more. She pursed her lips in a sad smile, then leaned forward and gave me a small kiss on my forehead. "Let me call the nurses in here. They'll probably want to know you're awake." I nodded in agreement, and she reached over my lap and pressed the call button on the bed's remote.

Mom had been right. The nurse who answered a few minutes later was thrilled to see my eyes open—as was everyone else who worked at the hospital, it seemed. Within a few hours, it felt as if the whole floor had been in my room to check on me, introduce themselves, and ask if I needed anything. Even as my eyelids started to feel heavy again, I could only ever start to doze off before someone else would come in the room to take my vitals or adjust my IV. I'd startle awake every time, and my mom would just catch my eye, her eyebrows turned upward in a silent apology.

I truly didn't mind it all that much. I was exhausted, but the constant distraction gave me something else to focus on. I didn't want to think about Dad, and if I was being honest, my memories of the crash were still cloudy and hard to sort through. The scenes I remembered were fragmented, and none of them pieced together in any way that made sense. We'd just been talking, and then . . . what had we crashed into? Or had something crashed into us? I remembered seeing a flash of light, but that must've been in my own mind. I couldn't remember anywhere it could've come from. And then there was the pain, and the adrenaline, and the fear. And then I was here. I had so many questions, so many gaps I wanted to fill in, but every time someone else mentioned the accident, I could see my mom withdraw a little. They'd say it was a miracle that I was awake and relatively okay, and the same heavy, pained look would flash in her eyes, a little as if she'd been slapped in the face. Of course she'd react that way, when Dad was just down the hall, still unconscious and hooked up to twice the machines I was now. So even after they'd leave, I would hold my tongue and keep my questions to myself.

Eventually, it grew lighter outside, and any sense of quiet I'd had during those first few hours ended with the changeover to the hospital's day staff. Out in the hall, people bustled back and forth almost constantly, and I caught myself staring at them through the window in my door more than once.

"I think the cafeteria's open again," Mom said after a while, glancing at her watch. I turned my attention from the TV show I'd been pretending to watch back to her. "Are you hungry at all?"

"Actually, yeah. Food sounds really good." I hadn't even thought about it until just now, but I was starving.

Mom nodded, then slipped her purse onto her arm. "I'm not quite sure what they've got, but I'll see what I can find and bring us back a few choices." She straightened and stood, and I smiled my thanks.

Just before she could leave the room, though, a knock sounded at the door. A tall man in a starched white lab coat entered, waving cautiously.

"Hello, girls," he said, his voice lilting with a slight accent. "How are we this morning?"

"Pretty good," I offered. Mom nodded politely.

He clasped his hands in front of him. "That's wonderful to hear. And Cassidy, it's so good to finally meet you. I'm Dr. Babu. I've been helping to take care of you and your father down the hall. I heard you were awake," he said, turning from me as he spoke to address the both of us, "so I wanted to stop by and see you before I started my rounds for the day. But it looks like you are just heading out?"

"I was just running down to get some breakfast from the cafeteria, but I can stay for a moment . . . ?"

"Well, I just have a few things I wanted to go over with Miss Cassidy, but now that she's awake, I'll need her permission for you to stay in the room." He raised his eyebrows in question, and it took a second before I recognized he was addressing me. I nodded hastily.

"She can stay."

"Excellent," he said with a smile. He turned back to me. "Well then, Cassidy, how are we feeling this morning, hm?" He found a small stool against the wall and rolled it over, taking a seat at the foot of the bed. I hesitated, trying to think of how to answer.

"I'm really foggy. It's hard to focus on things."

He nodded. "Any pain?" I shook my head. He wrote something on the clipboard of papers he'd brought in with him. "Good. The grogginess is probably from your pain medication. I'll have them lower your dose and see if that helps." He sorted through his papers for a moment before continuing.

"Now, has anyone spoken to you about your injuries?"

I shook my head again. Now that I thought about it, I hadn't even considered asking what all was wrong with me—I'd been too worried about my dad and how everyone else had been managing.

"Well, you've had a small concussion and bruised an area in your lumbar region—your lower spine—as well as broken two of the bones in your right foot." He paused, flipping through his papers for a moment before he found the images he was looking for. Removing the X-rays from the stack, he held them up one at a time in front of me so that the light from the window illuminated them faintly, and he circled my injuries with his finger as he spoke. "Now, neither injury is inherently serious, though you're going to be in a cast and need to stay off your leg for a few weeks. Your spinal contusion is very mild, though with that you might also feel some pain and tingling. If any of that changes or gets worse, you need to let us know."

"Tingling?" I asked.

Dr. Babu nodded, then cocked his head for a moment. "Have you been feeling any of that so far this morning?"

I spotted my mom's worried expression in my periphery and shook my head. "No, sorry, it's not that. I thought I remembered feeling this weird tingling in my back when we were in the car," I clarified. "I'm still only remembering bits and pieces of what happened after the wreck. Is that normal?"

The doctor nodded, frowning in thought. "It's certainly nothing out of the ordinary. As I said before, you do have a mild concussion. Beyond that, the wreck was a traumatic experience. People can often experience memory lapses around those moments. Still . . ." He paused, consulting his chart again before turning his attention back to my mom, then to me. "There is something else I should discuss with you. When you first arrived at the hospital, we ran a variety of tests to monitor your brain activity and make sure nothing more serious was going on beyond your concussion. We spotted a slight abnormality then—nothing we were too concerned about."

"Abnormal how?" I asked, interrupting his train of thought.

He shifted in his seat. "To be frank, I've studied neurology for almost thirty years, and I'm not sure how to describe it." He clicked the pen in his hand repeatedly as he spoke. It was starting to worry at my nerves. He must've noticed—a moment later, he stopped, then straightened. "It's quite possible that it was nothing, just a fluke in our equipment. But just to be on the safe side, I think I'll order some more scans. To be sure we haven't missed anything." The last bit he added as an afterthought, as if trying to comfort the two of us. "But you seem to be alert and in good spirits, which makes me tremendously happy." He smiled and nodded his head once in finality, then secured his stack of papers back onto his clipboard and stood. "I'll be back in later today to see how you're doing, but for now, I'll let you rest some more."

I called out a quick "thank you" as he closed the door to my room behind him, then glanced at my mom. Her jaw was taut, and she picked absentmindedly at the side of her thumb as she watched the doctor leave. Once the door clicked shut, she turned her attention back to me, any trace of nerves buried once more. "You're sure you're not hurting at all?" she asked.

I smiled. "I'm fine, I promise." Hastily, I switched topics. "He seems really nice."

She nodded, trying on a smile of her own. "He is." She glanced down for a moment, thinking about something, then met my gaze again. "I'll head down to the cafeteria and see what they have. You're okay?" I nodded again, giving her another smile. This time I must've convinced her, because she shouldered her purse and headed toward the hall. But as soon as I heard the door click shut behind her, the content expression I'd worn as a mask slipped away. I closed my eyes and covered my face with my hands. I'd never been great at telling when people were trying to hide things from me, but even I could tell Dr. Babu had been lying about an error with the equipment. Mom had obviously picked up on it too. Stumping the doctor was never a particularly good sign.

Over the next few minutes, I pondered what the doctor had said and took stock of my injuries for the first time that morning. Somehow, I hadn't felt the heavy plaster that weighed on the end of my leg until Dr. Babu had mentioned it, but taking a peek at it beneath the sheets now, I couldn't help but frown at how massive the cast looked on my leg. It was also about the extent of what I could see—I was awkward and uncoordinated, and just lifting the sheets to see beneath them tired out my arms. Thankfully, it wasn't too much longer before my door clicked open again. I offered a half smile as my mom entered the room again, this time carrying a beige plastic tray in one hand and balancing a small coffee in the other. "I'm back," she said in a sing-song voice. "And I brought you a couple presents."

Any of her worry and stress from earlier had seemingly vanished in her walk to the cafeteria and back. "It smells really good," I reassured her. I eased myself into a better sitting position as she carried the food into the room and began spreading it out onto the rolling table set up by the bed.

"I hope you've got enough to share."

The familiar voice came from the doorway, and I turned just as Andrew peeked his face around the corner. This time, my smile was genuine.

"I did say 'a couple presents,'" Mom whispered. She gave a quick wink.

"She found me wandering around in the lobby and decided to bring me up," he joked. He parked his wheelchair near the foot of my bed and grinned. Behind his smile, though, I could see the worry in his eyes, the dark circles underneath them. I realized Mom probably hadn't been exaggerating when she'd said he'd stayed with me all of yesterday, and I felt a warmth fill my chest at the thought . . . along with a subtle twinge of guilt.

"It's Wednesday, though. Don't you have class right about now?" I asked. He shrugged.

"I emailed the professor and told him I'd be missing lecture. Besides, I get three absences for the semester."

"Andrew . . ."

He shushed me before I could say more. "I care way more about you than I do vectors." I gave him a sideways glare, but he just waved me off. "You matter more. Besides, you getting in that wreck was the perfect excuse for me not to have to take my calc midterm yesterday, so I owe you one."

"Ha ha," I deadpanned.

He ignored me, just helped hold the coffee cup while my mom finished adjusting the table to the right height in front of me. When she finished, she brushed her hands on her pants and looked at the two of us. "Now, now, you two," she said. But there was a lightness in her voice that I'd had yet to hear since I'd woken up. "While you eat, I think I'm going to go check on your father in the other room. Andrew, I'm just down the hall if either of you need me. Or Cassidy, you've got your call button?" I held up the remote, and she nodded. "Good." She blew me a kiss as she headed out the door.

We watched her go, the lightheartedness dissipating the moment she rounded the corner. Once she was out of earshot, I turned back to Andrew. "How's she been handling all this?" I asked. He sighed.

"I mean, about as well as you'd expect. She's tough, your mom, but when she called me Monday night and told me . . ." He fell silent and spent a moment adjusting his glasses on the bridge of his nose. "I saw pictures of what the car looked like when they pulled you guys out. Cassidy, what happened?"

I opened my mouth to answer, then closed it again. "I don't know. I don't know if I just can't remember or if it happened too fast, but whenever I think of it, I just see this bright flash and the car spinning out of control. And I remember how bad it hurt." Even now, I winced a little at the memory.

The muscles in Andrew's jaw tensed for a second. A moment passed before he said, "I think they said a transformer blew at one point, so that was probably the flash you were talking about."

"I guess that makes sense." I paused, glancing at the assortment Mom had brought, and speared a piece of watermelon to nibble on. "Have you gotten to see Dad at all?"

He shook his head. "Not really? I mean, I've been past his room, and your mom told me what was wrong with him, but . . ." He sighed. "Mostly, I've been worried about you."

A warmth spread through my chest, but it was chased away just as quickly. Without having seen him, the reality of Dad's condition didn't seem to have sunk in. I kept forgetting about him, too concerned with my own injuries and the jumbled mess of memories in my head, only to have the fear and grief sock me in the stomach once more. The guilt usually followed a few seconds later.

"They want to run more tests," I finally said, breaking the silence that had elapsed. "I guess to make sure my concussion isn't worse than what they originally thought."

Andrew perked up. "What has them concerned?"

"I'm not sure. The doctor said I had 'unusual brain activity' when they brought me in, but he said it might've just been their equipment acting up."

He nodded, scrubbing at his chin and his nonexistent beard with his hand. "I mean, you seem fine now. You're confused about the crash, but that kind of thing is normal, right?" I nodded. "So I wouldn't worry about it. I'm sure it'll all be okay."

"Okay" was very much a relative term, and he sounded like he was trying to convince himself as much as he was me. Still, I forced an expression that I hoped was reassuring. Andrew watched me nibble at the fruit on my tray a moment longer, then leaned forward, a smirk suddenly tugging the corners of his mouth.

"Want to know what I just realized?"

I decided to play along. "What's that?"

"You're going to have to be off that leg for a while, aren't you?" he asked, gesturing toward my cast.

I just raised an eyebrow at him. "Your point?"

He scooted himself back a little from the bed, then leaned back in his wheelchair, popping a wheelie. "Welcome to my world, baby."

"Does this mean I can borrow your old chair then?"

"The red one?" He scoffed, wrinkling his nose. "Not a chance."

For the first time that day, I laughed, then popped the rest of my piece of fruit into my mouth.

All things considered, the rest of the day passed with everyone in relatively good spirits. They backed down my pain medicine, which helped with my grogginess and the uneasy stomach I'd had when I'd tried to eat breakfast. We convinced Mom to go home for a bit to get some sleep and a shower. And despite Dr.

Babu's concern this morning, the MRI he'd ordered of my brain had shown nothing more that was out of the ordinary. Toward the end of the day, the nurses had even helped transfer me into a wheelchair so I could go visit Dad in his hospital room—only for a few minutes, but I was grateful nonetheless.

Babu had also signed off on letting me start physical therapy, and the therapist had let me try getting around the room on a pair of crutches for a few minutes. The cold metal poles still leaned against the side of my bed from earlier in the day, though I had been told not to use them without supervision. It didn't really matter. Now that Mom and Andrew had left for the evening, I didn't have much reason to get around. So far I'd used them more for scratching my good foot or grabbing things from across the room when I couldn't reach.

In fact, I didn't have much to do, period. My phone had been lost or broken in the crash, and I wasn't recovered enough yet to even consider doing school work. I had flipped on a random TV show a while ago, but it was more background noise than anything else. I glanced up at it now—it had cut to commercial, and some ad for Halloween candy was playing on the screen.

I sighed. As much as I tried to ignore it, my back and my leg were starting to ache again, a deep throbbing that demanded my attention no matter how I tried to distract myself. I winced a little and tried to reposition, then grumbled aloud. The lumpy mattress of my hospital bed wasn't helping matters. For a moment, I contemplated the button next to my remote that would increase my pain medicine, my finger running circles over the ridge in the plastic.

Another dose would likely leave me muddled for the rest of the night. But the day was starting to catch up with me, and even though I'd spent all of yesterday passed out, exhaustion was weighing heavy on my eyelids again. Maybe sleep wasn't such a bad idea. I could brush my teeth and tie up my hair beforehand, try to get back at least some of my normal routine. Maybe the medicine would be enough to quiet the thoughts that had been vying for my attention all day and let me actually rest.

I traced my finger along the other remote until I found the button to call the nurse's station, then pressed it. The window in the door of my room gave a perfect view of the desk, and I watched for a minute or two as people bustled back and forth. It must've been between shifts. I sighed, drumming my fingers on the side of the remote and letting my eyes wander. The bathroom was pretty much right next to my bed, as were the crutches. It wouldn't be that much work to get over there on my own. Besides, the chance to actually use the toilet in privacy for once today was too good to pass up. I reached for my crutches and pulled one of them over into my lap, then wheeled my IV drip over and shimmied to the side of the bed as carefully as I could.

I readied myself for a moment beforehand, taking the crutch in my good hand and grabbing the IV stand in the other. I glanced through the window on the door that showed the hallway. One of the nurses was standing at the nurse's station, laughing at something with the man behind the desk. Another came by and joined them a moment later, a clipboard in her hand. I turned my attention back to the door to the bathroom in front of me. Just needed to be careful. I set the crutch down against the floor, then eased the rest of me down, the cold from the linoleum seeping into my good foot through the fuzzy, no-slip hospital sock I was wearing.

I risked a nervous smile as I balanced on the crutch and took a step, wheeling the IV drip forward as I went. Easy-peasy. I tried another, and I was already almost halfway to the bathroom door. On the third step, though, the IV stand's wheel caught on a cord on the floor. As I pulled it forward, it tipped onto its side, threatening to crash to the ground. Without thinking, I reached out and tried to catch it, and the muscles in my back spasmed in protest. I lost my balance against the other crutch and pitched forward, throwing my hands out in front of me just in time to—

I was back in bed, the crutch resting against my lap. My IV stand was where it had been before, up by the corner of the bed. It was as if I hadn't moved it out of place at all. The muscles in my back had stiffened, and my hands screamed, tingling with the worst pin-and-needle pricks I'd ever felt.

No, not the worst. I'd felt this before.

In the car wreck.

I gritted my teeth and rubbed my palms against my thighs, trying to get the feeling to pass. I was confused. Had I just imagined getting up? Imagined falling? I glanced out the window to the hallway again. The same nurse from before was still laughing at whatever story the man behind the desk was telling, oblivious to the loud crash I'd made against the floor. Another nurse walked up and joined them.

I froze.

It wasn't just another nurse. It was *the same nurse as before*. The one who had already been at the desk before I fell. I could see the clipboard balanced on her forearm. My eyes widened, and I glanced at the TV. Hadn't the cartoon duck on the screen said that same line just before this? And I still sat in the same exact position I had before I'd stood up.

Part of me wished I'd already pushed the button for that extra dose of pain meds—something to explain what I was seeing now. Because if this was all just déjà vu, it was the strangest version of the sensation I'd ever felt. As the tingling slowly dissipated in my hands, the feeling began to return to my fingertips and into my palm, and I frowned. My IV site stung a little all of a sudden. I turned my hand over and noticed a tiny bit of blood starting to seep around the needle. As if I'd yanked on the line somehow.

My thoughts came in slow motion. The ache in my back. The tingling feeling in my hands. The nurse reappearing. The line on the TV. Me still sitting on the bed, but my hand bleeding as if I'd fallen. This wasn't déjà vu.

Had I somehow pushed myself back in time?

CHAPTER THREE

I PUSHED MYSELF BACK in time.

The idea rattled around in my head. It drowned out any of my other thoughts. A moment ago, I'd tried getting up to get ready for bed. Now, the idea of sleep seemed laughable.

No, *this* idea was laughable. Rewinding time? It had to be my meds. The concussion. Sleep deprivation. Shock. *Something* more rational than time travel. Even so, my vision wobbled. I couldn't stop looking at my hands, turning them over in my lap, closing them into fists and releasing them. The tingling sensation had gone, but I could still remember the electric noise I'd felt, like radio static in my nerves. It was the same thing that had happened in the car the other night, albeit not quite as intense.

Suddenly, I had an explanation even better than "faulty equipment" for why my brain activity might have been less than ordinary when I'd first arrived at the hospital.

Time still felt like it crawled as I worked it over in my mind. I wasn't sure if it was seconds or minutes before I heard a quiet knock at the door, and the dark-haired nurse who'd been laughing at the desk earlier peeked her head in.

"What can I— Oh," she said, a bit surprised. "You're not supposed to be sitting up like this. Is everything okay? Can I help with something?"

In a panic and with my thoughts still reeling, I managed to mumble something about going to the bathroom. After I'd brushed my teeth and splashed water on my face, she helped me ease back against my pillow and replaced my crutches against the side of the bed—a little farther out of my reach this time, I noticed. I waited for the door to click shut behind her before I closed my eyes, and I stayed that way when someone eased my door open a while later and tiptoed in to turn off the TV set and check my vitals while I rested.

But I never slept.

The next morning, I faked a smile for Mom and made small talk with Andrew throughout breakfast. I even kept a straight face as a nurse replaced my IV site. "Looks like this one blew overnight, but that happens," she'd said. "Nothing to worry about." As she worked, I thought about it some more, and I realized I had to have been jumping to conclusions. There was no way I'd ended up with superpowers. Why would something like that happen to someone like me? And why now? The moment had been so brief, it must've just been my mind playing tricks—

"Still, you didn't fall at all yesterday, did you?" she asked.

"What?" I swallowed, working hard to keep my expression neutral. "No, not that I remember."

Except what if I had?

No matter what I did that day, a part of my mind kept drifting back to the question. I kept massaging my palms with my thumbs, trying to remember what I'd done in the moments leading up to everything. When I'd fallen, I'd tripped forward and thrown my hands out in front of me to catch myself. And hadn't I been pressing against the dashboard when my hands started tingling in the car? I fought the urge to try making the motion now as I sat in the armchair in the corner of my room, my foot propped up on a stool.

"When do you think you'll go back to class?" Andrew asked.

"Huh?"

"You know, assuming you actually get to go home today."

It took me a moment to process his question. "Oh. I'm not sure, honestly. I'd love to take until Monday, but missing a whole week of lectures . . ."

"Yikes. Yeah, didn't think about that."

I shrugged. "It's not a huge deal for most of my classes. I'm sure someone will be willing to share notes. But then there's all the readings and a couple papers I need to work on and—" I paused and scrubbed at my face with my hands. "Even if I don't skip tomorrow, my weekend is going to be so packed."

He pursed his lips. "That seems criminal."

I shrugged. "Thank you, American education system," I said drily.

He nodded, his gaze wandering to the window as he thought. "Still though, you'd think your professors would give you some extra time to get assignments done—beyond just the assignments you missed, I mean. It's not really fair if they expect you to . . ." Andrew kept talking, and I nodded along, but I was only half listening again. Part of me—a small part—wanted to ask him what he thought. I could feel the words dancing on the tip of my tongue. But what would I tell him exactly? How could I make it sound believable, when I wasn't even sure I believed any of it myself? I hated doing it, but at least for now, I kept quiet about the night before.

"Mom says they've changed Dad's diagnosis," I said instead. I tore my gaze from the leaf that was drifting along in the breeze outside and turned back to Andrew. "He's moved from being in a coma to a 'persistent vegetative state.'" The conversation I'd had with her had been one of the few things to pull my thoughts away from the incident the night before. The doctor had spelled out the differences between the two when he'd visited this morning. I think he'd been trying to make it sound like this was an improvement—something worth celebrating. Neither of us had felt like cheering after he left.

"I know. Your mom stopped me in the hall and told me." Andrew brought his chair closer to me and took one of my hands from my lap. "Have they said what his prognosis is?" he asked quietly.

"They're not sure. They said they can keep him comfortable and do physical therapy work so he doesn't lose function as much, but" —I paused for a moment, trying to keep my emotions in check— "it's a waiting game to see if he'll wake up again."

This time, it was Andrew's thumb that traced my palm. But his touch was different than my own had been. Softer, gentler. Kinder. "Cassidy, I'm so sorry. About all of this."

I tried to smile, but I couldn't quite manage one. Instead, I just nodded and looked back out the window.

As it turned out, I did end up getting discharged from the hospital that night. With my MRI showing no signs of concussion and my back healing even faster than expected, Dr. Babu admitted he had no reason to keep me lying around in a hospital room when he could just prescribe the pain medicine I needed and send me home to rest. But with everything else running through my head, the idea of attending a lecture in the morning gave me a pounding headache. After some convincing from everyone—Dr. Babu and the nurses included—I sent my professors a quick update and told them I'd be in to get the work I'd missed on Monday.

"You're sure you'd rather go back to the dorm?" Mom asked as I signed the discharge papers. "I'm happy to drive you to campus Sunday afternoon if you want to spend the weekend at home instead."

I adjusted my balance on my good leg and handed the last of the forms to the woman behind the front desk. "No, really, it's okay. I don't want you feeling like you have to be at home with me instead of here with Dad. He needs you more." I gave a small smile. "Besides, I've got Andrew to dote on me if I need anything."

She gave me a knowing look. "Yes, but you'd have to be willing to actually ask him for help if you needed it." Still, she relented. "Just text me when you get there, and let me know if I need to come get you or bring you anything. I'm only a phone call away."

"Of course. Love you, Mom."

"I love you too."

We hugged awkwardly around my crutches, tears waiting just underneath the surface for both of us. Even so, Mom's embrace held all the warmth and comfort it had carried since I was a kid. It thawed the last of my doubts about heading back to campus; *somehow*, it said, *everything will be okay*. Besides, as I clambered into the taxi waiting for me out front a few minutes later and waved good-bye from the window, my mind drifted to the real reason I'd opted to head back to the dorm for the weekend. There, I would be alone, and I could figure out what the incident last night with my hands had truly meant.

The taxi driver on my trip back to campus didn't offer much in the way of conversation, but I didn't mind. Even with nothing but the soft radio music to fill the space, the trip seemed to go by faster than expected, and amazingly, being in a car again didn't make me nervous. Even so, climbing out of the car in front of the lobby of my dorm was an odd experience. On the surface, this night seemed indistinguishable from the one when I'd last stood here—and yet so much had changed since then.

As I'd promised her, I texted Mom when I got there. She'd gifted me a new phone early this morning—a slightly older generation than the one I'd lost in the crash, though that kind of thing had never bothered me. I made a quick stop at the front desk to get a new keycard made, another possession of mine lost in the crash, then headed for the elevator. I almost had to laugh. Of course I would've broken my leg in the same year I moved to the top floor of a building. Still, as I punched the button for the seventh floor and waited, I decided it was probably an easier transition for me than most. Thanks to Andrew, I already knew where all the accessible entrances and elevators were around campus.

Finally, the door opened onto my floor, and a turn around the corner and a short walk to the end of the hall brought me back to my room. It was exactly the way I'd left it on Monday. My twin bed, tucked into the corner closest to the window, was still unmade, and my outfit from class that day was tossed haphazardly across the foot of it from when I'd changed for dinner at the restaurant. My laptop and textbooks were still laid out on my desk, though I doubted the computer had any charge left after not being plugged in at all these past few days. And the leaves of the small plant I kept in the windowsill were maybe slightly droopier but certainly no less green than before.

The room was fairly bare compared with some of the pictures I'd seen on social media from my high school friends. They'd all coordinated colors with their roommates and hung cute photos from their senior year on the wall, or they'd strung fairy lights across the ceiling and arranged cozy hammock chairs and fluffy rugs like something out of a teen's furniture catalog. I'd been willing to "splurge" on the extra cost for a single dorm, but when it came to decorating, I'd mostly stuck to an artist's sketch of Everett's campus and maps of cool historical cities I wanted to visit one day. On my dresser, I'd taped a couple of photos of my family and of Andrew and me. The rest of my belongings here—the extra bookcase, the fridge and microwave, the quilts and bedsheets—I'd scavenged from our basement or accepted as hand-me-downs from family friends. It wasn't that I had anything against the people with perfectly selected furniture or color-coordinated wall art that shouted who they were to the world; honestly, I'd just never known what mine should say.

With the lack of furniture, I didn't have as much clutter to maneuver around when it came to using my crutches, though getting to my bed was still a bit tricky in the tight space. I tap-tap-tapped my way around the chair and desk in the middle of the room, grimacing for whoever below me was hearing an impromptu percussion performance. "Sorry," I muttered aloud. Eventually, after a few minutes of cursing and awkward fumbling, I managed to squeeze my way around the mess. I heaved myself up onto the bed and leaned my crutches up against the footboard, then let out a heavy sigh. I was home.

And for the first time today, I was finally alone.

My heart pounded, and no longer because of the one-legged workout. I looked down at my hands and rubbed my fingertips against my palms. There was only one way to prove to myself the incident last night had really happened, that I hadn't dreamed it or imagined it in a medicine-induced stupor. I pulled my phone out of my back pocket and clicked it open to the clock. For a few seconds, I watched time steadily tick forward on the LED screen. Then, I set it down on the bed next to me. 8:57:36.

I sucked in a deep breath, then shoved my hands out in front of me.

For an instant, it seemed like nothing happened—except for the fire that started in my palms. I hummed and shook my hands back and forth to try and get the feeling to pass as I glanced at my phone. The clock ticked forward a second just as I did so, from 8:57:31 to 8:57:32. Five seconds. I let out a surprised laugh. After the feeling passed, I tried again. 9:01:03. Then 9:00:58.

I alternated curling my hands into fists and stretching my fingers as I tried to process it all. It was difficult to tell what exactly I was doing with each attempt—the numbers on the clock were moving backward, but was I? I chewed on my lip for a moment as I thought. Last night, I'd been a few feet from the bathroom when I'd tripped, but I'd ended up back on the edge of my bed.

So I needed to try doing something as I triggered it.

I glanced around my room, then spotted my trash can. I grinned and hopped toward it on my good leg, then used the desk to balance myself as I picked out a wadded piece of note-book paper. I let it rest in the palm of my hand for a minute. Then, once I was sure enough time had elapsed, I tossed it across the room, pushing forward with my palms again as soon as it left my fingers.

The movement knocked me off-balance a little, and I had to catch myself against the side of the desk to keep from falling. But as I did so, the paper ball rolled out of my hand and onto the floor.

It had been across the room. Then it had been back in my hand.

I hopped over to my bed and grabbed my phone once again. This time, I clicked it open to the photos app. My fingers fumbled on the screen as I searched through the settings—they were almost starting to feel numb with how much they tingled, but I didn't care. Finally, I found the setting to switch to selfie mode. I set it to video, then balanced my phone against the lamp on my desk. The angle wasn't great, but it would do for now. I took a steadying breath and rewound time again.

I glanced back at my phone. It wasn't even recording any-more. *Too quick?* I frowned, hitting the button to try again. This time, I counted to five before I moved my hands. They were starting to really sting, and it took a moment for the pain to subside enough for me to remember to end the recording. Once I did though, I picked my phone up with trembling hands and went to watch it back. On the screen, I watched myself set the phone up, then bounce in place as I tried to distract myself from the tingling sensation. I watched the whole thing elapse, until the me on screen approached the camera again to end the video. There was no motion of me pushing my hands outward, no skip between frames or odd glitch where I appeared on the screen. To my phone—and I could only assume to the rest of the world—the things that happened before I moved time back never actually happened at all.

I kept experimenting and trying out my new abilities until late into the night. I tried different movements to see if I could trigger the time jump in other ways, moved things only to see them move back instantaneously, watched time tick forward and leap backward on my phone's clock and on the wristwatch I dug out of my jewelry chest. I only stopped when my head was swimming too much to concentrate and my hands were prickling all the way up into my wrists. I hadn't realized how exhausted I'd become. I didn't even bother changing into pajamas before I crawled into bed—though this time, I did at least get to brush my teeth on my own. And when I turned out the light, I was asleep almost before I finished pulling the blankets up over myself. It was a deep and dreamless sleep, but even there I could feel the strange sensation lingering in my palms. It was as if they were reminding me that it had all been real.

The next morning, I awoke to sunlight casting prisms around my dorm. I blinked my eyes until I could focus them, then glanced at the time on my phone's screensaver. It was already almost noon. I had a few texts from Mom and from Andrew asking how I was doing. I groaned and rolled over. For a moment, I contemplated covering my head with my blankets and dozing for a few more hours. But I was starting to get a bit hungry, and Dr. Babu had warned me to keep on a regimen with my pain medicine. I sighed and tossed my covers off, then reached for my crutches.

It took me a bit longer to get ready for the day than it usually would, mostly on account of me trying to figure out how to shower with a cast. But in the middle of the day, there was no line for the bathrooms, so I was able to take my time brushing out my long, coppery hair and braiding it back away from my face. Once I finished, I headed back to my dorm and made a peanut butter sandwich, then sat down to work. Now that I was back on campus, it wasn't quite as easy to ignore how far behind I'd fallen in my classes. The list of overdue assignments was daunting, as were the hours of lectures I was going to need to make up at some point to even understand them. Andrew was right; I probably would get extensions for almost all of it, especially for the work I'd missed this week. But somehow that didn't make me feel any better. I pulled out the first of my textbooks and flipped open to the proper page.

I hardly moved from my desk for the next few hours as I tried to make a dent in my to-do list. I managed to check a few assignments off at least, but as hard as I tried, I couldn't seem to make myself focus. I put on soothing study music in the background. I brewed some tea in the microwave to put myself in the right mindset. But I still found myself rereading passages two or three times before I actually could pay attention to what they were saying.

I couldn't help it. Every time I picked up my pen or turned a page, I thought about my discoveries the night before. The painful tingling had long since subsided from my hands, but even now I could still feel a slight ache in my knuckles when I moved my fingers. It was that stiffness you'd feel when your joints had been out in the cold too long and were finally starting to thaw, or when you had exercised muscles the day before that you didn't usually work. It was all I could think about—that, and what I should do about it.

I finally gave up just around 4:30, when I could see the colors in the sky shift outside as the sun sank closer to the horizon. I'd at least been sort of productive on my day off, and there was always the rest of the weekend to work. I closed my laptop and stretched, then drummed my fingers on my desk. Andrew's history discussions were usually on Friday afternoons, and I hadn't heard from Mom in a while. I assumed she had spent the day at the hospital with Dad. Dinner was up to me.

Well, there was always the ramen place downtown. I didn't quite feel like eating at any of the dining halls, but my peanut butter sandwich from earlier hadn't been particularly filling—and the popcorn I'd snacked on a few hours later hadn't helped much, either. It was still pretty early in the afternoon, but maybe the walk would give me a chance to clear my head and think about something else. When I got back, I could decide whether to keep working or to call it quits for the day.

I chewed on my lip as I considered it, but after another moment, I nodded to myself. Grabbing my crutches, I gathered my things and headed for downtown.

Something I'd failed to consider previously: Getting around on crutches took way more effort than I'd realized. It also took way longer than I was used to, which became apparent as I headed toward the restaurant. Even though I'd thought I'd left plenty early, the sky was already burning crimson when I arrived and sat down. I ate quickly and paid, but by the time I headed back out the door, the streetlights had come on, and the nighttime sky had put an extra chill into the breeze. As I stepped back onto the sidewalk, I couldn't help but shiver a little.

It wasn't just the breeze that made me shudder. Unease was starting to coil itself in my chest for some reason I couldn't quite put into words. Maybe it was the memory of the plea from my dad right before our crash. But there was something more to it too. Something I couldn't quite explain. Whatever it was, it made me wish I could move just a little bit faster on my trek back to the dorm.

At least tonight I didn't feel like I was walking alone. The first Friday back from fall break, college students were out in droves, either heading to cafés to study or heading to bars to actively avoid it. I passed by several groups of students I recognized from Greek life events on the campus quad, their outfits and hair and makeup all nicer than anything I had ever been able to pull off. There were several other people out too, most of them enjoying the semi-decent weather before they were forced to don puffy coats and thick gloves or stocking up on last-minute Halloween decorations before the trick-or-treaters arrived in a couple weeks. I furrowed my eyebrows. With everything else going on the past few days, I'd almost forgotten about the holiday, the parties—that was, until I overheard two young girls approaching the crosswalk I'd just passed.

"What are you going as?"

"I can't decide. I want to go as a scarecrow, but I don't know if I'm going to have time to do my makeup after school lets out."

"A scarecrow?" Her friend made a face, and she pulled out her phone to explain.

"No, trust me, it's really cute. Here, I've got this video—"

"Lily!" Her friend grabbed her arm and stopped her just before she walked right into me. The girl—Lily—blushed in embarrassment.

"Sorry," she muttered.

I chuckled. "You're fine." I waited until the two had passed, smiling a little at her friend's hushed teasing. Just as I started to move forward again, though, another sound stopped me in my tracks. From a couple blocks away, I could hear people shouting, their voices indistinct but laced with urgency. I turned toward the noise, my heart starting to hammer in my chest again. Another sound joined the shouts, this one growing louder. A car engine, maybe? No, it sounded like a motorcycle revving. I squinted at the road up ahead. Something crested over the horizon, but it was much bigger than a motorcycle. It looked like . . . a city bus. And it was moving much faster than city buses were supposed to.

Suddenly, I could hear the name people were shouting.

"Phase!"

The hero's sleek black motorbike crested the hill just behind the bus, coming up quickly along its side. The bus careened out of control, barreling straight through an intersection and barely avoiding another car in its path. Phase kept pace with it, swerving on her bike to avoid getting hit herself. Once she got close enough to the front, she reached an arm out toward the tires. I watched her fingers, the only part of her not clothed in black, stretch outward, and suddenly the scent of burning rubber filtered into the air.

Or rather, *melting* rubber.

The bus began to slow, but it also began to swerve even more dangerously than before. It came close to clipping the side of Phase's bike, and I gasped as she jerked out of the way, losing her balance for a moment and grabbing hold of the handlebars again to regain control. She righted herself, then reached a hand out again. This time, it only took a few seconds before the tires burst.

People screamed as the sparks flew from underneath the bus, its metal frame now scraping against the pavement less than a block away. The rubber from the tires exploded out from underneath it, and Phase veered out of the way as the projectiles flew toward her. But the bus was still sliding downhill, and though it was slowing even more now, with the tires gone, it had lost any semblance of control. I watched in horror as it slid toward the crosswalk I'd just passed, toward the pole for the traffic light hanging above it. Toward the two girls from earlier who stood just beside the road, frozen in fear.

I didn't even think. In one swift motion, I threw my crutches outward and shoved my hands in front of me.

Five seconds.

I didn't have long to get my bearings. I leaned forward on my crutches for a better view, hearing the front tires go on the bus just as I spotted them. They were moving closer to the crosswalk, trying to get a better view of what was going on.

"Lily, wait!" I yelled, starting toward them.

Four seconds.

Lily and her friend turned at the sound of her name, trying to find who'd shouted. I raced toward them as fast as I could, my arms and hands aching with the effort. Somewhere up the street, I heard Phase's motorcycle almost go out from under her as she avoided debris from the tires.

Three seconds. Two.

The girls had spotted me now, and both wore the same look of concern on their faces.

"Get out of the way!" I pleaded. I tried to gesture with my head as I moved, but they didn't understand, and the screaming that started behind them drowned out my warnings and drew their attention back to the street.

One second.

As I reached the girls, I dropped one of my crutches and stretched my arms out, scooping them back away from the road. When I did, I lost my balance, sending the three of us toppling to the sidewalk.

"What the—" Lily's friend started. But the grinding and scraping sound behind us shook the street, trapping the last word in her throat. With my ears still ringing, I turned to look over my shoulder. The bus had pressed up against the traffic light, pushing it off-kilter. What was left of the bus' front bumper hung over the sidewalk, only feet from where we lay on the ground. It had come to a stop right where the two girls had been standing.

I turned back to the girls. Lily's eyes were wide and unblinking, and her friend had tears in her eyes. They both were staring at the bus. "Are you girls okay?" I asked. The sound of my voice drew their attention back to me, and after a moment, they slowly began to nod. "Good." I didn't fully believe them, but I wanted to give them a moment to process what had just happened. I reached for one of my crutches on the ground and began to stand. As I hopped back up onto my good leg, though, I faltered a little. Everyone was staring . . . at me. Their shocked gazes bore holes into my back, and my cheeks turned a violent shade of red.

After a few seconds, a man walked up and offered me my other crutch. I mumbled a sheepish "thanks" and adjusted my balance. The silence that hung in the air was oppressive.

"Miss, are you okay?"

"I'm fine, but check on them." I tipped my head toward the other girls still lying on the ground. He hesitated for a moment, but he must've decided he trusted me. With a nod, he knelt down in front of the two girls.

Our short exchange must've been a cue to everyone else. A few murmurs started among the crowd, and people began clamoring to help passengers off the bus, to make sure everyone else on the street was okay. Phase's motorbike had skidded to a stop a few paces in front of the bus, and she still stood astride it now, directing someone to call 911 and scanning the scene for anyone else in need of help. I took the opportunity in all the chaos to slip away unnoticed.

After a while, as the lights and sounds from downtown began to fade away behind me, I released a breath that had been trapped in my chest. What had just *happened*? Not just with the bus, but with me. I hadn't meant to use my new ability like that, especially in front of so many people. But it had happened so fast. It was like my instinct had taken control of the situation before I even had time to realize what I was—

A noise came from just behind me. I could hear it over the clicking of my crutches against the pavement. Footsteps.

My mouth suddenly went dry. I was on the short stretch of road that spanned between the downtown district and Everett's campus. The lighting here wasn't as bright as it was elsewhere, and with all the commotion that had just happened downtown, I doubted any cops were patrolling the area like they usually would. I picked up my pace, staring straight ahead at the edge of campus.

"Wait, please! I just want to talk."

The woman's voice wasn't one I recognized. Whether from the adrenaline from earlier I still had pumping through my blood or my father's warnings replaying themselves in my head, my skin crawled. I was suddenly hyperaware of the ache that lingered in my foot beneath my cast, at just how vulnerable it made me. I ignored her and kept moving.

"What you did back there—how did you know where the bus was going to crash?"

"I don't know what you're talking about." I shook my head as I walked, not even bothering to turn around. "I saw the bus was out of control. I saw the girls standing near the street. I pushed them away. It was just good timing."

"That bus swerved at the last second toward that light pole," the voice said. "You knew *exactly* where it was going to crash."

I scoffed, but my palms were growing sweaty on the handles of my crutches. They still tingled from earlier. "That's impossible."

The woman was quiet for a moment. "They're new, aren't they? Your powers?"

"What?" I asked incredulously. I stopped in my tracks and turned around. The lampposts on the edge of campus were just a few feet ahead, but their light barely reached to where I stood. I could only make out the outline of the figure who'd stopped a couple of steps behind me. "Look, I'm sorry, but you've got the wrong idea," I pleaded. I had to work hard to keep my voice steady, my expression at least somewhat composed. "I'm just as ordinary as you are."

"Now *that* I believe," the woman said. I could hear the playfulness in her voice. Slowly, she stepped forward, moving into the hazy glow from the campus lights. Her black jeans and leather jacket looked a bit scuffed and well worn, but the piping that ran up her chest and along her shoulders still shone bright blue and vibrant red. The light reflected off her black motorcycle helmet as she slipped it off and tucked it under her arm. She shook her bouncy curls free and grinned, holding out a hand—the only part of her not clothed in all black—for me to shake. "I'm Mia," she said.

But I already knew her by a different name.

"You're Phase," I whispered.

Chapter Four

T HE NEXT MORNING, I stood outside the door to one of the apartments on the north side of campus, working up the courage to raise my hand and knock. I could feel my heartbeat in my stomach. It was stirring up the butterflies that had been there since late last night. I took a deep breath and let it out slowly, then rapped on the door.

A moment later, it swung open. The woman inside was only a little taller than me, with a warm complexion and natural inky black curls that stretched out around her shoulders. She beamed when she saw me. "Cass! I'm so glad you made it," she said. "I was worried the elevator was going to be a little hard to find." Phase—or Mia, I guess—beckoned me inside, and I followed her through the doorway. Even though I'd known her for less than twelve hours, somehow I knew the place screamed "Mia." You could tell that most of her furniture was secondhand, but almost all of it had been repainted or refurbished to match. Her walls were decorated with bold-colored artwork and a collection of newspaper clippings, the back of her front door with a blue, pink, and purple flag. The farthest wall of her living room included a balcony door that looked out onto campus. Being on the third floor, the view stretched all the way to the tall spire of the administration building. I knew her apartment complex was one of the oldest and less popular ones in town, but glancing around now, it was hard to really understand why.

As my gaze continued drifting around the room, it landed on a black motorcycle suit and helmet shoved into a corner near Mia's desk. The butterflies from before took flight again, and I swallowed.

"Here, I'll find you a place to sit," she said, pulling out one of the chairs at her kitchen table. I thanked her and sat down, leaning my crutches against the wall. "No worries," she said. "How did that happen, by the way? If you don't mind me asking."

"Oh." I faltered a little. "I was in a car crash."

Mia waited for more, but I didn't really have the heart to elaborate further. Thankfully, she seemed to get the message. She grimaced in sympathy. "I'm sorry." I nodded and looked down, studying a scuff on the floor by her shoe. After a moment, she tried a different tactic. "I was going to make some tea. Do you want anything to drink?"

"I'm fine with tea," I said. She nodded, then went over to the cabinet. I watched as she pulled two mugs down from the cupboard, waving her hand absentmindedly at the kettle across the room while she rummaged for the cups. It started to whistle in only a few seconds. Still, it took me another moment to connect the dots.

Mia finished pouring the mugs before she looked up. Too late, I tried to clear the shock from my expression. She met my gaze, then laughed to herself, and I felt the color in my cheeks deepen. "Couldn't help myself," she said. She handed me my cup, then sat down across from me with her own. "It's a great party trick, right? If only I could actually use it at a party."

I chuckled politely, then glanced down at the tea bag floating in my mug. Again, silence took up the third chair at the table. At least the steam could help hide my embarrassment this time. Eventually, I sighed. "I'm sorry. I'm being a horrible guest," I said. I turned my gaze back to Mia. "This is all just so strange to me. So much has happened in the past week, and now meeting you . . ."

"No, no, it's okay," she said. "This is new to me too. I mean, I've had to tell people I'm Phase before, but I guess I've never really done it the other way around." She paused, thinking, then seemed to decide where to begin. "Well, I'm Mia Dominguez. I'm a grad student in the journalism school, at Everett, obviously," she said, gesturing to her view out the back window. "I mostly do public safety reporting—basically the on-the-ground, local stuff. And I've had my powers for about three years now, I think? I made myself into Phase a little bit after that, and that's pretty much been my life ever since." She shrugged. "Not much free time anymore to do anything else."

I smiled. "I'm a freshman still at Everett. I guess I'm not technically in the official school for it yet, but the goal is to go into anthropology for my major."

"Honestly, pretty similar to journalism, in my opinion," she said, winking. "So you're living on the other side of campus then?"

"In the dorms, yeah."

Mia chuckled and wrapped both her hands around her steaming mug. "Ugh, I remember that," she said. "I mean, don't get me wrong, the dorms had their upsides. But I was so happy to be out of there after that first year."

I shrugged. "It would be nice to have my own bathroom again."

"And be able to actually cook your own food," she added, then sighed. "But what about you? Your powers, I mean. I've been thinking about it ever since last night, and I know there was no way it was just luck."

I glanced down again, this time at my hands. "I . . . think I can go backward in time. I've only been able to do it for a couple seconds at a time, but if I push my hands outward" —I raised my hands as if to demonstrate, then caught myself— "I end up exactly where I was five seconds ago."

"And then you can change things," Mia added.

"Right. But no one realizes it, I guess."

Mia nodded, more to herself than to me. "How long? I mean, how long have you been able to do that?"

"What day is today?" I asked, half-sarcastically. "I found out just a couple days ago. After this" —I gestured to my crutches and to my cast— "happened."

She paused, thinking about something. She swirled the tea bag in her mug, watching it spin for a moment. "But last night, you saved those girls," she finally said. "You barely knew what you were doing, but you knew enough to save them."

"I didn't even really know what I was doing last night. It just sort of happened, and . . ." I trailed off and shrugged. "I mean, don't get me wrong. I'm glad I was there. But so much of that was luck."

"Maybe." She shrugged, then turned serious. "But I don't think it would have to stay that way."

I frowned. "I'm not sure I'm following," I said.

"How much longer are you in those crutches?" she asked. As I started to calculate, she rolled her eyes. "I want to train you."

I stopped. "Train me for what, exactly?"

She gestured to the suit she'd stuffed into the corner. "To be a superhero."

"Whoa, whoa, whoa." I held up my hands in defense, then closed them into fists and lowered them again. *I have got to learn to stop doing that.* "I mean, I'm flattered. And that would be . . . amazing." I laughed. "But that's not me. I'm not a superhero."

"Not yet," Mia said. "Hence the training part."

"I don't just mean 'not yet.' I can't—" I stumbled over my own words, trying to formulate my thoughts. "I don't think I'd even be able to help that much. No one's going to want to talk about someone who can rewind time for five seconds."

Mia shook her head. "Honey, they're already talking." My confusion must've shown on my face again because she pulled her phone out of her pocket and clicked open to her social media feed. She scrolled for a second until she found what she was looking for. "Ah, there we go." She set the phone down on the table and turned it toward me. On the screen was a video someone had shot on their phone. "Play it," she said. I tapped the screen.

It took me a moment to figure out what I was watching, but I soon realized it was a video from just after the bus crash the night before, from someone who'd stood on the opposite side of the street from where I'd been. "Oh my god," the person filming said. "What just happened?" He asked the question again, this time with an extra expletive in the middle. He zoomed in on the bus, but then his camera focus drifted just a few feet away, to Lily and her friend. And me. "Did she just push those girls out of the way?" I watched myself find my footing again as the stranger from yesterday handed me my other crutch, then turned to the girls. The person filming let out another curse. "She's on crutches! And she just pushed them out of the way of the bus! Oh my god."

As the video played out, Mia reached across the table and swiped away from it, then clicked on another post. This one was a photo of the same scene from yet another angle, captioned, "Seriously, talk about right place, right time." She scrolled down, and on another post about the crash, a commenter had posted, "Ok, but did anyone else see the girl save those two kids?"

"There are so many of these," Mia said, sliding the phone back over to her. "I kept seeing posts last night about you having a sixth sense or deserving a medal for saving those two. I mean, you're getting more attention than me." She laughed.

I opened my mouth, but I realized I didn't know what to say. I closed it again, and my face fell into a confused frown. Mia continued. "Look, I know this is a lot to think about, and I promise I'm not pushing you into anything. But if your only reason for saying no is that you don't think your . . . abilities are good enough, you're wrong." She smiled softly, her eyes shining with the gesture. "Just think about it. Please."

I hesitated, my chest tightening. It was a strange sensation, a mixture of fear and doubt and . . . hope. Hope that she was right. After a long minute, I nodded. "I'll think about it."

To my own credit, I certainly did think about what Mia had said. The rest of the day, our conversation looped in my mind, and thoughts of the incident with the bus the night before made my palms tingle. I kept catching myself balling my hands into fists and stretching my fingers out, trying to work through the feeling. And as I sat in my dorm that night and stared at the history textbook in front of me, I tried my hardest to focus on my reading. But it wasn't working. The words on the page kept blurring together until I closed the book and let out a heavy sigh.

I was honored by everything Mia had said about me and humbled that she'd trusted me with her identity. But she had to be wrong, right? I was no hero—at least no more than anyone else. Maybe that one social media post had been right. I'd just been in the right place at the right time. It was luck. That's all it was.

But even then, something about her offer nagged at me. What if I could help people? The idea, as faint of a possibility as it might've been, tugged at my heart. For the first time, I kind of wanted to be more than the quiet, bookish girl in the back of the classroom, hiding just outside of the limelight. A part of me—however small it was—kind of wanted to be like Phase.

My phone buzzed against my desk, and I startled a little at the noise. I kicked myself at the overreaction, then answered. "Hello?"

"Hey, you," Andrew said, his voice sounding tinny through the phone's small speaker. "How's the homework coming?"

I groaned and pinched the bridge of my nose with my free hand.

"That bad, huh?"

"I can't focus on anything right now. I swear I've been reading the same paragraph for the past hour."

"Maybe it's time for a break?" he questioned.

I looked out my window at the darkening sky. The stars were just starting to show their faces again from behind the clouds. "If I take a break now, then I'm not going to go back to anything."

"Well, then, is there anything I can help with?"

"Not really," I said, my frown audible in my voice. "It's mostly a lot of readings and lecture notes I have to work through." I was skipping over the whole moral dilemma I'd been given this morning about whether I wanted to help a superhero save lives, but that was probably for the best. "It's okay. I'll figure it out."

"I know you will," Andrew said. "Listen, I've got to go—I just wanted to check in with you real fast. But I'll talk to you here in a bit, okay?"

"Sure. Talk to you later." I listened for the phone call to disconnect, then leaned my elbows against my lap and hung my head. How would he react to this? How would my parents? I'd hardly kept anything from them growing up. How could I keep a secret this big, this important—especially now? Mom was already dealing with so much, and keeping something like this from her . . . The thought pressed against the weight that had already balanced on my shoulders since that afternoon, and my headache flared. I pressed my fingers against the space just above my eyes, willing it to go away.

I must've dozed off like that, because it felt like only a moment later when a knock sounded at my door. I jumped a little at the sound, knocking over my crutches that had been leaning against my desk. I muttered a curse under my breath. "Coming!" I hollered, picking them up off the floor and making my way across the room. I took a quick glance through the peephole before I opened it, but I hadn't needed to. I opened the door and offered a small smile to the person waiting on the other side.

"You said you couldn't take a break, but I figured you could at least use some dinner." Andrew grinned, nodding at the takeout containers he'd balanced in his lap. I opened my door a little wider and moved aside so he could come in—a tight fit with the size of the rooms here, but we'd found a furniture arrangement that sort of worked back at the beginning of the semester. He made his way in and set the plastic bag on an unoccupied corner of my desk. "I was heading back from the bookstore and passed that ramen place you like so much, so I stopped and grabbed some. And I promise I won't bother you if you'd rather work while you eat. Just figured you could use some company."

My stomach turned a little, and I moved to sit down on the edge of my bed. Flashes of the night before passed through my mind—the squeals and grinding from the bus's tires, the screams from the onlookers, the terror on the girls' faces once it was over. I remembered the panic that had crowded my chest as I raced toward them. What if I hadn't gotten to them in time? Misjudged the distance they were from the curb?

My reaction must've shown on my face, because I watched Andrew's own fall.

"Or if you want to be left alone, that's fine too."

"No, no, it's not that. It's just . . ." I floundered a little. "I just don't feel great. My meds are getting to me, or I'm tired or something."

He furrowed his brow as he studied my face for a moment. "You look stressed. And kind of pale."

"I'm feeling a little nauseated, honestly," I said. It was hard for me to tell if the feeling was from my anxiety about everything going on, my headache, or my erratic sleep schedule the past few nights. I frowned. "Sorry about dinner."

"Don't apologize. It's okay—I should've asked." Andrew picked up the bowl and moved it over into my mini fridge. He took his own food and placed it back in the takeout bag. "Maybe you should get some rest."

"Nah, it's okay. I'll push through. I can sleep later, but I want to make some headway."

He shot me a judgmental look. "Cassidy, come on. Trying to focus on any of this when you're tired isn't going to help. Besides, there are only so many seconds in a day."

I snorted at the irony in his statement. "Yeah, right," I muttered, then clapped my hand over my mouth. It didn't matter. Andrew's eyes widened, and I back-pedaled. "Wait, that wasn't—" I cringed, closing my eyes. "Sorry. I didn't mean that to come out that way."

"It's . . . okay." The corners of Andrew's mouth turned up in a comforting smile, but his eyes still betrayed some of his hurt. "You've been through a lot this week," he said. "With the car crash and the hospital and your dad, you're allowed to be stressed."

I swallowed against the lump forming in my throat and nodded. He turned his chair awkwardly in the tight space, then leaned forward to hug me. I returned the gesture, all the while screaming inwardly at myself. Here I was wishing I could take something back, when too late, I realized the obvious solution would've been to rewind time and actually change my reaction. But my five seconds were up.

If I couldn't think on my feet now, why did I think I'd be able to when lives were on the line?

After a moment, Andrew pulled away and took hold of one of my hands. "Seriously, it's okay. All I'm saying is that your leg isn't the only thing that deserves a chance to heal from that crash." He gave my fingers a slight squeeze, then let them fall back into my lap. "I'll head out so you can focus—and maybe get some rest." He maneuvered his chair again until it faced the door. As he reached for the handle, though, he stopped and turned toward me one last time. "You're strong, Cassidy. I know you'll get through this."

I wasn't exactly sure why the click of the door shutting behind him stung so much, but it did. I growled at myself and fell backward on my bed. I hadn't meant to hurt him. I stayed there for several minutes, staring at my ceiling as our conversation replayed in my head. The more I thought about it, the more I wondered why I hadn't just told Andrew the truth back at the hospital. Maybe it was the whole concept of secret identities that had made me hold my tongue, or maybe it was simply the fact that I didn't quite know *how* to tell him. But the decision Mia had asked me to make was one that could change my life, for the rest of my life. It wasn't one I was going to be able to make by myself.

Of course, that raised a second, more nerve-inducing dilemma. I sat up, the queasiness in my stomach roiling again. If I was going to tell Andrew, how was I going to convince him I'd gained superpowers without him wanting to send me back to the hospital for another MRI of my brain?

And how was I going to do it when showing him would mean rewinding time and erasing the act of ever showing him in the first place?

"I'm gonna need a plan," I muttered to myself. This was going to be another long and sleepless night.

It was early the next morning when I stood outside Andrew's dorm. Far earlier than I was normally known to be up and moving. Maybe that was why Andrew looked so surprised to see me when he answered the door. He still wore his pajamas—an old pair of sweatpants and a T-shirt—and his hair was still mussed in the back from his pillow. Under other circumstances, I would've commented on how cute it was. "Cassidy? Is everything okay?"

"Can I come in for a sec?"

His jaw stiffened, the way it normally did when he was nervous. I wondered if he could tell how much my own gut was twisting right now. "Sure. Come on in."

I made my way inside and waited for the door to close behind me. Andrew's roommate, Ben, was still in the room, and he waved as I came in. He was the only one who seemed oblivious to the tension in the air.

"Hey, Cassidy!" he said. "You're an early riser today."

I tried a chuckle, but my stomach was still knotted too tightly to keep it from sounding forced. "Guess so," I managed.

"Listen, I was sorry to hear about what happened with . . . everything." He tipped his chin toward my leg. "Are you doing okay?"

"As good as can be expected, I guess," I said with a shrug. "Thanks though."

"Sure thing." He paused, glancing between the two of us. It seemed he was slowly starting to pick up Andrew's tense expression and my failing attempts at pleasantries. "Well, I'll leave you two alone. You look like you want to lose the third wheel, but you're both too polite to say anything." He pursed his lips a little in a tense smile, then weaved between us to grab his coat by the door.

"Thanks, man," Andrew said as he headed out the door. Ben only nodded, and a moment later, the door eased shut behind him. Just as it did, Andrew and I turned our attention back to each other. I opened my mouth to speak before he could.

"You said last night that I could ask you for help. When you called on the phone?" I took a deep, shuddering breath. "Well, I'm asking." Andrew's features seemed to shift, but I held up a pointer finger before he could say anything. "But first, I need to show you something."

With shaky hands, I pinned one of my crutches underneath my arm and reached for the small box in my back pocket. I brought it over to Andrew's desk, then dumped its contents into my palm. Even without looking, I could feel Andrew's quizzical stare at my back. I ignored him and began to shuffle the playing cards. They arched beneath my thumbs once. Twice. Then I flipped them over and began looking at each one.

"Cassidy, what is this?"

"Shh, hang on," I pleaded. I flicked them quickly between my fingers, repeating each one under my breath as it passed. *Ace of hearts. Three of clubs. Eight of clubs. Jack of spades.* I repeated three more cards to myself, then added one more to the total. It was more than I'd managed to memorize last night, but I needed him to believe me.

"Seriously, what the hell is going on?" Andrew asked. Worry wove itself into his voice. I looked up at him, my eyebrows turned up in a silent apology. But time was up anyway. Before he could say more, I dropped the cards onto the desk and shoved my hands forward.

The cards fell into a neat pile against my fingers, bending beneath my thumbs. I took a deep breath to steady myself.

"Cassidy, what is this?" Andrew asked the question again, just like he had before.

I closed my hands around the deck, careful not to look at them, and turned my attention to Andrew. "This is going to sound strange," I began.

Andrew shrugged. "You're in my dorm room before eight on the weekend, acting cryptic, and playing solitaire," he countered.

"Please. Just trust me." I handed him the deck of cards, and after a moment, he took them. "You know every time you shuffle cards, it's a completely new combination that's never been seen before? Because there are so many cards in a deck, it's basically always going to be a unique shuffle?"

Andrew frowned. "Sure . . . But since when do you care about statistics?"

I ignored him, gesturing to the deck in his hands. "Ace of hearts. Three of clubs. Eight of clubs. Jack of spades."

"What are you talking—"

"Those are the first four cards in that deck. Then it's the seven of diamonds, the five of spades, the two of hearts, and the nine of . . . clubs, I think." Andrew's frown deepened, and he flipped the deck over in his hands, pulling the first eight cards in the exact order I'd listed. He returned the cards to the stack and looked back at me.

"Now you shuffle it."

"Cassidy . . ." he said, sounding exasperated. And maybe a tad concerned. I just looked at him expectantly, then watched the cards flutter against one another in his hand.

"Now read them out to me." He shrugged, but after a second, he did as I asked. Before he'd finished, I moved my hands again, a familiar prickle traveling through my palms.

As Andrew read off the cards and their suits, I interrupted him, listing off the next five cards in his hand.

His mouth opened a little in surprise, but after a second, he composed himself. "So, what? You know magic now?"

I laughed a little, an empty sound, then shook my head. I studied my shoes. "Something happened to me in that crash. I realized it the other night, but I guess I didn't believe it, or I didn't know how to explain it." My voice quivered in my throat, echoing my nerves. "I rewound time," I said softly.

"You what?"

"I rewound time." The words came a little louder this time. "I don't know what happened exactly, but since the crash, I can push myself backward in time. Only by a few seconds, but . . ." I looked up at him, took note of his guarded expression. My anxiety creeped up another notch. "It's how I knew what the cards were going to be. The weird brain scan that Dr. Babu was talking about, the one with the faulty equipment? I think—"

Andrew sucked in a breath and looked away, his gaze losing focus as he stared off somewhere behind me. He ran a hand through his messed-up hair. I could tell he was formulating sentences in his head. Trying to figure out what to say. To choose his words carefully so as not to upset me.

My heart wasn't hammering anymore. Now it just sank. "I'm sorry. It sounds crazy. And the cards were . . . a stupid idea, I know. But I couldn't think of how else I could tell you." I squeezed my eyes shut. "I didn't even want to tell you. But Friday there was this bus crash, and someone saw me pull this girl out of the way. And now everything's so . . . complicated."

"A bus crash?" he asked quietly. I opened my eyes. His eyes flicked back over to mine, his expression just a little less guarded than before. "I heard about that. Ben mentioned it last night. He said he heard Phase showed up. You were there too?"

I nodded. I watched as he absentmindedly adjusted his glasses, then readjusted them, chewing this over in his mind. There was more I wanted to tell him, but I was trying to gauge the waters, to figure out how much of my story he believed. I bit down my tongue in order to keep quiet. If I hadn't been on crutches, I would've started pacing. Finally, though, he looked up.

"Look, Cassidy. I'm trying to understand what you're saying, but—"

"Please believe me," I muttered, the words slipping out before I could stop them.

He softened. "I'm trying to," he said. Yet just as quickly, his expression grew serious again. "But you have to know how this all sounds."

"What else can I do to prove it to you?"

"I don't know," he huffed. He turned away from me and ran his hands through his hair again as he thought. "Maybe just give me some time."

I scoffed inwardly. *How ironic.* Outwardly, I bit my lip, fighting against the flurry of emotions that were swarming to the surface. So many words ran through my head, so many things I wanted to ask or say. It took all my effort to close my eyes and simply nod. "Okay," I said. "I—I'm sorry. I shouldn't have said anything." I turned to head out, not able to look up from where I stared at the floor in front of me. As I reached the door, though, he spoke again.

"Cassidy, wait." I paused but didn't turn around. "I didn't mean—I didn't mean for you to leave." He sighed, and I could hear the layers of pain and desperation in his voice. This was hurting him as much as it was me.

"It's okay," I told him. I should've known it would go like this. Still, I hesitated at the door. My fingers still stung, enough so that the handle of my crutches felt like it was made of needles. Maybe he didn't believe me, but . . . "Can I just ask you something?" I took his silence as a yes. "I want to be able to help people," I said, choosing each word deliberately. "And someone I met thinks I can do that. She *wants* me to. But I'm not sure if I can." Anger boiled in my core, at myself more than anyone else. I wished more than anything I could change all of this, take back everything I'd said and start over. But that's not how life worked. Even for me. We only ever got a few seconds to decide things that could change our lives or the lives of the people around us forever. I only got five seconds, one choice, to try and alter. And, well . . .

"What are you asking, Cassidy?"

I turned to face him again. "What difference can one choice make?" I asked.

One second passed, then another. I could hear them ticking away on the alarm clock he kept beside his bed. They counted out the time and the growing space between us. Finally, though, he answered.

"It can make a world of difference."

As I stepped back out onto the sidewalk in front of Andrew's dorm, I allowed myself a moment to think. I leaned back against the rough cement wall beside the entryway and closed my eyes. I sighed. My breath still caught in my chest, but it was starting to come a little easier.

I'd told Andrew. And he hadn't quite believed me—but he'd said he would try, and that was something to hold onto now, I guess. More importantly, he'd reminded me of something I'd failed to consider since I'd first talked to Phase.

A world of difference . . .

After another moment had passed, I opened my eyes and pulled out my phone, tapping on the familiar blue icon and scrolling until I found what I was looking for. One of the videos Mia had shown me yesterday morning. I tapped on the "play" button and watched the bus barrel toward the light pole. This time, I focused my attention on the two girls. Their faces were grainy and pixelated on the screen, but I could make out enough of the image to jog my own memories of that night. Lily's wide-eyed, numb expression. Her friend's quivering lip and teary eyes. In another reality, the one before I had stepped in . . . I didn't even want to think about that.

But in this one, I had stepped in. As the video automatically replayed itself, I turned my attention to myself this time. There was a moment, however subtle, when my demeanor changed. I saw my face shift and my muscles tense. I remembered the adrenaline coursing through my veins in that moment. The clock that had started to count down in my head as I raced toward the girls.

I remembered the decision I'd made without even thinking about it—to go back in time and stop the tragedy I'd already almost seen happen. Only now, I realized the decision I'd truly been making. Mia hadn't needed to ask me yesterday morning to think about working with her. I hadn't needed to ask Andrew if he thought my power would be enough. In that instant, with those girls, I'd already made my choice.

I swiped out of the video screen and over to my phone's contact list. I scrolled a bit until I found the number I'd saved a few days ago, then hit the "call" button and held it up to my ear.

On the second ring, the line clicked on. "Hello?"

"Mia, it's Cassidy. I thought some more about what you said."

"Yeah?"

My voice rang clear and confident, and I was surprised to realize it matched my true emotions. "I'm in."

CHAPTER FIVE

A FEW DAYS LATER, I sat against the wall and leaned my head back, working to steady my breathing. A little more than a week ago, I'd still been Cassidy Sinclair. No one special—just another student at Everett, whose biggest worry had been failing her midterms. Then had come the car crash. The one that had put my father into a coma. That had given me abilities I couldn't explain. Now I stood in Phase's living room, morning sun just starting to cast golden rays onto the floor of the apartment, training to become a superhero.

Saying "a lot had changed" would've been the biggest understatement of my life. It seemed the only thing that hadn't was my name.

I'd been here with Mia since about 5:30 in the morning. Now, it was about two hours later, and my muscles ached. My arms felt like rubber, and even my legs protested a little. I reached a hand down and adjusted the Velcro on my walking boot. It was a nice change from the crutches, albeit earlier than I'd expected. Dr. Babu had seemed impressed at my last appointment with how quickly I was healing. I was just happy to be able to use my hands again when I walked.

"Is your foot okay?" Mia asked, nodding toward the boot.

"It's good so far," I reassured her. It felt weird to put weight on it again, but the ache was one I was willing to ignore for now.

"Then are you about ready to go again?" She grinned, slipping the strike pads back onto her hands and hitting them together. I groaned.

"Am I allowed to say no?" I heaved myself back onto my feet and took my place in the center of the room. With all the furniture pushed aside, the place managed to seem a lot bigger than when I'd first visited. Mia had laid down yoga mats as well to try and muffle our footfalls. I found my spot in the taped-off "arena" she'd marked on those mats, then adjusted my stance and held my arms at the ready.

"Just like we've been practicing," she said. I nodded. She waited a beat, then flashed one of the pads toward me. I threw a jab, and she responded by turning the other pad toward me, which I answered with another punch. We continued for a few minutes, dancing around the room and each other. I wasn't quite as light on my feet as she was, nor as fast to react. But I was able to hold my own for the most part. At least, I thought so. Every few hits, Mia would critique my form or say something to goad me into fighting harder. I could tell she was holding back still. She was slowing things down so I could keep up and think about each move individually, and though I understood why, part of me wondered how I'd manage if she were really trying.

Maybe not as well as I wanted to believe. After a couple of minutes, I missed one of my swings, glancing off the side of the pad and knocking myself off-balance a little. I righted myself quickly, but Mia waved me off as she reached for her water bottle, signaling I could rest. I dropped my hands to my sides.

"That was pretty good," Mia commented before she tipped the water bottle up to her mouth.

I shot her a skeptical look.

"What, that last one?" She shrugged. "We've been at this a while. You get a pass."

"I mistimed it. I thought you were going to be moving slower than you were."

"I guess that means I know you weren't using your powers," she said. One corner of her mouth turned up in a tilted smile. "Speaking of" —she set her water back down, then leaned against the edge of her dining table— "why don't you step it up a notch and show me what you've *really* got?"

I turned toward her, searching her face to make sure I understood correctly. "We're using our powers?"

"Let's start out with just yours for now. Mine are . . . a little less welcome in indoor spaces when I'm in a fight," she mused. "I'd like to not get evicted."

Oh. Right. I nodded, then glanced down at my palms. I hadn't tried rewinding time since I'd talked to Andrew. I squeezed my fingers into a fist and then stretched them outward, and my heart beat a little faster in my chest.

"We'll take it slow," Mia promised. Her expression softened the slightest bit. "Before we do anything, just remind me what it's like."

I thought for a moment. "For me, it's this . . . instant playback. Like the footage they use in football games? It's like someone rewound everything, except I'm the only one who remembers anything. And it's only five seconds. That's all I've ever managed to go."

"'Instant playback'? Do you mean 'instant replay'?"

My ears burned. "I thought that's what it was called."

Mia chuckled a little. "Not quite, sports fan, but you're close enough." Her nose scrunched with her smile. "Is there a limit to what you can change?"

"Not that I've found, really. Whatever can happen in five seconds, I guess."

"And I won't be able to tell?" she asked.

"Did you remember the bus?"

Mia nodded to herself, considering. "Fair point. Okay, then here's what I want you to do. We're not using the pads this time. You're going to try and block my hits for sixty seconds. Rewind as many times as you need. If you can get some of your own jabs in, great, but just focus on blocking."

I nodded, maybe a little more confidently than I felt, and brought my arms up to block like before. A second passed, two, and then Mia leapt toward me. Her swings came almost faster than I could recognize them, and any technical practice I'd had left my mind. I batted a jab at my shoulder away with one hand. She answered with a hook from the other direction, and I ducked to the side just before it could reach my jaw.

A deep pain rippled through my ribs from one of her hits I'd failed to dodge. It forced the air from my lungs in a sudden rush, and I stumbled for a second.

"Rewind it," she told me. I shoved my hands outward.

My hands tingled as I batted her hit away this time, then danced to the side of her swing at my jaw. I swatted her hand away from my ribs, then took a step back, trying to open the space between us. Wrong move. Mia crossed her foot behind mine, tripping me on my good leg. The yoga mats did little to cushion my fall onto my back. I muttered a curse, then pushed my hands through the air in front of me.

I blinked a few times, trying to fight the vertigo from being upright again so suddenly. I almost forgot to move away from the hook and the second blow to my ribs. I stumbled a little as I moved away this time, dropping my hands to rebalance myself. Mia took the opportunity, striking toward my stomach.

This was turning into the least-fun memory game I'd ever played. My fingers were growing numb from the electric bolts shooting through my arms as I tried the third time. Jab toward shoulder. Hook toward jaw, then ribs. A small hop backward this time to keep out of reach of her legs and arms. This time, I made it farther in the fight, swatting her leg away as she brought a knee toward my stomach, then sweeping my own leg behind hers as she readjusted her stance. It knocked her off-balance in the same way her move had knocked me down earlier. She caught herself before she fell, but a fire burned in her eyes when she looked at me. Her smile invited a challenge as she swung another hit at my ribs.

I guess I wasn't quite up to the challenge yet.

When I rewound the seconds this time, I held up a hand in defeat, using the other to cradle my side. "Time out," I wheezed. My hands seared, and I could feel my ribs turning colors to a deep shade of plum. I stood up a little straighter and began to pace, wringing my palms to get feeling back.

Mia straightened, and worry crossed her features. "Jesus. What happened?"

"You hit harder than I thought. And I think I keep my injuries when I rewind."

"To be fair, you were supposed to be blocking," she offered. "But I meant with your hands." She pointed as I shook them back and forth in front of me. As best I could, I explained to her the sensation I got when I rewound time. Mia frowned.

"Well, that's not great." I just winced in response. Before either of us could say more though, her phone buzzed from across the room. She went over and clicked it on, frowning a little as she read her message.

"Newspaper stuff?" I asked.

"Uh . . . sort of. Maybe Phase stuff. We'll see." She looked up from her screen. "It's almost eight o'clock anyway."

"I guess I probably need to get going then." I took a few more seconds to recover, then gathered my things from the corner of the room. By the time I was finished, Mia was almost done packing her own bag, and I waved bye to her over my shoulder as I headed out the door.

Back in my dorm room, I had just enough time to change out of my sweaty exercise wear and into clean clothes before I had to leave again to meet up with Andrew. I wrinkled my nose as I tossed my leggings and socks into the laundry bin. I'd already visited the laundry rooms once this week—maybe it was about time I bought some new workout clothes instead of relying only on what I'd bought for gym class back in middle school.

By the time I finished changing and made it to the student center in the middle of campus, Andrew was already waiting for me. He'd parked his chair by a set of large bay windows that stretched out over the sidewalk to create a covered patio for one of the dining halls. From here, they gave a perfect view of the students milling about outside and of the university's pride and joy off in the distance. Even from afar, it was an opposing monument: a white slab building with a domed top, encircled by windows and capped with a bronze spire. The faculty had a fancier name for it, probably the same as one of the founders of the school, but none of the students could ever remember it. To us, it was just the physics building—and a towering testament to the chunk of our tuition money that the school used for upkeep.

"Morning, you," I offered as I came up beside him.

He turned to meet my gaze and smiled warmly back. "Morning to you too . . . finally."

I knew he was joking, but guilt still crept into my throat. "Sorry it took me so long. I had . . . a thing."

He nodded. "Training?" he asked, keeping his voice low.

"Yeah," I said with a grimace. "I think my bruises have bruises." I adjusted my backpack strap away from the sore spot on my ribs at the reminder. Andrew went quiet, his gaze drifting back to the window. Maybe he was just nervous about talking about it in public. Still, something about his expression made me pause. I had wanted to tell him about getting to use my powers, but I held my tongue.

"You know, I keep trying to picture what I think she looks like," he said after a minute had passed, "but nothing seems to fit. So it's like she's just constantly wearing the helmet in my head."

I stifled a laugh, and Andrew's grin returned.

"Oh, your mom texted me this morning by the way. She asked if I could ask you to call her. Apparently you weren't responding to her messages, and she was getting worried."

Of course she was. I chuckled again, but this time, the feeling fizzled out of me before it reached my chest. Any other time, it would've been my dad telling me to call her. Andrew took my hand in his and squeezed. "I told her you were retaking a test this morning, but that you'd call her later." His voice was softer, tiptoeing around the subject.

I sighed. "Thanks. For covering for me."

"Of course," he said. He gave my hand another squeeze, then glanced at his phone. "I should head to class. Wanna walk with me?"

I still had some time to kill before my next class, so I agreed. The two of us made some small talk as we headed toward the next building over, but nothing of any importance. Mostly, we just enjoyed the morning quiet—the birds chirping, the wind rustling the leaves in the trees or scattered on the ground—and being in each other's company. When we reached Andrew's calc classroom, I gave him a peck on the cheek, then continued toward the lecture hall on the other end of the building, where my first class was.

When I arrived, a muffled sea of voices was already spilling out into the hallway. I wasn't exactly sure which class it was that met before mine, but it always sounded dreadful. The professor's voice droned on in every sense of the word. I hadn't started showing up early until I'd been forced to maneuver the crowds of students while on crutches, but even in just that week, I'd fallen asleep to his monotone a few times., I sighed and settled onto a bench on the neighboring wall. Pulling my laptop and earbuds out of my bag, I set up my makeshift workspace and opened up a reading I'd been trying to finish.

Unfortunately, the earbuds only worked to drown out the distractions coming from the outside world. They did little to help the monotonous buzzing coming from my own mind. Every few minutes, I pulled my hands away from my laptop to stretch my fingers and circle my wrists. This morning's practice still lingered in my palms like radio static, and the rest of me felt as if I'd been run over by one of the campus shuttles. I was glad Mia was working me so hard, but it was an unwelcome reminder of how out of shape I truly was. Add my powers into the mix, and I was starting to regret not opting for the nap idea earlier.

After a few more minutes of re-reading the same two paragraphs in my reading, I gave up, closing the laptop and slipping it back in my bag. The lecture hall wouldn't be emptying out for another ten or fifteen minutes. Not enough time to do anything productive. I picked up my phone out of habit, but I let my finger hover above the screen before clicking on anything. *Well,* I thought, *there is one thing I could do.*

I pursed my lips, then opened the phone's keypad. The line rang twice before she picked up.

"Hello?"

"Hey, Mom." I fiddled with the cord to my earbuds as I spoke, rolling it between my thumb and pointer finger. "Andrew said you'd wanted me to call."

Her voice immediately went up in pitch. A forced cheeriness. "Hey, sweetie. I just wanted to know how you were doing. You haven't been calling." Even through the fake smile in her voice, I could tell she was frustrated.

I sighed. "I know. I'm sorry." And I was. "I've just been so tired. I'm trying to catch up on everything I missed in my classes, but . . ."

"That's right. Andrew told me about that. How was your test?"

"Huh? Oh . . . it was fine." I hesitated, then chuckled a little. "Actually, my hand's still aching a little."

"Lots of writing?"

"Yeah, sort of." The conversation faltered, and I listened to the line go quiet for a few seconds. My mom sniffed. She'd been crying, I knew. "How's Dad?" I asked quietly.

For a moment, I thought maybe our connection had dropped. But then I heard the waver in her voice. "Still the same. The doctors haven't noticed any change."

I closed my eyes. Pain stabbed at my chest again, but it didn't come from any bruise.

"He's getting visitors, which I think he likes," she continued. "The neighbors sent flowers, and the nurses said a man called yesterday to ask how he was doing. I think he must've worked with him in the physics department, but they didn't get a name."

"That's nice at least," I offered. But my words no longer sounded convincing, even to my ears.

Mom's composure was slipping too. "Yes, it was," she said, but her voice had grown strained and stuffy, and I knew she was suddenly feeling as alone in that hospital room as I was sitting on this bench.

I was starting to wonder if me calling had truly been a good thing for either of us.

"Do you want to come see—" She started to ask something, but as she spoke, her voice was drowned out by the growing murmur from within the lecture hall. A few seconds later, the door opened, and students began filtering out into the hall-way. *Saved by the bell.*

"Sorry, Mom, the class before mine just let out, so I've got to go."

"Oh. Well, that's okay, sweetie. I'm glad you called," she said. Loneliness still clung to her words.

"Me too. Love you, Mom."

"I love you, too." The phone call ended, and as I slipped my earbuds into my pocket and shouldered my bag, I found myself glad I got to choose which moments I relived.

The morning's lecture seemed to drag along even more than usual. I was looking at the clock at the front of the lecture hall every fifteen minutes, only to see the minute hand had only moved ahead by two. It wasn't that I had anywhere in particular I wanted to be; I just wanted a chance to escape from where I was now. To somewhere I wouldn't have to try to pay attention to a boring lecture. To where I wouldn't instead be stuck in my head about the conversation with my mom, my thoughts about my dad. At this point, with as exhausted as I was from training this morning, I'd even just take somewhere with more comfortable chairs.

When the professor finally dismissed everyone for the day, I was one of the first out the door.

Back out in the crisp breeze, I felt a little better. I let myself pause as I drank the cool air into my lungs. Then I turned down the road that headed toward my dorm. The area was quiet this time of day. Most people were in class or at the dining halls in the center of campus. I normally would've been too, especially after a breakfast of only a banana and half a granola bar, like I'd eaten this morning. But all I really wanted to do today was sleep. It was better at least than overanalyzing Andrew's distant look this morning, or the relief I'd felt that Mom hadn't finished asking her question about me visiting Dad.

I was kicking a stone along with me as I walked, watching it skitter ahead of me on the sloping sidewalk. It had stayed with me for a while, dancing just in front of the toe of my boot. Then, about halfway down the street, my phone buzzed. I stopped in my tracks, accidentally sending the rock sailing. I watched as it bounced into the grass near the curb. I pursed my lips a little tighter, then pulled out my phone.

Hey. You busy?

It was Mia. I sent back: *Not in the slightest. What's up?*

I watched the speech bubble that popped up as she typed, then got back: *Can you meet me at the student newsroom? You know where it is?*

I knew the building. It was fairly nondescript, tucked away by some of the larger, more historical buildings on campus, back in the direction I'd come from. I passed it every Monday morning on my way to the library. I told her I'd be there in five minutes, then turned and headed back up the hill.

The journalism school was much more interesting on the inside, I had to admit. Stepping through the set of double doors at the entrance a few minutes later, I found myself in a spacious common area, dotted with couches, beanbag chairs, and a couple of sets of long tables and chairs. The walls were lined with individual workstations, each with a desktop monitor and keyboard, and in the corner nearby, a wire stand held copies of the newspaper's newest issue. Everything here was very, *very* blue. The carpet and chairs were somehow all a matching shade of cobalt, one of Everett's school colors, making the plain walls and white tabletops a relief to my eyes.

I scanned the place for Mia. There were only a few other students in the room. A small group had gathered at one of the far tables and spoke in hushed tones, and another girl lounged in one of the beanbag chairs, ignoring the notebook in her lap and scrolling through her phone instead. A few of the monitors at the back of the room were also occupied, but Mia was nowhere in sight. As I surveyed the area, my eyes landed on a metal plaque hanging to my left. SANTINA ENQUIRER, FLOOR 2.

I felt a tap on my shoulder and nearly leapt from my skin. I turned to see Mia, one of her hands raised up in front of her face as she tried to hold in a laugh. "Sorry. Had to step outside to get something and saw you come in," she explained. "Couldn't resist."

I managed to shrug off the startled feeling enough to give a small laugh. "I'm guessing you're on the second floor?" She came around to stand at my side as I gestured to the plaque.

"Oh, yeah. This is just kind of a study spot. A lot of the digital kids like to film down here, but I feel like most people just end up taking naps on the couches." She shrugged. "Anyway, that's not what I wanted to show you." Without saying more, she beckoned for me to follow her, then headed toward the door by the wall placard.

We entered into a concrete stairwell, cold and dusty. The door tossed shadows along the wall as it shut behind us, though it was hard to believe there were any shadows at all—the bulbs above us hummed with the effort of even the faint glow they gave off. The only other light filtered in through the window of the door the next flight up, but Mia turned to lead me downstairs instead. I frowned and followed her. At the base of the stairs, we walked into an alcove just off to the side of the building's basement entrance. Then, she stopped.

I waited, then laughed a little, hoping it would hide the knot of discomfort forming in my stomach. Quiet as it was, the sound still pinballed off the walls. "What's with the shady meeting place?" I whispered. That was when I noticed the thin package she held at her side. Mia grinned so wide her eyes shone.

"I thought about what you said earlier this morning," she said, her voice low, "and it gave me an idea." She handed me the package. "Try them on."

I looked at her for a second, raising my eyebrows, then at the package in my hand. It was a plain mailing envelope, so the outside held no clues as to the contents. But I could feel an odd shape inside. I opened the envelope on its torn edge and slid the contents out into my hand. It was a pair of fingerless gloves. I frowned and slipped them on, tightening the Velcro on the back. They were a deep shade of plum, with thick white padding on the palms. Comfortable, but . . . "I'm going to be honest—I'm confused." I looked back up at Mia.

"Now try rewinding time."

Suddenly, I understood. My eyes widened, and I looked down at my hands again. I turned them over, studying them. Then, I pushed them outward.

Everything felt the same. I was still looking down at the gloves on my hands. Turning them over in front of my face, stretching my fingers.

"Now try rewinding time."

Mia spoke again, exactly the same way she had the first time. I looked up at her. "I think I just did."

"And?"

Both hands raised in front of my mouth, as if saying it aloud would prove me wrong. "I didn't feel anything."

Mia let out a surprised laugh of her own, then clapped a hand over her mouth at the echo. "Nothing?" she asked, her voice a whisper. "I was just guessing . . . They're an old pair of rock-climbing gloves, but they have an insulated grip on the palms. Wait, try it again."

This time, I took a glance at Mia's watch, counting to myself and noting the second hand as it ticked around the circle. As I watched it, I made the same motion as before. Instantly, the seconds hand leapt backward.

Now I was the one whose smile reached from ear to ear. I met Mia's gaze and nodded at her. She stood up a little straighter, then held out a hand. "Nice to finally meet you . . . Playback." I raised an eyebrow, and she shrugged. "It had a nice ring to it," she admitted, "even if it wasn't the right word."

I felt the embarrassment return to my cheeks again, but at the same time, a sudden swell rose in my chest. I paused, trying the name out in my head. Cassidy Sinclair. Playback.

I reached for her outstretched hand and shook it. Scratch what I'd said before: It looked like my name had changed after all.

Chapter Six

J ust as Mia's hand fell away from mine, something buzzed against my leg, the sound bouncing off the walls around us. I startled at the noise, then laughed at myself. I couldn't help it; excitement spilled out of me. *Playback*. I pulled out my phone and glanced at the screen before I answered.

"Hey, Andrew."

"Hey . . ." came his voice on the other end. "You've got a weird echo. Where are you?"

"Oh, sorry. I'm in a stairwell." I caught Mia's eye and mouthed the word "boyfriend," and she just waved me on, a smile still tugging at the corners of her mouth.

"Ah. Explains why I don't recognize it then." I could hear the smirk in his voice, and I rolled my eyes. "Do you have a second? Can I share some good news?"

The smile that leaked out into his voice made it hard not to feel another surge of optimism. "Yeah, go for it."

"Apparently the physics department is getting this really cool equipment later this year. We just heard the announcement. An alum is donating one of his prototypes to the lab—I guess to try and bring back interest in particle acceleration? We'll literally be the only ones in the world with this tech."

"Wait, particle acceleration? As in what Dad researched?"

"Yeah." The word stretched out a little as his voice quieted. "I guess the work he published was a big reason for Everett getting the donation over other schools."

"That's . . . wow." My attention drifted to one of the shadows in the corner as a familiar hollow ache reawakened in my chest. I found my grin again, but it was just a little smaller this time. "That's amazing."

"Everyone's really excited," Andrew said on the other end. For a moment, there was a pause on the line, just like with my mom that morning. Then, he cleared his throat. "I've got to head to my next class, but I . . . figured you'd like to know. You know?"

I scuffed my boot against the ground, smiling sadly. "Yeah, I know. Thanks."

"Of course." He went quiet again, then asked, "Did you want to meet up tonight? I was thinking dinner at your dorm?"

"Sounds great," I said. He said something else, probably a suggestion for what we could eat, but I replied without really processing it. My thoughts had already drifted somewhere else. We exchanged a quick goodbye before he hung up, and I waited for the line to fully disconnect before I put my phone away.

"I didn't know your dad studied particle acceleration," Mia said. She looked curious, but a grimace quickly erased it from her features. "Sorry, I didn't mean to eavesdrop. I just over-heard—"

I shrugged. "You're good."

She smiled a little, her eyebrows knitting together in sympa-thy. At this point, she'd heard bits and pieces of my account of the car wreck. I hadn't been able to convey the whole story, but she'd heard enough to know that night had taken away as much as it had given me. "You okay?" she asked me.

I nodded. "I'm okay." It was the truth, though the answer was relative these days.

Mia nodded and pursed her lips as if she understood. This time, it was her phone that broke the silence. She glanced down at the screen and *tsk*ed. "My editor," she said. "He's wondering where I am."

"Oh?"

"Nah, it's nothing big." She shrugged. "I'm on general as-signment duty today, so I'm supposed to be listening to the police scanners in case anything interesting comes through."

I raised my eyebrows. "Isn't that kind of all the time for you?"

She laughed. "Ironic, right? Listen, I actually have more I want to show you than just the gloves, but the rest'll have to wait until you get the boot off. Until then, bring those tomorrow. We'll see if we can make you into less of a punching bag with a few more practice sessions."

More to show me? I wanted to ask, but Mia had already started back up the steps, and I got the sense she wanted her surprise to remain that way. I followed her lead, pausing at the landing for the first floor. "Thank you again. This is . . . amazing." I smiled as I reached for the door handle, but Mia blocked it with her own hand before I could open it. I furrowed my brow, and she pointed her chin toward my hands. My cheeks flushed as I undid the gloves and slid them into my backpack.

"You'll get more aware of it, don't worry," she promised with a laugh. "And no problem. I'm glad they help." She moved her hand and started up the second flight of steps, giving me a final wave over her shoulder. I answered back, then turned to make my way out into the daylight.

Even after Andrew's phone call, I somehow felt better and more awake than I had before. The campus seemed brighter. *I* felt a little lighter. Maybe it was the fact that I'd been able to get out of my own head, even if only for a few minutes. Or maybe it was stress about the pain in my hands that I hadn't realized I'd been shouldering until I wasn't anymore.

That night, I ate dinner with Andrew up in my dorm—sandwiches from a small deli on campus. My excitement had come in spurts throughout the day, spiking each time I remembered the gloves or my interaction with Mia in the stairwell. Now, though, it was back in full force. I wanted to tell someone about everything that had happened, and except for Mia, he was the only person in my life I didn't have secrets from.

"So this new equipment you guys are getting," I started, picking up a pepper that had fallen off my sandwich. "Do you know what it is exactly?"

He shook his head. "No, not yet. But it's supposed to be a really big deal. I guess they got a huge grant they're putting toward the research with it as well, but all I really know is the connection to what your dad used to study."

I smiled, though I wasn't sure how well the gesture reached the rest of my face. The conversation with Mom from earlier in the day pushed its way back into my mind. Andrew paused, looking at me. Reaching over, he placed a comforting hand on mine, then pulled me closer, scooping me toward him until I leaned my head on his chest.

We stayed like that for a moment, neither of us speaking. Then, after a moment— "I've got to be honest," he said, pursing his lips so he spoke out of the side of his mouth, "when they told me about the grant, I was kind of hoping it was going to be a table and microscope I can actually reach from my chair, but ya know . . ."

I laughed a little, then looked up at him. "Want to take bets on whether you actually get any sort of accommodations in the lab before you graduate?"

"Ha! Are we talking the university's version of accommodations, or ones that actually work?" he asked. His voice rumbled against my ear from deep in his chest. "I guess I should be fair. The professors are pretty good about things for the most part."

I smiled, letting the room fall silent again. I knew he was trying to distract me from thoughts about my dad. But I also wasn't going to fight him on it. "I actually had something exciting happen today too," I offered after a little while. "I mean,

I guess it's not the-Nobel-Prize-goes-to-Andrew-Simmons-level exciting, but *I* think it's pretty cool."

"Oh, yeah?" he asked, leaning back and cocking an eyebrow. "Wait, does this have to do with *you* or with . . . the other you?"

We both laughed, and I told him about using my powers this morning, the gloves, and my new name.

"A name?" He frowned. "Like a nickname, or . . . oh. Oh!"

I nodded. "It's 'Playback,'" I told him.

"Playback." He tried the word out on his own. There was a silence, as if he were thinking about something. But then, I felt his lips brush against my forehead. "I like it," he whispered.

A smile broke out on my face. This one was genuine, I realized. And though sadness and worry had already made their homes in my heart over the past week, as I sat there, a different feeling started to grow alongside them. It wasn't enough to chase them away entirely; I doubted anything ever would. But its warmth was enough, for now, to quiet the pain just a little.

A week and a half later, I stood in Mia's living room once again. I rolled my neck, then readied my hands. Even standing still, my right leg felt lighter. It was finally boot-free—not quite according to my orthopedist's instructions, but with as cumbersome as the hunk of plastic was to deal with, I'd decided I'd worn it long enough to call it good. Mia grinned, her hair bouncing as she hopped in place on the tips of her toes. I waited for the lunge that I knew was coming, and our dance began. Her hands flashed in my periphery as I ducked, blocked, and jabbed, running through the moves I already remembered. As the fight started to change, I shifted tactics, opening up the space between us to give myself more reaction time. I made note of how she reacted to different moves: a knee was slapped back down, a palm strike was caught and twisted away, a hit connected but was answered with one of her own. It didn't matter how often I rewound the clock anymore. With my new gloves, I had as much time as I needed.

The dance continued for longer than it usually would—even longer for me—but eventually, I slipped up. I swung toward Mia a little wider than usual, and she caught my wrist, using my own momentum to pin my arm to my back. I leaned back on my heels, trying to maintain my balance, when she quickly caught hold of the other arm, holding it in place against my back. I struggled to break free of her grasp, but without my arms, I couldn't rewind and try again. After a few seconds passed, I sighed. She released her grip. "Time's up," she said with a smile.

"Yeah, yeah." I rubbed at the sore spot on my wrist. "Just once, I wonder if I'm going to win one of these."

She shrugged, then smiled. "If it helps, I'm not really going easy on you anymore."

"I can tell," I said. But I answered her smile with one of my own. "Should we go again?"

"Actually," she said, "I had something else I wanted to show you." She disappeared for a moment around the corner, and

I heard rustling from somewhere in her bedroom. A few moments later, she came back, a large cardboard box in her hands. She stopped and held it out to me. "I know; a bit early for Christmas."

I raised my eyebrows at her, but I took the box. It was an old package that had obviously been through the mail, the tape already sliced on top, the shipping label halfway peeled off. I moved to balance the package on the back of the couch, then opened the flaps.

My mouth fell open, but no sound came out. Slowly, I pulled out the contents and, one by one, held them up to examine them. Mia stood just off to the side, her arms crossed. I looked back at her, and she smirked. "I told you, 'once you got your boot off.'"

"Where did you get it?" I finally managed.

"Just a friend." She shrugged but didn't say any more, and I didn't pry. She stepped closer. "Well, what are you waiting for?" She gestured to the suit in my hands. "Let's see how it fits."

A few minutes later, I stood in front of the vanity mirror in the bathroom. The suit was a perfect fit. My eyes traced the zigzagging pattern that ran across my chest, the lines from reinforced stitching and extra padding that traveled up my arms and legs. The top bore the same colors as my gloves: a shade of deep plum underneath, with white fabric on the shoulders and collar. The pants were darker—a dusky eggplant that faded down into gray, almost black, to blend in with my shoes. Even with it still in a messy braid from my workout, my copper hair was a shock against the fabric.

"Don't forget the most important part," Mia added. I turned to face her. She held out the last item that had been in the box. It was the simplest piece by far—just a small piece of dark purple fabric, with a white ear loop on either end. Mia gestured how to put it on, and I copied her instruction, pulling the cloth over the bottom half of my face and securing it behind my ears. "How does it feel?" she asked.

I looked back at the mirror. Everything about me seemed more confident. My shoulders seemed broader. I think I even stood taller than normal. I was watching a reflection, but it wasn't mine. "Different," I finally decided. "A really good different."

Mia laughed. "Well, you look good. And different," she said. "It fits you—and I don't just mean the size." She paused, looking me up and down once more. "Congratulations, Playback. I'd say you're ready."

I cocked my head at her. "'Ready'? You don't mean . . . ?"

"You're as prepared for the real thing as I was when I started. Probably more so." She shrugged her shoulders. "There's only so much of this stuff you can learn with pads and yoga mats. Eventually, you'll have to move beyond practicing and be part of a real fight. I mean, most of the time, you don't even get a choice. You just . . ." Her thought trailed off. Her gaze wandered away, somewhere toward the wall, though I could tell her mind wandered farther. "Training helps, but your adrenaline's going to step in, and you'll just have to trust yourself."

A second or two passed before she pulled herself back from whatever memory she'd been lost in. She took a breath and met my eyes again. "Besides," she said, forcing a smile, "even when I try to make it tough, I'm always going to pull my punches with you. The bad guys won't." She patted her hand against my shoulder, then turned away to grab her water bottle.

My eyebrows knitted as I watched her. With her back turned, she seemed to hesitate a moment, long enough that I debated whether I should say something. This was a side of her I'd never seen before, one that seemed almost . . . haunted. Vulnerable. But the moment passed before I got the chance. As Mia turned around, she took a swig from her water, looking up at the clock as if nothing had happened. She made a small noise in her throat. "I didn't realize how late it was. I probably should head to the newsroom soon."

Whatever window into her past had peeked open a moment ago, she had just closed it tight once again.

I took my own look at the clock—one of those modern art pieces with a colorful, vaguely round disk and hands that stretched out beyond its face—and tried to work out the time it read. When I finally did, I muttered a weak curse. "I need to go too. Like, right now." I pulled off the mask and hurried to the corner where I'd stashed my other belongings.

Mia turned to watch me as I worked, leaning her back against the wall. "Wait, did you have something after this? Do you have to get to class or something?"

I undid the side zip in the jacket of my suit and pulled it over my head, replacing it with the Everett hoodie I'd been wearing on the way over. "No, not a class. I'm supposed to retake a test this morning with my history professor." I slipped off the rest of the costume piece by piece as I talked, stuffing it all into the bottom of my backpack.

Mia clucked her tongue. "I hated history. Probably a good thing I don't have your powers." I paused, shooting her a curious look from across the room. She answered with one of her own. "What? You can rewind time, and you're telling me you've never thought about using it to sneak an extra peek at the answers without anyone knowing?"

I bit my bottom lip to contain a laugh. "Well, for one, only five seconds, remember?" I held up five fingers on my free hand as if that was answer enough. I used the other to grab my water bottle and stuff it into my bag, then zipped the whole thing closed and stood. "And two . . . no. I just never really thought of it, I guess."

Mia just shrugged. "You're a better student than me. That would've been one of the first things I tried."

I just chuckled under my breath, still not entirely sure if she was serious. "Maybe it is a good thing I've got these powers instead of you," I joked.

"Maybe so."

Her words ended with a smile, but there was something else in her tone that didn't seem like she was joking. I tipped my head to the side, waiting for an explanation. But none came. She didn't even seem to be watching me anymore. After a moment, I nodded, then swung my bag over my shoulder and headed toward the door. "Thanks for the suit," I said softly. "I'll see you later."

She glanced up without missing a beat, and if her grin had gone missing a few seconds ago, she didn't show it. "Good luck," she called after me.

I made it to Professor Wasserman's office in almost record time, all the way there feeling hyperaware of the odd lumps of fabric and padding that pressed against my back through my back-pack. The image of my reflection in the mirror had imprinted itself on my memory, and I wasn't quite ready to let it go. But I did have a history exam to take, and the details of post-1950 civil rights movements were probably more important. Begrudging-ly, I tried to push the suit out of my mind.

The teacher's assistant was waiting for me by the time I ar-rived. He sat in one of the brown leather chairs in the main department office, the kind that had cracked and grown stiff after years of use. All the furniture here looked like it belonged in a history textbook of its own. When he saw me, he stood, and the chair groaned and squeaked in protest underneath him.

"Cassidy! You made it just in time," he said. "You ready to head back?"

I nodded and followed him down the hall. At this time of day, most of the offices we passed were still locked from the night before, everything dark inside. Even the ones that were open seemed only half-lit, as if the occupants were still trying to decide if they wanted to work this morning or sleep. When we finally reached Wasserman's room, it was mostly the same, though thankfully the small corner table set up for me sat underneath a tall yellow reading lamp. I took a seat and set my bag down just beside me, then reached in for a pencil.

"Oh, hang on. Let me get you a Scantron for the multiple choice." The TA set his coffee cup down and began to rifle through a stack of papers on the professor's desk.

Coffee. *Crap.* I'd meant to text Andrew on my way over to remind him I'd be missing our usual Monday meet-up.

The TA sighed. "I thought I'd brought one in here, but I can't find it," he said. He set down the papers he'd been searching through, then looked up at me. "I'm going to run and get one from next door."

"While you're doing that, is it okay if I send a text real quick?"

He nodded. "Sure. But I'll need you to turn your phone off and keep it in your backpack while you're taking the test."

"I will," I promised. As he disappeared around the corner, I pulled my phone out and typed a brief message to Andrew, watching to make sure it sent. Once it finished, I held the button to shut my phone off entirely. Wasserman had always promised us she was incredibly strict about her "no phones" policy, and I didn't want to risk the TA being the same. I tucked it back in my backpack just as he arrived with the bubble sheet.

"All right," he said, handing it to me. "You should be set to get started."

The test was more difficult than I'd anticipated. About halfway through, my knee began to bounce and my pencil to tap against my leg as I tried to remember names and dates. I glanced up at the clock, trying to gauge how much time I had left. But as I turned back to the page, all I heard was the seconds hand ticking away.

One.

Two.

Three.

Four.

Five.

Not going to lie, a tiny sliver of me considered what Mia had said earlier. I mean, the note cards I'd made the night before were right there in my backpack . . .

No. I'm not going to cheat. I grumbled inwardly and shoved the thought away. Over the rest of the allotted time, I managed to scrape together answers I thought were at least halfway decent. I scribbled my chicken scratch onto the paper right up until I noticed the TA in my periphery, his hand held out to collect the pages.

"Sorry, but I'm really going to need to take it. Class starts in about ten minutes."

Reluctantly, I scratched in a final few words on the sentence I was writing, then handed him the papers. He tucked them into his own stack of work as I packed away my things. "I'll try and have this graded before the end of the day," he reassured me. I think I muttered some semblance of thanks, but as I opened up my bag and stole another glance at what was hidden inside, my thoughts were already wandering far away from any exam.

Wasserman's office wasn't too far from the lecture hall, so the TA and I managed to arrive just before the rest of the crowd. I took my usual seat toward the back of the room and set up my laptop on the small desk. I even sent in a correct answer to the attendance question, though I'd had to make a lucky guess at the answer. But my efforts in note-taking only went as far as watching the cursor blink at the top of a new document. I simply couldn't focus on anything she was saying. All through the class, I could feel the weight of the suit in my bag as it pressed against my leg. My mind drifted to what Mia had said about my "graduation." Surely she couldn't be serious. There was no way I was ready yet, right? And then there was the warning she'd had, the one about not getting to choose my fights. I still wasn't sure I knew what she meant, but the look on her face when she'd said it . . . I still wanted to ask her about it, but some memories carried barbs, and whatever this was, it had seemed like one of them. I wasn't sure if I'd yet earned the right to test its sharpness.

Even when I was focusing on the presentation slides at the front of the room, the dates and facts blurred together with those I'd crammed the night before. I'd always struggled with taking tests in school, but the one I'd taken this morning had me feeling even worse than usual—enough so that when I noticed my TA waving me to the front of the room at the end of class, my stomach turned sour. *Maybe I should've stolen Mia's idea*, I thought as I headed over.

"I got your scores added up during class, so I figured I could at least tell you your grade now," he said. "You got a 74 percent."

"Only a C?" I asked. The sour feeling spread.

"I know it's probably not what you wanted, but it should help your grade for the time being. And if you'd like, you're welcome to meet with me during office hours if you need to go over what you missed. We can even try and set up a time outside of then, if that works better."

I nodded, but in truth, I had no idea when that would be. Training with Mia, catching up on other work I missed, all my other classes, stressing about Dad . . . Even if I could bear to focus on the work for any length of time, I had no idea how I'd manage to fit it in with everything else. "Thanks," I mumbled. He nodded, and I turned and left.

After history, I'd gotten used to heading to the library to get some work done before my next class. Today, I just wanted to sit in the café and try to make myself feel better with a drink that was more sugar than coffee. I made it about halfway there before I remembered my text to Andrew this morning. I'd never checked to see if, or what, he'd responded. I pulled my phone out from my backpack and paused, waiting for it to power up all the way.

Before I even got the chance to open up my messages, the thing started buzzing in my hand. I glanced at the screen and frowned a little. "Hey, Mia," I answered.

"Cass!" Her voice came out high-pitched and slightly frazzled on the other end. "Where have you been? I've been trying to call you."

"Sorry, I forgot to turn my phone back on. Is something wrong?" I felt my heart thud a little louder against my rib cage at the thought.

She ignored my question. "Where are you?" she demanded.

"Uh, heading toward the library."

"Okay. Meet me there in five, and be ready to go. Wear the suit." The line clicked off.

For the briefest moment, I could only stand there, processing what she'd said. But as her words settled in, I shifted into another gear. I started toward the library, my feet pounding against the sidewalk. I slipped around the corner of the building to the back, behind the dumpsters for the café. Once I was sure I was hidden, I pulled out the suit and began to change.

I heard Mia before I saw her. I stood just beside a mass of cardboard boxes where I'd stashed my backpack, adjusting the Velcro on my gloves, when the zip of a motorbike grew louder. I peeked around the corner as the sound shifted to a low, powerful thrumming. Mia sat atop the bike, having donned Phase's outfit—the leather jacket, the heavy black combat boots, and the helmet that concealed her features from the rest of the world. She spotted me, then waved me forward, ignoring the onlookers who were starting to gather. "Climb on," she shouted above the sound of the bike. I did as I was told. Once I'd found my seat, I wrapped my arms around her middle to hold on. Then, we were off.

CHAPTER SEVEN

THE RIDE THERE WAS short and silent, save for the rumble of the motorcycle beneath us. I kept a death grip on Mia most of the way. A rush of adrenaline surged through my blood, but I hadn't fully decided yet whether it was anticipation for whatever we were about to face or just my fear of falling off. One traumatic, life-altering roadway accident was enough for the semester.

When we finally began to slow, I took in the scene in front of us. I knew this place. It was a natural food mart on the south end of the city, the kind of place that only sold products from its own brand name, for prices higher than I could afford. Police cars had encircled the small parking lot out front, their lights flashing. Mia tucked her bike in a few spaces away from the farthest one, then shut off the engine.

"I heard about this over the police scanner in the newsroom," Mia explained in a low voice as we approached the store. "There are two or three guys holed up inside. They tried to rob the place, but someone spotted a gun and called the cops, and they panicked. Now they're holding everyone inside hostage until the cops let them leave with the money."

"What should we do?" I asked.

"We're going to get them out." She turned to a pair of officers as we reached the front of the store. "How many are inside?" she asked them.

The first man cocked an eyebrow at her, his gaze trailing up and down her suit. He looked at his buddy, the younger of the two, and scoffed. "I guess people are out trick-or-treating already?" Mia just tipped her head to the side in response, then twitched her fingers toward the coffee cup the second man held in his hand. He startled, almost dropping it on the pavement. In an instant, the liquid inside had turned solid, and the ice's temperature had dropped low enough to make the walls of the cup bead with sweat. He glanced at the cup, then at his partner, then back at Mia. She repeated her question.

The first man stammered. "Look, this is an evolving situation. We—we can't allow civilians to interfere—"

"Three men inside, at least one armed," said the second cop. "Dispatch says there are about ten hostages, but there could be more."

A second passed as Mia and the first man stared at each other. The cop's neck grew ruddy, as did his ears. Finally, she turned back to the younger one. "Can we get in?"

"There's a back entrance where they load and unload the trucks. We don't think they have anyone there, but they've got eyes on all the other entrances."

Mia just nodded. "Thanks for your help," she said. She turned to the first man. "You too," she said, a little less sincerely this time. She walked past them, heading toward the side of the building. Unsure what else to do, I followed.

"Hey, who's she?" The second cop called out as I passed.

Mia didn't even turn around. "Playback. She's with me."

The two of us moved quietly but quickly around the building until we found the area the officer had talked about. He was right; the loading dock was empty and unguarded, except for a few more officers watching the doors from a distance. As we approached, I heard one of their radios come to life. "Officers on the north side, be advised. We're letting Phase and Playback through." It was cop #2, his voice broken up a little by the static.

"Excuse me?" one of the officers said before unhooking his own radio. I watched, but Mia just tapped my shoulder and waved me forward.

"It's always like this, like we need a proving ground and an entire city hall debate about whether we can help, even when they already know who I am." The two of us stayed crouched, creeping forward below the truck docks toward the maintenance door on the far end of the wall. "Sometimes it's the same cops throwing a fit, and they can't even do their own job right half the time."

"I can make one guess as to why," I whispered back, and she groaned in agreement.

"I should've done a whole silent act when I first put on the suit," she muttered. "Maybe then they wouldn't be able to tell I'm a woman."

At this point, we'd reached the steps and the door on the other end. We moved up the stairs with careful footfalls, our shoes barely making a sound. Once at the top, Mia reached forward and tried the handle. Locked. Mia pursed her lips, setting her shoulders just a little. Then, she raised her hand again, this time holding it in front of the deadbolt. The lock began to shift colors, glowing red, then white. The metal warped and bubbled outward, then began dripping down the doorframe. As it hit the pavement, it sizzled and popped, leaving scorch marks. She tried the door again, and this time, it swung open, catching just a little on the lump of once-molten metal.

I was biting back my excitement. This was only the second time I'd seen Mia use her powers for something other than heating or cooling someone's drink, and the first time up close. I could still smell the heat in the air, like fireworks just gone off. But as I began to creep toward the entrance, I felt a hand on my shoulder. I turned. I could feel Mia's eyes on me even through her visor.

"I'll take care of the robbers. Just get the hostages out. Lead them out this door, and the cops can handle the rest. Got it?"

I nodded. Mia studied my face for an extra second or two. Satisfied, she led the way into the back stockroom of the store.

In here, my eyes took a moment to adjust from the bright light outside. As the spots cleared, I took in the place. The shelves weren't quite what I had pictured for these kinds of stores—I wasn't sure what I *had* pictured, I realized, but maybe something more outwardly organized than it seemed. There were wire shelves packed high with indiscriminate cardboard boxes, the stacks tucked in three or four deep. In place of endcaps, there were pallets of food, each plastic-wrapped to almost the same level of obscurity as the boxes. The whole place was a maze.

There. After a few agonizing seconds, I'd spotted it—a set of swinging doors on the wall to our left. Mia and I moved toward them together. Slowly, we peeked our heads through to the other side. I could hear two men at the front of the store, and a third stood off to the side, watching out the window at a side entrance in the liquor section. Mia and I moved forward until we could make out what they were saying.

". . . don't have a choice. Once those cops showed up, we were done."

"So why don't we just give up now? Ricky, we've got hostages, man. This isn't what we planned." I could make out a young guy with a thin frame and the scruff of a beard on his chin, pacing nervously. The first one to speak—Ricky—put his hands to his head as he thought. In one of his hands was a gun.

"Probably best to listen to your friend there, Ricky." The familiar voice came from somewhere in front of me. For some reason, I still turned around, as if I'd expected a second Mia to be waiting behind me. But no, she'd snuck forward while I'd been listening. Now, she stood in front of the two men, her arms raised as if gesturing for them to calm down.

This was my chance, I realized. As she distracted the men, I could help the hostages escape. I scanned the room, daring to crawl out another few feet to get a better angle. Finally, I spotted someone, the back of his head just barely visible over the service counter from where he sat at the front of the store. I just had to pray Mia could keep their eyes focused on her.

"Who are you supposed to be?"

Mia feigned hurt, moving a hand to her chest. At this point, the other two men had trained their eyes on her. "You don't know who I am? Really?"

"Ricky, ain't that Phase's costume?" It was the third man, the one who'd been at the windows. He had a shorter and slightly stockier build than the other two, with buzzed hair the same color as Ricky's. He also looked the most like he didn't belong, as if he hadn't even wanted to be here to begin with.

"Shut up, Aaron." Ricky shifted on his feet, posturing once again. I continued forward, moving out from behind one of the checkout counters and into the open. "Look, lady, no one here's playing the hero, all right?" He pointed his gun at her, then gestured with it in the direction of the other hostages. "Why don't you—"

"Wait a second, who's that?!"

Aaron had yelled the question in my direction, panic lacing his voice. But I didn't give anyone time to respond. I shoved my hands forward.

I reappeared behind the checkout counter, my heart hammering in my chest. This time, I made sure to wait for Ricky to continue before I crawled out from my hiding space.

"Why don't you get over there with the rest of them before I have to make a mess?"

Mia clucked her tongue. "Well, you see, there's just two things wrong with that. First," she said, "playing the hero's kind of my whole thing." Aaron and the other lackey looked nervously at each other, then back at her. "And second, I think I'm going to make a bigger mess than you."

Without warning, Ricky cried out, dropping his gun. It clattered against the ground, smoke rising from the grip. Before anyone had time to react, Mia reached a foot forward and kicked the weapon far behind her, sending it sliding down one of the aisles. As Ricky clutched his singed hand, Mia raised her fists, glancing between the other two. The man at the front of the store began to go after the firearm. "I wouldn't," Mia warned. He stopped in his tracks, looking back at Aaron for help.

Under the cover of the chaos out front, I had managed to reach the service counter. As I came around the corner, every face turned to me, all of them etched just as much with fear as with confusion. My gaze met with each of theirs in turn. The middle-aged businessman. The old lady with wispy white hair. The young mom. Her son, who couldn't have been more than four years old. I tried to smile underneath my mask, hoping it spread up into my eyes and comforted at least some of them.

"While she keeps them busy, why don't I get you guys out of here?" I whispered.

The others nodded eagerly. I stole a glance behind me to make sure the coast was still clear, then turned back. "All right. Then here's what we'll do." I laid out my plan. Admittedly, I was making it up on the spot, but I managed to sound confident enough. I would go out first to make sure it was safe, then have them follow in groups of three. There were eleven of them, which meant four groups. Not ideal, but my nerves were already stretched taut as it was, and I didn't want to risk moving a group any bigger than that at a time, especially when I was their only form of protection.

"Is everyone ready?" I asked. The question was just as much for myself as it was for them, but they nodded, most of them tensed to move as soon as I gave the okay.

Except for one. The little boy was frozen on the spot, his lower lip quivering as he maintained a death grip on his mother's hand. I hesitated, then moved a little closer.

"Hey, buddy," I whispered to him, giving him a small wave. "Do you like superheroes?"

He looked at his mom as if for permission, then nodded at me.

"Well, that's good," I said. "Because my friend over there is a great superhero. And she's gonna stop the bad guys. But she and I need your help with something. We need help getting you, and your mom, and all these people out of here. Do you think you could be like a superhero, too, and help me with that?"

His eyes glistened with monster tears, but to his credit, he was managing to stay silent. He seemed to be thinking hard, but finally, he whispered back. "Okay," he said.

I squinted my eyes with my smile, hoping it showed through my mask. "Awesome. I'll need you to be brave though, and really quiet, just like we're being now. Can you do that for me?" He nodded again. I held out my fist for a knuckle bump, and I saw the tiniest hint of a smile play across his cheeks as he returned the gesture. I turned to the rest of my group. "Okay, first set of three. Remember: I go first."

As I peeked my head around the counter once more, I allowed myself a nervous breath. *It'll be fine. You've got this,* I told myself. *As long as Mia can keep them occupied.* I could hear her a little farther away from where we were now, her voice sounding winded and strained even as she continued taunting the men. She seemed to be leading them deeper into the store, I realized. She was giving us a chance to escape.

With the front of the store empty, I crept back over to the checkout lanes, ducking behind the counter the employees usually used. Once there, I waved the first group of three on: the boy, his mother, and another kid who looked to be barely out of middle school. They tucked in behind me just as I waved the next group on. As they followed suit, however, things started to get crowded, and I realized my plan wouldn't work quite as well as I'd hoped. I closed my eyes and willed myself to think for a moment.

How long would it take for them to run from the checkout lanes to the cover of the aisles?

I turned to the three store employees who'd just arrived behind me, one a woman with worry lines already carved into her forehead and cheeks, the other two fresh-faced high school students. "You three know your way through the back exit." It was a statement more than a question, but they whispered their confirmation all the same. I let out a breath. "New plan. Have you heard of the game, 'Red Rover'?" I explained what I had in mind in hushed tones, though a chill was starting to creep down the back of my neck. It had gone quiet on the other end of the store. I didn't hear the robbers—and I didn't hear Mia, either.

The store employees waited for their cue. I waited for mine.

One second.

Two seconds.

I scanned the room, daring to raise my head above cover. Once time was up, I shoved my hands forward.

"Go. Now."

The three closed the distance to the grocery aisles without a sound. I turned and found the other group, still waiting to leave from behind the counter, and waved them forward.

The store employees and I worked in tandem. I would bring a group over to the checkout lanes, and another three would run to the aisles, clearing just enough room in our hiding space for the next group. I poised myself to bring the last group of three to my side: the elderly woman, the businessman, and another woman who looked about my mom's age.

"Help!"

The scream came from one of the employees across the store. My adrenaline surged, and I whipped my head around just as Ricky grabbed the arm of the little four-year-old, wrenching him from his mother. The boy's wails filled the store, stopping Mia in her tracks as she rounded the corner.

I rewound everything, then shoved past everyone toward the aisles. I had to get between Ricky and the boy. "Run!" I told everyone, just as Ricky rounded the corner, his glare dripping with vitriol.

"I've about had it with you costumed freaks," he spat. He marched toward me. I stood my ground, even as his hands curled into fists. I didn't dare turn my eyes away—after all, I was all that stood between him and the owners of the hurried footfalls behind me. When he swung, I caught his fist easily in my hand.

Well, the first one, at least.

I saw his second blow coming too late to block it, and I felt it ripple through my core just as I rewound.

I doubled over, all the air trapped outside my lungs. I heard Ricky's voice again, and the sound of his boots echoing off the ground as he came toward us. I stumbled forward, still coughing and sputtering. Somehow, I managed to block his path just before he reached the others. I batted his punches away a little less gracefully this time than I'd done before, just as Mia rounded the corner.

"Come on, man," Mia said. Her shoulders drooped in exasperation. "I thought we talked about this."

Ricky didn't seem to want to play along with her gibes. He spun to face her, leaving me to finish finding my breath. "What did you do to Emil?" he asked through gritted teeth.

She raised her hands, palms out—a show of submission, but also in another effort to mock him, I was fairly certain. "Your buddy? He's fine. Probably cooling his feet." She paused as he lunged at her, blocking his attacks. "It's a shame you wore those boots—wooden soles, and all." In a quick move, she grabbed at his hands and spun him around, hugging his wrists together against his chest. She met my gaze, grunting as she tried to keep him in place. For the first time, I noticed how she favored one arm as she fought, her jacket slashed near the collarbone. I wondered if the wound went any deeper.

"You good?" she asked.

I nodded, finally filling my lungs. "Yeah, just perfect." I straightened a little. "You?"

She tipped her head as if to shrug. "I'll be fine. Listen, skinny one's down, but I lost the brother. He sliced me and ran."

"Which way?"

I could hear the aggravation in her voice. "I think toward your exit."

My feet nearly slid out from under me on the slick linoleum as I ran to catch up with the others. They were nearing the stockroom now, trying to herd everyone in the right direction as silently as possible. I reached the older employee at the front of the group and skidded to a stop, panting just a little. "One of them has a second weapon," I warned her.

"Then let's not waste any more time," she answered.

I positioned myself alongside the group as she and the other employees ran forward, holding the doors to the stockroom open for everyone. As the customers filtered through, the younger employees continued through the stockroom, guiding everyone through the dark and confusing network of shelves and boxes to the exit and to the officers waiting on the other side.

As the final person crossed the threshold into the storeroom, Mia's boots pounded up the aisle just behind me. "Are they out?" she asked.

Before I could answer, a voice boomed from the other direction. "Where do you think you're going?" We both spun on our heels, standing face to face with the third robber, Aaron. He held his switchblade in front of him, his whole arm quivering in what looked like silent fury. His eyes gave away the truth though: He was terrified.

Mia stepped forward, trying to put herself between him and me. "Aaron, the hostages are gone. The police are right outside. This doesn't have to get ugly. Just let us go, and we can talk through this."

"No. No." He shook his head back and forth with each word. "You're not going anywhere. I'm getting me and my brother out of here."

"Aaron, please—"

But before Mia even had time to finish her sentence, he had turned, his eyes focusing on me. Time slowed down—not in the sense that I had made it slow, but that my body took over while my mind worked to keep up. Aaron's arm swung outward, his teeth bared as he screamed. A flash of metal moved toward my center. Air rushed by my ears, and I tried to dodge away from his swing. But I lost my footing. My limbs flailed as the tower of water jugs I'd fallen against gave way, and I did the only thing I could think in that instant.

Five seconds.

"You're not going anywhere. I'm getting me and my brother out of here."

I shot a nervous glance at Mia, my heart pounding against my ribcage. My gaze flicked in the other direction, to the water jugs at my side.

"Aaron, please—"

I watched his body weight shift, his arm pull back as he readied his swing. I angled myself closer to the tower of water this time, playing chicken with his blade and my own memory. I forced myself to wait a fraction of a second more . . . and in the final instant, I side-stepped.

The force he'd used sent his blade plunging into one of the giant, five-gallon containers. Water spurted out from the gash, pooling on the floor around us. "Phase!" I yelled, leaping back.

But she already knew what to do. I watched the liquid grow cloudy as it froze, ice creeping outward and up the shelf, into the remnants still housed in the bottle. Aaron's hand became encased in the delicate glass, and his feet lost any traction beneath him.

The two of us bolted for the exit. By now, the rest of the hostages had made it outside, and the door to the loading docks was propped wide open—a beacon of light at the end of a dark tunnel. We ran until our feet hit pavement once again, and only then did a small swarm of vested SWAT officers trade places with us, heading into the building to clean up our mess.

I squinted in the bright light, blinking a few times. It took me a moment before I could make out the scene in front of me, and still another before I could process it all. There was a sea of uniformed officers a few paces away from the building, all of them scrambling. Amid the organized chaos—emphasis on the "chaos"—were the faces I'd seen inside. They were here, safe. We'd done it. We'd gotten everyone out.

My gaze finally settled on the older employee, who stood just off to the side, talking to one of the officers—the one whose coffee Mia had turned into an ice cube earlier. He kept his eyes trained on her as she spoke, his pen scribbling across his notepad without slowing.

"You all did a brave thing, getting everyone to the exit on your own like that."

The woman shook her head. "It wasn't us. That was all her."

His pen stopped, and his forehead wrinkled. "Who? Phase?"

"No, the other one. She got everyone out. It was like she could see things before they happened. You should've seen her—she stopped one of those a-holes from grabbing that woman's kid. Just caught his fist right in the air."

Mia elbowed me lightly in the side. Apparently, she'd been eavesdropping too.

The cop just nodded slowly, hesitating for a moment. Then, "Okay, ma'am. I see." Condescension coated his words, and the grin I wore behind my mask flattened just a little.

A commotion behind us tore my attention away. The SWAT officers were reemerging through the same doorway we'd just exited. This time, they brought the three robbers in tow. All were handcuffed and wearing the same dejected expression—and varying degrees of embarrassment. Ricky's bravado was gone, and the fabric of Aaron's jeans had grown dark and wet along one side where he'd slipped on Mia's ice. But they at least had all their clothes. Emil wasn't so lucky. His shoes threatened to flap off his feet with each step, causing most of us present, cops included, to stifle a laugh.

"Tennis shoes. Rubber soles," Mia whispered. I could hear the smile she wore underneath the visor.

I'm not entirely sure what sparked the next moment. Maybe it was everyone's laughter, or it was retaliation for what had happened inside. But I watched Aaron's face pinch. His shoulders rose, and he threw his weight away from the officer who led him to the patrol car. He moved toward Mia, tackling her to the ground before anyone could react.

"No!" I screamed, throwing my hands out. My shout found itself caught between one reality and the next. I watched everyone coming down the steps again and heard the snickers and giggles from behind me. Mia looked to me. "What is it? What happened?" Worry laced her tone, but I ignored her. As the trio approached, I stepped forward, just in front of Mia.

"Hey!" I shouted in Aaron's direction. He stopped in his tracks, the picture of bullish rage. I softened. "Don't. I know what you're thinking. Don't make this worse for you."

"Shut up," he growled. He tacked on a curse for good measure, the word more spittle and growl than sound. This time, when he made his move, his sights stayed on me. But he didn't make it as far. His foot hit my own outstretched leg as he ran, and he tumbled to the ground once more.

The SWAT officer who'd been leading him ran forward, but for a moment, no one else moved. They didn't seem to know how to react.

It was a tiny voice that finally broke the stillness. "Mom, look!" The little boy's whisper was more of a yell, though he surely didn't realize it as he tugged on her sleeve. "It's the superhero girl!" He pointed, and I could feel the warmth of his smile from across the lot. He was pointing at *me*.

Suddenly, a different sound echoed off the building and in the air: applause. People began clapping—everyone who'd been in the store at first, but after a while, a few bewildered cops even started to join in. And Mia . . . I saw her in my periphery, celebrating just as much as the others. Pride radiated off of her, spreading out from her in waves until it settled in my own chest.

A title settled on my tongue again, one that hadn't seemed right before, not even after that incident with the bus. I'd pretended, sure, toying with the word when I'd repeated my name under my breath or put on the suit this morning. But this time, for the first time, it felt true.

Hero. I was a hero.

Chapter Eight

"I DON'T KNOW HOW to explain it. I just felt so ... so powerful." I grasped for the right phrasing. "Like everyone there was seeing me for the first time."

I sat across from Andrew that evening, nibbling thoughtfully on a piece of pepperoni I'd plucked from my pizza. We'd commandeered a table on the far end of the dining hall, trying to avoid the throng of Greek life students who'd stopped by before the parties and events they'd planned for the evening. Truthfully, until the rude cop's comments in the parking lot, I'd lost track of the date. It seemed fitting though—a new superhero making her first appearance on Halloween.

"They *were* seeing you for the first time," he pointed out.

My face flushed. "You know that's not what I meant."

"I know." He met my eyes, and one corner of his mouth turned up just slightly. "Maybe you were finally seeing yourself."

I paused, considering. Was he right? Maybe, but he continued before I had the chance to decide. "Anyway, I win." I must've looked confused, because his smirk grew, twinkling in his eyes. "I saw you first."

I groaned. "Oh my god." He just laughed, clearly far too proud of himself. As his laughter died, though, an emptiness seemed to settle between us again. I was starting to notice it more—the hesitant silences and delayed responses. There was an odd twist in my stomach each time it happened. I was trying not to pick apart every interaction we had and examine the pieces, especially when I wasn't sure anything was wrong in the first place. I studied him now from behind my eyebrows, watching as he adjusted his glasses, took a drink from his cup. Maybe he was just tired from classes and working in the lab. Maybe I was just stressed because of everything I'd been through recently. Maybe I was allowing a wound to fester in my mind that hadn't even existed before I'd started to scratch at it.

Still, the longer we sat there in silence, the more I could see his expression growing serious. After a moment, he looked up at me once more, and I couldn't help the twist that wound itself a little tighter.

"Look, I know you said you were just helping to get those people out, and that you were careful, but . . ." He trailed off, sighing when the right words didn't come to him in time. "I hate the thought of you being put in danger you're not prepared for."

Relief swept over me. "Andrew, weren't you the one who encouraged me to do this in the first place?" I countered, suppressing a chuckle.

"I said I believed you could make a difference, I'm pretty sure. I don't know if you can say I *encouraged* you." He clasped his hands together in front of his mouth, then just as quickly unclasped them, taking my hands in his. "I just want to know you're safe."

I'd felt my anxiety building again just a moment ago, but with this gesture, it dissipated entirely. His thumb rubbed tiny half circles on the backs of my fingers, and I closed my eyes, just for an instant. Whether it was because I felt comforted or guilty for making him worry, I wasn't entirely sure. I opened my eyes again and gave his fingers a small squeeze.

"I'll be safe. I promise." I took my hands back, then flashed a smile. "Besides, I trust Phase."

He nodded slowly, his gaze falling to the table as he pondered this. "Well," he said, "if you trust her, then I guess I can too." Turning back to me, he answered my smile with a small one of his own before taking another bite of his pizza.

The next afternoon, I ducked into an empty side street between two of the buildings downtown—one a restaurant, the other a hole-in-the-wall music venue that was probably only kept in business because of Everett students. I checked around me one last time, then deposited my backpack into an overturned milk crate. Kneeling down, I unzipped the main pocket and pulled out my suit.

For what felt like the first time in a while, I actually had a moment to myself. My classes were done for the day, and though I had readings and an essay I could've been working on, nothing was pressing. Andrew was doing work in the lab, and Mia had an article she was writing for the paper. "Apparently, there's a new superhero in town," she'd said when I ran into her that morning, her nose wrinkling with a knowing grin. I couldn't help but smile myself. Talk of Playback was everywhere overnight, mostly thanks to social media. One of the reporters who'd been on the scene yesterday had managed to get footage of me stopping the robber when he lunged at Mia, and it seemed to have gone viral. Between that and the statement police had released later that evening, the city was abuzz with excitement. And, truth be told, a fair bit of confusion. My powers weren't the easiest for bystanders to comprehend. Luckily, I knew a journalist who'd promised to help with that.

After all, mine wasn't the first superhero profile Mia had tackled—just the first where she wasn't having to interview herself.

I zipped up my jacket and finished fitting my mask over my face. If I had some time to myself, I was going to enjoy it. And right now, things in my life were much simpler and more exciting as Playback. Anyway, the mask was more of a precaution. I just wanted to try something on my own, and with where I was going, I wasn't too worried about being spotted.

Once I was dressed, I turned and headed deeper into the alley, toward the entrance on the opposite street. The back of these buildings jutted up almost against the next, and here on the corner of the structure, old bricks hung just beyond the edge.

These larger limestone slabs were supposed to be decorative, making the buildings seem more timeless to match the ones on campus. But I had a different idea in mind, courtesy of Mia's suggestions about my test the other day. I wasn't quite the type to cheat with my powers, but that didn't mean I couldn't still have fun with them. There was something I'd always secretly wanted to do since I was little. No way could Cassidy ever get away with it, but Playback . . .

I adjusted the Velcro on my gloves. *Mia did say they used to be for rock-climbing*, I thought as I found my first foothold. "Besides," I muttered to myself, reaching a hand back and pressing it against the wall of the building to hold myself in place, "if it doesn't work out, I can just rewind." I was choosing to ignore the fact that any injuries I sustained would carry over with me when I relived those seconds. I hoisted myself up farther and took hold of another brick.

It took much longer than a few seconds—and a lot of grunting and cursing—for me to shimmy my way up to the top. But eventually, my plan worked. At least, the first part did. Letting out a breath, I steadied myself, then reached a leg out to the windowsill around the corner. My hand was next, grasping onto the top of the window with just fingertips. I grew stiff and achy with the effort, but as I brought my other limbs over, I found my balance. Just one more gap to cross . . .

I eyed the ledge of the balcony. Stretching a leg out, I could just reach the tip of it with my toe. I stalled like this for a few more seconds, steeling my nerves. Then, I let go and leapt sideways, landing with soft feet on the wide banister wall. Momentum carried me forward another step, onto the patio. Quiet laughter bubbled up inside of me. I'd done it. Standing from my crouch, I dusted my hands, then moved toward my actual end goal: the clock tower at the other end of the balcony.

The place I stood now had once been home to a luxury restaurant and bar. I vaguely remembered my parents going there one year for their anniversary. My mother had styled her hair and worried over her dress for most of the day, until Dad had pulled her into his arms and promised her she looked beautiful. He'd gotten dressed up for the occasion as well, even putting on cologne, which was how I knew as a little girl that the place was fancy. I'd always loved the smell of Dad's cologne, but he only ever wore it on special occasions—to weddings or Christmas Eve services, or on extra special dates with my mom.

The restaurant had closed a few years after that. As a college town, the owners eventually realized the majority of people spending time at bars had much smaller budgets and much less refined tastes when it came to getting buzzed. They'd tried remodeling to get a fresh group of young patrons interested, switching to solar panels to power the lights on the patio and advertising creative brunch options on the weekends. But when a sports bar cropped up a few streets away, the space here became less popular, then vacant altogether.

The clock tower was another story, though not all that different, now that I thought about it. The tower had been here when the courthouse had been on this side of town, but when college students had moved in, it had moved farther away to give campus space to expand. The clock tower was a landmark though; it had stayed. And except for when the city announced it needed maintenance, I was fairly certain it stayed *empty*.

The door at the base of the tower was padlocked, but the access ladder I'd thought I remembered was still here on the outside of the structure. I took hold of the rungs and climbed, much more easily than I had with the bricks before. Once at the top, I swung myself through the open window and inside.

It was small and cramped, with the tarnished bell that stretched to about half my height taking up a majority of the space inside. The wooden platform I stood on was only a few dusty boards across all the way around—I could maybe take two steps toward the center before I would reach the edge. I couldn't stop the grin that reached across my face from behind my mask. Maybe it was childish, but it had always been a dream of mine to see what was inside the clock tower. And I loved it. With a gloved hand, I reached out and felt the cool metal of the bell against my fingertips. I studied the thick rope that hung from the clapper and imagined the vibrations the whole instrument would carry when it pealed.

The irony was not lost on me that the one with the power to manipulate time was choosing to hang out in a clock tower. But I didn't particularly care. The space up here, limited as it may have been, was peaceful. Understated. The perfect place to sort through my thoughts . . . or to think about nothing at all. I pulled my attention away from the bell and walked the length of the platform, setting my boots down gently against the floor until I reached the staircase down to the ground level. The wooden boards protested slightly after so many years of neglect, but even with their creaks and groans, they held my weight. I turned and walked in the other direction, trying to keep each step within the imprints I'd already made in the dust.

The corner closest to the ladder was shrouded in shadows this time of day. I hadn't noticed it before, but as I came closer, I noticed a blue tarp peeking out, just enough to draw my attention. I stopped in front of it. The plastic sheet bore its own layer of dirt and grime, but underneath it looked like a stack of cardboard boxes. I hesitated, but curiosity got the better of me. I took hold of the tarp and dragged it off the pile.

Years of pollen and grime billowed into the air, and the cardboard stack tipped toward me. I heard them tumbling at the same time my nose twitched. Reflexively, I threw one hand out against the boxes, burying my sneeze in the other elbow.

I stayed like that for a moment, and a frown creased into the space between my eyebrows. No crash. No second dust cloud. I turned toward the pile, and this time, my mouth fell open. The boxes were suspended there, as if hanging from wires anchored into the ceiling. They were frozen mid-fall, and as I leaned to one side and then the other, a familiar tingle whispered across my fingertips. I rubbed the pad of my thumb against the feeling absentmindedly. My jaw still hung slightly agape. And then, just as unexpectedly, the illusion was broken. I leapt back as cardboard tumbled to the floor, spilling a string of holiday lights and banners at my feet.

My attention drifted from the mess on the floor to my hands. A few more seconds passed, but all I managed was a hushed, "Well, that's new."

In my head, I was already retracing my steps from right before the boxes had tipped. That had been me, right? But I'd only ever rewound time for myself. Could I actually manipulate more than just my own timeline?

It looked like I had my answer, but I wasn't given a chance to test the theory just then. A teeth-chattering crack sounded from down below, echoing with hisses and pops of electricity. The discordant noise was joined almost instantly by a chorus of shouts and gasps. I tore my attention away from the mess I'd made and moved over to the window. Leaning out, I could just make out some of the scene down below. A couple stumbled back from the sidewalk and into the street, clutching at each other. They barely noticed the cars that slammed on their brakes to avoid hitting them; their looks of surprise were trained on something else. I craned my neck and braced myself against the ledge, trying to find a better angle. But even while I couldn't make out the spectacle, others down below were clearly starting to notice. I watched as people began to gather and point, and one woman's nervous shriek reached my ears.

Worry sent my heart slamming against my ribcage. I spun on my heels. The staircase descended to a locked entrance at street level; that was how I'd reach whatever was down there.

My footsteps fell heavy on the wooden stairs, echoing in the large tower. But only part of the way down the first flight, a pressing weight formed in my stomach. Hazy light filtered down from the windows above, but it stopped here. The rest of the stairs were still swallowed by shadows that could've carried on indefinitely—certainly far too long for me to climb down them all, no matter how much faster I willed myself to go.

I growled in frustration and shoved myself back in time.

Back at the top of the stairs, I looked around frantically, the few seconds I could buy myself ticking away in my head. The way I'd come in was no more of an option than the stairs had been . . . which left only one other choice. I turned toward the bell. *Well, it's only the second dumbest impulse decision I'll have made today.* I shrugged the anxiety off my shoulders, backing my heels up against the exterior wall. I lined up my sights, took two steps, and leapt, reaching for the rope that hung from the bell's center. The rope went taut in my hands as it took on my weight. But the bell remained silent. I glanced up with a smile, and the pads of my fingers fizzed as I pulled them away from the clapper. *Theory proven.* I adjusted my grip and began clambering down the rope toward the ground floor.

As I lowered myself deeper into the tower, my vision left me. But the muffled commotion from outside traveled through the walls. It pushed me faster. And when my feet finally stumbled against something solid underneath me, the shouting and yelling carried clearly to my ears. My hands found a metal section of the wall—I could only assume it was the door—and I fumbled for the handle. Just as the door swung open, a new sound bellowed from behind me in the tower, drowning out everything else.

The bell's chime was enough to disorient everyone on the street, and I used the extra seconds to scan the crowd in front of me. Everyone still seemed to be staring at something on the sidewalk beside the tower. I followed their sights, and as I rounded the side of the building, something in the air made the hairs on the back of my neck prickle. I saw what they'd been staring at. Up against the back corner was a strange metal structure, pieced together out of car parts and salvage from the scrap heap. It looked like an archway, and I would've thought it was some sort of modern art installation—except for the fact that it felt like the air around it was electrified. I shuddered, and an all-too-familiar sensation crept up my fingers and into my wrists.

I spun back around just as the ringing above me stopped. "Run!" I shouted. I felt their eyes on me—everyone was noticing me standing there for the first time. But their panic won out; they did as they were told, following my gestures as I waved them onto the next street over. Truthfully, I fought the urge to do the same. I forced myself to stay within the block as I helped people out of their cars and herded them away. But I'd felt the air like this once before.

Right before a car crash that nearly killed my father and me.

The memory sent my heart thumping in my ears with something other than adrenaline. I clenched my fists and unclenched them reflexively, and as I watched the final few people round the corner to safety, I turned my attention back to the structure behind me.

My expression darkened. In the faint glow of the structure and with the shadows cast by the clock tower, I could only make out a silhouette—but I could tell I wasn't about to get past its owner without a fight.

"I don't know what you think you're doing, but you have to shut it down," I tried. "This is going to kill people."

"You're dealing with things beyond your understanding." The man's voice was deep and gravelly in his throat. "Leave. Now." Though I couldn't make out any of his features, his demeanor screamed danger. This wasn't a man you wanted to cross paths with—and I just had.

"I can't do that." I took a step forward, and the man reached for something behind his back. When his hand reemerged, something silver glinted in the low light. A short blade.

"I wasn't asking," he threatened.

My eyes flicked toward the knife, but I didn't shy away. I looked back toward him. "Neither was I."

I knew what would happen the second the words left my mouth. The man lunged for me, and I dived for him, ducking low as he sliced the air. I managed to dodge the blade and swatted at his arm, but he recovered faster than I'd anticipated. I pushed myself back in time with the blade only centimeters from my core.

My movements were faster, more forceful the second time around. Still, I couldn't help the air that escaped from my lungs in a sharp huff when the blade came for my stomach this time, barely brushing past the padding of my suit. As we continued our dance, I tried to match each of his movements with one of my own. But I was sloppy and panicked by comparison, even as I replayed the fight a third time, then a fourth. Mia and I still had never practiced with weapons. I had no idea what I was doing. I was just trying to survive the encounter.

This time, I managed to keep his hands away from me as we volleyed. I would bat the blade away from my body, watching it from the corner of my eye and following its momentum to find where to block next. Except the man seemed to know what I was doing. After a moment, he moved his arm high up toward my collar bone. Then, his fingers let go of the knife, dropping it into his outstretched palm below. Before I had time to process what had happened, his arm arced back around, and a final slice brought the knife down above my head.

On instinct alone, I threw my hands up. My crossed forearms took the weight of his swing as it crashed against me. I gritted my teeth, and my knees threatened to buckle. I looked up. The point of his blade waggled inches from my eye.

"Stay out of my way," he growled.

It was his strength against mine, and I shook with the effort. Blood rushed in my ears and pounded from behind my eyes. I almost didn't notice when the machine's hum shifted into a piercing, grinding whine. But he did. In a panic, the man shoved his weight forward, and my legs and arms gave way. I dived to the side. Metal sang as it brushed past my ear, close enough that I could feel the whisper of its breath on my neck. Then, something much harder struck me on the temple.

Stars filled my vision, and my world went askew. Before my sight had cleared, I felt a rush of air beside me, and I watched the man's outline shrink away into the distance. I gathered my limbs beneath me. I had to get out of here. Had to find that man. I took a few steps forward, my legs wobbly but slowly gaining back their strength. As I found my balance once more, I broke into a run. I rounded the corner where others had fled, but if the mystery attacker had gone this way, he'd long since been swallowed by the crowd.

Before I could figure out my next move, the grinding from behind me grew louder. The asphalt beneath my feet trembled, and I threw my arms out instinctively for balance. The move only made my dizziness worse; I didn't realize immediately that I'd rewound. By the time the seconds caught up with me, though, the whole earth seemed to be shaking, buildings rattling above us as people screamed. I tried to direct everyone away from the structures and toward the center of the road—that was where you were supposed to go in an earthquake, right? I guess it didn't matter, as hardly anyone could hear me at that point. I helped the woman next to me to crouch low and cover her head, and I crossed my fingers that Mia had heard what was happening by now. *Please, let her be on her way. She'll know what to do.*

That was when the grinding stopped, and the street behind us exploded.

CHAPTER NINE

I ARCHED MY BODY over the woman next to me, trying to shield her. I braced for debris or a shockwave of some kind. I squeezed my eyes shut, gritting my teeth. I felt a scream rising up from my core, but if it escaped, I couldn't tell. Instead, the roar of the explosion filled my ears, drowning out everything until my hearing left altogether. In its place came a persistent ringing, louder than my thoughts. And then finally, silence, and the quiet whimpers and cries of the woman next to me and the others I'd helped evacuate.

I wasn't sure how long we stayed like that, but eventually, I straightened, craning my neck to try to get a view of the wreckage. The blast had sent plumes of smoke and dust into the air and onto the road, layering everything in thin white gauze. The buildings were all still standing, but debris was scattered across the sidewalk. It was impossible to tell where it had come from. Loose papers fluttered in the wind, and except for a lone car whose hazard lights blinked on and off, there was little to interrupt the stillness.

It was all a horrifying contrast to what was taking place here, a block over. As everyone recovered their senses, the chaos began anew. People screamed and cried, taking stock of their things and the people they were with. A few examined their injuries. Amazingly, most of what I saw near me were scrapes and bruises. My stomach roiled at the thought of finding worse.

After a moment, or maybe more—it was hard to process exactly how long it had been—I stood and pulled out my phone. The screen was cracked. *Of course it was*, I thought. But I couldn't seem to muster any sort of frustration or disappointment after what I'd just experienced. I clicked into my contacts and dialed Mia's number.

The only answer I received was a busy signal.

I tried again, bouncing from one foot to the other as I waited. Still nothing. And as I glanced around at the sea of worried faces in front of me, I was starting to think it wasn't just my cell having issues. I chewed my lip for a moment behind my mask, debating. It wasn't a surprise service was down—everyone for blocks was probably trying to contact someone. The police. Their loved ones. Their friends.

Another moment passed, and I began to weave my way through the crowd. I wasn't sure quite where I was going, but with each step I took, something drove me to move faster. I could feel eyes and murmurs following me, but I pushed them out of my mind. I only slowed once. An Everett University hoodie lay abandoned on the sidewalk, and I paused, picking it up and dusting it off hastily. I tucked it under my arm and kept moving. The number of people thinned, and I broke into a jog. Then a run.

My feet carried me someplace while my mind raced to keep up, but as I neared campus once more and rounded the corner, I realized where I was headed. I ducked around the side of a building just for a moment to pull the hoodie I'd rescued over my head. I peeled off my mask, scrubbed at the dirt on my face with my sleeve, and tucked the mask and my still-gloved hands into the pocket. When I entered the street once more, I tried my hardest to steady my breathing and followed the familiar path up to Mia's apartment.

As I climbed the stairs to her floor, a frown creased my brow. Everything was quiet in this building. Not in the same tortured way it had been in the street, but in the way it had been in the moments before everything had taken place. It felt wrong to see things so sleepy, so casual. Then again, I reminded myself, a few minutes ago—up until I'd left that clock tower—it had been just another Tuesday for me too.

I let out a breath when I finally stood in front of her apartment. I undid one of my gloves within my pocket, then rapped on her door.

"Hey, you made it. Thanks for agreeing to an inter—" Mia's smile fell. "Cassidy. You're bleeding." My expression asked a silent question as I raised a hand to the bruise forming on the side of my head, then to the tip of my ear. I winced, and as I pulled back, my fingertip was dotted with a single drop of blood.

I stared at it for a moment, until Mia broke my trance. "What's wrong?" she asked.

Another breath shuddered from my chest, and I met her gaze again. "You . . . you need to come with me. There was an explosion."

She blanched. "What?"

"By the clock tower. Everyone was evacuated, I think, but I'm not sure."

"Police? First responders?"

"They're probably on their way," I said, my voice still sounding a little foreign to my ears. "But it's chaos. Phone lines are down. No one knows what to do. I don't—"

Mia put a hand on my shoulder, a fire burning in her eyes. "Come on. Let's go."

She ducked around the door for a second to grab her keys and was back in the hallway in a flash. As we turned toward the stairwell however, another sight froze us both to the spot. My mouth opened, but I couldn't think of a single thing to say.

Mia did. It was just one four-letter word, muttered under her breath, but it was as apt a response as any. My gaze darted to her, then back to Andrew, who was stopped in the middle of the hallway, currently mirroring my dumbfounded expression with one of his own.

"Cassidy?" he asked. I could see the cogs turning in his mind. "You know Mia? But she's reporting on . . ." He trailed off, then raised a hand and pointed at Mia. "You're . . ." He stopped himself, moving his hand to his mouth as if to trap the rest of the thought. But it didn't matter. We both knew.

He knew.

He sucked in another breath, but Mia stopped him before he could say any more. "I'm so sorry, but something came up," she gritted, her voice clipped. "Can I reach out to you later and we can reschedule the interview?" Without waiting for his answer, she wrapped a hand tightly around my wrist and yanked me along, past Andrew and toward the stairs. As we passed, a strange sense of shame burned my stomach. I couldn't help but take one last glance over my shoulder at him, his face still wearing the shock of the secret—Mia's secret—he'd just uncovered.

Silence kept Mia and me company as she donned her suit and I replaced my mask, though whether it stemmed from Andrew's discovery of her secret or the gravity of what we were facing, I wasn't sure. It was fine with me. Guilt still wormed its way through my insides. So did confusion, worry, shock, and a host of other feelings I was too distracted to identify. But whatever awkwardness existed between us dissipated when we reached the clock tower. Mia brought her bike to a halt, and I could hear her sharp inhale behind her helmet.

The scene seemed worse now than even a few minutes ago. With the dust settled, the devastation left behind was in full view. A few people's clothes were torn and shredded, and shattered glass from storefront windows that had blown out now littered the street. In the distance, something smoked in a pile beside the clock tower. The door still hung ajar from where I'd exited; one of its hinges looked like it had bent. People danced from one foot to another, unable to stay still, while others still crouched near the ground, as if frozen in place. Wordlessly, the two of us climbed off the bike and headed toward the epicenter.

Our arrival seemed to spark a new wave of chaos. Before we'd even taken two steps, someone shouted our names, and people ran up to meet us or cried for our help. My attention flashed from one panicked and scared face to the next, all of them surrounding us, begging us to do something. Mia melted back into Phase without any hesitation. She turned from one person to the next, directing them on what to do, how to help. She spotted a toddler standing alone in the street, tears creating tracks in the dirt on his face, and scooped him into her arms without a second thought. But I didn't know what to do. I couldn't help it; I stilled. Phase paused, looking at me.

"Playback?" she asked.

I tore my eyes away from what was ahead and looked at her. "I . . ."

"I know. It's okay." She paused to shift the little boy in her arms. "Just do what you can." She held the child out to me, and he reached his arms out expectantly. A second ticked by, and then I took him. His small hands clasped at the collar of my jacket behind my neck, and another hand, Mia's, brushed against my arm. I looked back at her, and she nodded. Then she turned back to the crowd.

I closed my eyes and took a steadying breath. A small sniffle made me open them again, and I looked through the mop of blond hair at the wide blue eyes staring back at me. *Do what you can.*

"Hey, buddy," I finally said. "Wanna help me find your parents?"

He answered with the tiniest nod.

As we started to comb through the sea in front of us, I kept up a small string of questions: What was his name? How old was he? Did he have any brothers or sisters? They were just as much a distraction for me as they were for him. "Are we looking for your mom or your dad?" I asked.

"Um . . . bof," he mumbled, the end of the word "both" sounding like an "f" as he scrubbed a chubby fist against his face. I nodded, turning back to the crowd. But I didn't really need to search for long. As someone in front of us moved, a woman's cry of relief reached our ears above the noise. The boy in my arms turned toward the sound, then started crying again. Before I even could react, the woman and the man next to her sprinted toward us, and the boy's dad scooped him out of my arms.

"Oh, Adam," the mother sobbed, her tears preventing anything more coherent. The boy's father turned to me.

"Thank you," he whispered, hugging the boy fiercely.

I just nodded, unsure that anything more needed to be said. As they turned their attention entirely on little Adam, I let myself be swallowed back into the fray.

I waded slowly through a sea of survivors. The desperate looks on their faces imprinted themselves in my memory; even when I closed my eyes, I saw them pleading for help and for answers. But this wasn't like the grocery store. I'd practiced and prepared for the fight—never the aftermath.

Focus on one person, then the next, I had to keep reminding myself. Any more than that, and my thoughts and anxiety started to spiral. At some point, I stopped counting time in the seconds that passed and instead with the different people I helped. I noticed the police and first responders when I instructed a woman on keeping pressure on the small gash on her head. I realized the scene had started to disperse when an EMT and I hooked another woman's arms around our shoulders, helping her limp on a swollen ankle toward clearer ground. As we set her down for a moment to rest, I heard a familiar voice call my name from around the corner.

"You okay here?" I checked with the two of them.

The woman on the ground managed a faint smile, and the EMT offered a thumbs-up. "Go ahead. We've got this," she said.

I nodded, then jogged toward the noise. Phase waved me over to the entrance to a small shop just across from the tower, her shoulders set. "We need your help with this one," she said, her voice sounding grim. I followed her inside. Crossing the landing was like stepping into an apocalypse. Glass and dust crunched underfoot, and I had to step carefully to avoid the drywall and rubble that had fallen in the blast. Several police officers huddled at the back of the room, behind the counter. They glanced up as we approached, looking about as pleased with us being there as the group had looked yesterday at the grocery store. Ignoring their condescending frowns, I followed Phase and tried to put on an air of confidence I didn't really have.

When I reached the back counter, I saw what she'd called me for. An older man lay on the floor, pain contorting his face. His arm was pinned at an awkward angle beneath a large shelf that had fallen and a heavy brick slab that looked like it had once been part of the counter. He whimpered a little at the sound of my arrival, but he was wedged beneath the debris in such a way that he couldn't see any of us. I recoiled a little at the sight.

"Sorry," Mia muttered softly beside me. I could hear her own distress in her voice. She continued a little louder, so the others could hear. "We need to get him out, but we have to make sure nothing shifts the wrong way. Can you . . . ?"

I nodded, an idea forming. I turned to one of the officers. "Actually, if you can lift everything, I can keep it out of your way for a few seconds."

"Huh?"

"Just trust me," I reassured Mia. "And be ready to grab him." I looked back to the officers and nodded. Two of them lined up on either side of the man, getting a hold of the shelf first. The third stood just behind them, his weight leaning against the brick, ready to tip it out of the way. I took a deep breath, and they counted each other off.

"One . . . two . . ."

On "three," the men grunted and huffed, lifting the objects only an inch or two. It was all they could manage, but it was enough. I reached an arm out, placing a hand against the shelf and feeling the static dance across my fingertips. At the same time, Mia reached for the man, dragging him out from underneath the pile as he yelped in pain. The officer who'd tipped the brick slab away held his grip until he was clear, then let it slip back into place. It was all done in the matter of a second or two, and then everyone stepped back, panting and staring at the heavy shelf that was suspended in time. It floated there, then slammed back down, nearly breaking in half and sending a small plume of dust into our eyes.

Most of us coughed, except for Mia. She looked up at me from where she knelt by the man. "That's new," she commented.

I shrugged. "I said the same thing."

Together, we helped the men clear a path for the EMTs and firefighters to load the man onto a stretcher—after we'd gotten him clear, he'd complained of neck pain that made us too nervous to try to move him again. Mia and I watched from the side of the room as they wheeled him away. Once they were gone, I took a heavy breath. I couldn't help it any longer. I collapsed into a nearby chair, letting my head droop.

"Hey," Mia said after a moment, breaking through the quiet. I looked up at her. "How about we call it for the day?" She nodded outside, at the sun that was starting to dip toward the horizon once more. "They've got it handled from here. Besides, you and I should probably clean ourselves up a bit." She gestured to her suit, now coated in a thin layer of dust and drywall. I glanced at my own, marred with a few new scuffs and stains from all I'd been through over the course of the day. I sighed and nodded, then let Phase help pull me back on my feet.

"Tell me again what happened?"

I paused my scrubbing, looking to the ceiling while I recounted what I could of the events before the explosion. The sound I'd heard while inside the clock tower. The strange structure I'd seen in the alley. The man who'd guarded it.

"And you said you didn't get a good look at him?" Mia asked.

"No, not really. Not at his face, at least."

Mia frowned, her hand hovering over the hole in her suit she'd been sewing.

"What is it?" I asked.

She set her needle down, looking at me a moment while she thought. "Nothing," she muttered. "It's just weird."

I nodded in agreement. It was later that night, and the two of us sat in her bathroom, me cleaning the dirt and stains from my suit in her tub, Mia sitting on the toilet lid and repairing a few minor holes in hers. It was something I probably could've done with a soapy rag on my own back in my dorm, but I think we both preferred the company tonight.

I dipped my rag back in the soapy water and wrung it out. Since that afternoon, words had hammered against my chest alongside my heartbeat—things I wanted to say but didn't know how to. I *hadn't* been able to say them earlier, when we'd been downtown. Now, I guessed I was just too nervous. As I tried to work up my courage though, Mia cleared her throat.

"I know today was . . . a lot. For both of us." I turned to her, and she pursed her lips, not really looking at me. "But you did good. Really."

I swallowed my guilt and shook my head. "I froze."

"So what? I would've too, back when I started." She shrugged. "You have powers, Cass, but you're still allowed to be human."

I nodded, letting her words sink in. "About what happened before . . ." I started.

She cut me off. "It was an accident. And someone was bound to find out at some point. I mean . . ." She trailed off, her attention drifting to the work in her lap. In the silence, she snipped the thread she was using and set aside the excess.

"Why was Andrew coming here in the first place?" I asked.

"That big grant for the physics department. I'm writing a feature on it for the paper, and we'd set up an interview, but I forgot the newsroom is under construction. The elevator's out of order all week." I watched her focus on the leftover thread for a moment, brushing a finger across the raw end. At her touch, the fibers melted together. She looked back at me. "I didn't even realize at first that you knew him, but by the time I did, it was going to be more suspicious if I backed out."

"And of course he wouldn't have ever realized who you were," I said, "until I walked right up to your door."

Mia sighed, drumming her fingers on her leg. "I'm not gonna lie . . . it sucks. But you were doing what you had to. I'm not mad you came to get me."

"Still. I'm sorry."

We continued our work over the next few minutes, neither of us really feeling the need to fill it with anything except the sounds of snipping thread and sloshing water. Beyond the weight of the conversation, the day itself was starting to catch up with both of us. But after we'd finished with our suits and hung them to dry, as I'd gathered my things and suggested heading back home for the evening, Mia voiced one last reassurance aloud.

"He knew about Playback already, right?"

"Yeah. He did."

She nodded, glancing back into the corner of the room where her helmet was tucked just out of view. "You trust him," she finally relented, sounding tired. "So I do too."

CHAPTER TEN

I N THE DAYS FOLLOWING, the three of us moved past the awkward encounter in the hallway and faked our way back into the status quo as much as we could. Andrew now carried both our secrets, but as more time passed, he and Mia were coming to accept the fact. Slowly.

I was happy they were getting along, and that I had one less secret to keep from the people I cared about. Still, it didn't make my "status quo" much easier to face than it had been before.

The weekend after the explosion downtown, Mom picked me up from campus in the early morning and drove me to the hospital, so I could visit Dad for a few hours in the afternoon. As we drove, I stared at the world that flew by out the window, my mind wandering somewhere along the brush on the side of the road. Mom had said the trip would be good for all of us. The nurses had told her even though Dad was in a coma, he might be able to hear people talking to him. I wasn't sure if I wanted that to be true. I ached with how many stories and secrets I'd kept inside since the accident, how much I wanted to tell him or ask for his advice. But the thought of him being conscious this whole time and unable to let anyone know? It made me shudder to even think about.

We'd been silent for much of the trip so far, with Mom shooting me worried glances in between watching the road. Finally, she spoke up. "Is everything okay with you and Andrew?" she asked.

Her bluntness caught me off guard. "What?" I gave a surprised laugh. "Yeah, everything's great between us." *Other than the fact that he found out my superhero friend's secret identity.* "I mean, he's been busy with the lab, and I've been busy with schoolwork and . . . everything else. But we're good." I gave a small chuckle. "He told me to tell you he misses your cooking."

Mom's face turned up in a half smile. "I'll have to make some gumbo for the next time I come up to campus." Her expression faltered a moment later. "You just seem . . . quiet lately. That's all."

I bit my lower lip, turning to watch the road. "Things have been hard."

"I know." I heard her shift in her seat behind me. "None of this is fair to you or to your father. I wish there was something I could do, but I'm . . . lost." Her voice wavered on the last word. I turned back to her. "I just want to know you're okay."

"I'm . . ." I sighed, not sure how I wanted to finish the sentence. "There's some things I'm figuring out right now, I guess. But I'm okay."

"Promise me?" she urged.

I promised.

I watched a weight roll off her back, and her posture relaxed in its absence. She blinked back tears, reaching a hand across the console. All this time, I'd been grappling with what had happened inside that car a few weeks ago. What had changed because of it. But only now did I fully consider what it had been like to the one family member who *hadn't* been there. Mom had been on the sidelines for everything; she was still there now. I wished there were something I could say to fix things, some way to take us back to the way we'd been before.

But that wasn't how Playback's powers worked.

So instead, I reached out and took the hand she offered and, with a squeeze, tried to close some of the distance between us.

To my surprise, the city was just as desperate to move on with life the way it had been before—only somehow, it was succeeding at it more than I was. People seemed horrified for a moment by the explosion, but then that moment passed, and everyone went back to their old lives as if nothing had happened. This was just what they did, Mia told me one day with a shrug. Maybe it was because of what it took to bear the gravity of a situation like this for much longer. Maybe it was because they couldn't see it once the rubble was cleared, or because they were so used to these kinds of events happening that they had become just part of the landscape. The important thing, she reminded me, was that we'd been there. *I'd* been there. And we'd done what we could to help. "That's what they'll remember most," she'd said.

The next few weeks seemed almost boring by comparison. I traded in my morning practice sessions with Mia for time spent patrolling downtown, and in between classes, the police scanner app she'd helped me download became the background music to my study sessions. (It was the same one they used in the newsroom, she'd told me. I was starting to understand the appeal of having a journalism job as a cover story.) We didn't see each other quite as much anymore, at least not as Cassidy and Mia. The longest conversation I could remember was when we'd been cleaning our suits the night of the explosion.

When we were masked, it was a slightly different story. Playback and Phase had a tendency to meet up in the evenings as they moved through the city. Those nights were my favorite. We helped an old man who was living on the street find an open warming shelter on a night when the temperature dipped. We helped cool things down—literally, in Phase's case—in a parking lot drug deal that had threatened to turn ugly. We even got to step in when a few guys who'd had too much to drink began harassing a group of sorority sisters outside a bar. The look on the men's faces when the two of us had stepped out of the shadows behind those three women ... Well, let's just say they'd sobered up pretty quickly.

None of it was all that eventful, yet even those small scuffles had seemed to dissipate over the past few days. Throughout the week, my walks through downtown had ended without any excitement, and I'd changed back out of my suit each night feeling almost unsettled by so many hours of quiet. Mia had admitted the same. Maybe everyone was just putting in that last push at work before they left town for Thanksgiving or before the chaos of the holiday shopping season. But the two of us both felt on edge about it all, as if we were just waiting for the eye of the storm to pass before the hurricane returned. If that was the case, it was certainly taking its time, I'd noted. Our rounds of patrolling today had helped an elderly man find his way back home after making a wrong turn but not much else.

Tonight, at least, promised to be more interesting.

"Looks like the crowd is starting to pick up," Mia remarked. We stood in a small alleyway off one of the main streets in the city, watching. The sun was just starting to dip lower in the horizon, and the light that was left had transformed into liquid honey. It dripped down buildings and pooled on the brick pathways that had worn smooth over years of footsteps, and it drew people outside in growing numbers. It was even busier than usual; tonight, the city was kicking off its holiday lights season.

"Have you normally needed to be here for this?" I asked. I stood farther back from the entrance to the alley. Pros of having a flashy purple suit: It was instantly recognizable. Cons of having a flashy purple suit: It was instantly recognizable. I was relying on Mia's all-black getup to blend in better, and on her commentary to keep me in the loop.

"No, not really. I come because the chief asked me to one year, but it's just for show— Oh, hang on." Mia crouched forward, as if she were trying to get a better angle. "Something just ahead maybe. In front of the parking garage."

"What kind of something?"

"Mm, not sure. Let me see if I can take a quick peek." She moved backward, deeper into the alley, and slipped off her helmet and jacket. She held both out to me. I shot her a skeptical look, one that was likely lost in the shadows and behind my mask; still, I took them both from her, freeing her hands to tie her hair up in a quick knot and straighten her T-shirt. She huffed in finality. "Be right back," she promised. Then, she walked out onto the street, leaving me crouched in the alley with her things. I sighed and balanced them on a nearby box, then crept forward a few steps to take her spot at the entrance.

From here, I could see what she'd been talking about. People milled about in a large clump, but nothing really seemed out of the ordinary. Families with small children laughed and joked, and groups of students seemed to be standing around and gossiping with one another. Still, something bothered me, and I couldn't quite put my finger on what it was. I turned my attention back to Mia and followed her movements as she skirted around the edges of the crowd. I got the feeling disappearing had never really been a strength of hers. Even without her suit, she carried herself with an air of authority. People couldn't help but notice her.

A few minutes passed while Mia wove her way through the throngs of people. I stayed in a low crouch as I watched, hoping she was deducing things better from up close. All I could make out were her curls as they peeked out above the sea of faces, bobbing along with the traffic's slow-moving current. Eventually, they reemerged at the front of the crowd, the rest of Mia's outline appearing along with them. The light outside had lessened in the time that had passed; the pools of honey from before were now dusky amber, and shadows carved harsh lines across the scene. Her face appeared serious in the late afternoon light, but she made eye contact with me from across the way and shrugged. Nothing out of the ordinary.

As she started toward our makeshift hideout again, a slight commotion rose behind her. The muscles in my legs tensed. I watched a few people stumble to the side, and a man in a large trench coat knocked into Mia's shoulder from behind. "Hey!" she called out, catching herself before the rest of her met pavement. He just kept walking, as if he hadn't heard her. She frowned after him for a moment, a flash of confusion or frustration crossing her features. But whatever emotion it was disappeared as quickly as it had come, and she continued toward me until she was concealed once again between two buildings. "Aside from Friendly there," she said, jabbing a thumb toward the crowd over her shoulder, "I didn't see anything. Just a bunch of people clogging up the sidewalks." She shrugged, at as much of a loss as I was, then reached for her outfit once again.

A beep sounded from Mia's pocket as she zipped her jacket once more, making the two of us jump. The scanner app on Mia's phone crackled to life. "Requesting backup," a strained voice said. "Officers down . . . the roof of the Second Avenue garage."

My eyes widened. Mia, her face concealed once more underneath her helmet, turned toward me. "The fire escape on the bookshop next door. Go. I'm right behind you."

I didn't need to be told twice. I leapt out from the alleyway and began weaving through the crowd, startling a couple students I recognized from my history class. Just as I reached the fire escape, metal latches clanged and sizzled above me, melting into small pools that dripped onto the platform below. The ladder unfolded itself at my feet. Before the gasps and murmured names had reached my ears, I was climbing, staying careful to avoid the areas that still glowed red hot from Phase's handiwork.

The parking garage's roof had been built almost flush with the bookshop, so the leap from one building to the next was manageable. Still, I kept my eyes trained ahead of me as I jumped, not able to afford to slow down. Dirt and gravel crunched underfoot once, then again as my feet, then Mia's, found purchase on the concrete. It didn't take much more searching before we found the officers who had made the radio call. We had to weave around stacks of construction supplies to get to them—materials and tools were spread across the space, blocking off most of the parking spaces on either side of the roof.

"Are you two all right?" Mia asked, running to meet the two policemen. One of the officers had leaned against the stacked wood pallets of cement blocks and metal rebar. He clutched his side, and tinges of red had leaked out to stain his fingers. The other officer stood to greet us, but he seemed shaky on his feet. He bore a large gash on his forehead, and blood trickled down just past his ear.

"He just . . . he came out of nowhere. The roof was closed to the public. No one was supposed to be up here because of the renovations," the second officer said.

Mia reached her hands out to support him, then eased him back down into a sitting position next to his partner. "Who?" she asked him.

"We couldn't see his face," rasped the first, his voice strained. "All we saw was the long green coat."

I whipped around to face Mia. "Phase. The guy in the trench coat."

She shook her head. "No, wait!" she called. But I had already spun on my heels, searching the ground below for the man who had bumped into Mia. About two blocks away, I spotted a flash of army green slip around a corner. I shoved myself back in time.

It wasn't much, but I'd given myself a five-second head start at least.

Mia's warning echoed behind me, the same words and cadence as before, but I didn't stick around to argue or explain. I ran for the opposite side of the building, in the same direction as the man. A streetlamp, arched over the sidewalk and the patrons below, stretched to about the same height as the roof of the garage. As I came to the edge of the building, my feet lifted away from the concrete lip, and I reached my hands out in front of me. I managed to wrap my arms around the light post just in time. I grunted at the impact, but my suit took the friction as I slid, and my feet found solid ground a moment later. I jumped away from the post and continued down the road, finding a shortcut between two buildings parallel to where the man was heading.

With the sun setting, night oozed out from between buildings and behind structures, and shadows escaped their usual daytime confines to play tricks on my eyes. It was hard to maintain my pace and keep from stumbling on uneven ground or discarded beer bottles in the process. Still, I kept my eyes trained on the slivers of sunlight ahead of me. I counted the blocks in my head as I went, trying to guess how far I was behind the man. But how sure was I that I could even catch up to him?

I felt the wall before I saw it. As I exited back out onto an empty sidewalk, I slammed into it at a full sprint, stumbling a few steps while I worked to right myself. Except . . . the wall stumbled too. Metal clanged against the ground, and thin copper pipes bounced and rolled around my feet. I turned so the silhouette in my periphery took form, and my adrenaline surged. I locked eyes with the man in the trench coat.

"I told you to stay out of my way." The words came from deep in his throat, so low I almost couldn't make them out. A shiver worked its way down my spine.

"What?" I asked. I'd never seen this man before in my life. But that voice . . . I racked my brain to try and place it, to understand why just the sound of it turned my blood to ice water. "It was you that day by the clock tower," I realized. For the first time, I took in the sight of him: patchy and worn-through military jacket, grubby pants, heavy boots. His hands were rough and calloused, curled into fists that showed off scars and scrapes on his knuckles. His dirty—literally dirty—blond hair, with hints of gray showing through, hung just past the tops of his ears, and his eyes made silent threats behind his bushy brows. I forced down a shudder. I was staring into the face of a wild animal.

He didn't answer me, but I knew I was right. "You blew up half a block. You just attacked two cops," I continued. My words were steady, but they were helping hide my taut nerves. "Tell me why."

He shook his head, almost laughing. "*You* wouldn't understand." The rest of his sentence leaned on that first word. For a moment, I was actually offended.

"What the hell is that supposed to mean?"

But he wasn't in the mood for a conversation. He lunged forward, and I ducked hastily, turning so my shoulder would slam into his middle and absorb his momentum. The man folded inward for a second at my blow, holding an arm to his stomach. But just as quickly, he righted himself. His eyes darkened. His gaze darted away from my face for an instant, and I followed it to the copper tubes behind me.

So I had part of an answer. I turned back, and this time, I was the one to make the first move. I dashed forward and leapt into the air, and as my feet lifted off the ground, I drove a knee into his chest, sending him stumbling back a step. He swung an arm out blindly in my direction. I reacted at just the right moment, feeling the impact in my forearm instead of in my face. Still, it didn't lessen the sting.

I shook the pain from my arm, then raised my fists again. He was bigger than me, and obviously stronger. Yet I was faster, and I had time on my side. With every few swings, I watched for openings in his movements, and I rewound to exploit them as much as I could. A kick to his exposed side. A knee to the groin. I was getting cockier, but I didn't really care. For the first time, I didn't feel like I was using my powers just to stay in the ring. I was fighting—and it felt like I was *winning*.

As the man hastily scrubbed his eyes—I'd thrown a handful of dirt in them when he'd knocked me onto my back a second ago—I reached behind me for one of the loose copper tubes he'd dropped earlier. I had something I wanted to try. Drawing back, I brought the tube over my shoulder, putting as much force into my throw as I could muster. Just as it left my hand, I let it brush against my fingertips, and my skin buzzed with static where it touched. I pulled my arm away. The pipe stayed suspended where it had left my hand, floating in the space between the man and me. He was upright again, a savage look in his watering eyes, and the small smirk I'd been wearing dissipated. I matched his glare with one of my own, and then I struck the pipe with my other palm. It sparked through my glove as I released it with all the momentum it'd had before, plus the force of my second strike. Without waiting, I took another step to close the distance between the man and me, and as the tubing struck his wrist, I tried to hook a leg behind his knee and bring him down.

His shout of pain from the pipe's impact was drowned out in my ears by my gasp of surprise. His opposite hand squeezed around my ankle, throwing it out to the side and sending me tumbling to the pavement. My head cracked against the ground. I felt a welt grow behind my braid, and my eyes watered.

"No more games," the man said, leaning in close. I raised my hands in front of me to try again, but he caught them beneath his injured arm and pinned them back against my chest. His other hand pointed his knife to my throat. His weight made it hard to breathe, and I coughed, each one sending bolts of pain through my head. His icy eyes bore into mine for another second. Then, he pushed against me to get up from the ground. The extra pressure constricted my airways, and when it released, I gasped for breath, each lungful of air scraping against my throat. A heavy boot landed inches from my face, and I scrambled to right myself. But he didn't care anymore. The man had already gathered most of the copper pieces into his arms again and was now moving farther down the road.

The sound of footsteps pulled my attention away from the man. I saw a familiar silhouette drawing closer from between the buildings, the same direction I'd come from. "That way," I called, pointing a finger up the road. Phase turned as if to follow him and skidded to a stop, her hands already raised. But by that point, the thief was just a smudge against the dim backdrop. Too far away for Mia to reach with her powers. She growled a curse I couldn't quite make out, then turned and reached a hand out to me.

"Are you all right?" she asked. I took her hand and pulled myself to my feet, wincing a little.

"I've been worse," I said.

"You've been better," she countered. "You should've listened to me."

I ignored her, reaching a hand behind my head to feel the bruise that was there. With my other hand, I picked up one of the copper tubes the man had left behind, offering it to Mia. "This is what he wanted from that parking garage."

She studied it for a moment. "Copper," she commented, mostly to herself. "So probably a get-rich-quick scheme? But then why would you take it in broad daylight?"

I shook my head. "This wasn't for money. It was the same man from the other day," I told her. "The clock tower." She looked up from the pipe.

"I thought you'd said you couldn't see the man's face then."

"I recognized his voice," I assured her. "It was definitely him."

It was hard to gauge her reaction through her helmet. I watched as she looked down at the pipe still in her hand, rolling it thoughtfully between her fingers. Finally, she looked back at me. "Let's get you back home. I want to take a look at that." She pointed at where I still gingerly cradled my head, then stuffed the pipe under her arm and began leading us back in the direction of campus.

A few hours later, I sat propped against my pillows in my dorm room, holding a sandwich bag filled with cool water to the back of my head. The last of the ice had melted probably half an hour ago, but I barely noticed. Or cared. Besides my headache, I was still nursing a sour mood, and I had little motivation to try and fix it, especially at 12:30 at night.

I'd told Mia about the man I'd fought earlier. She'd walked me back here and checked me for a concussion after my fall, listening to my play-by-play of everything that had happened. But no matter how much I tried to convince her, she wasn't willing to accept it was the same man I'd fought before. "Did he ever *say* he was at the clock tower that day?" she'd asked when I kept insisting.

I'd racked my brain, trying to remember the conversation. "No," I'd finally admitted, frowning in thought, "but he definitely didn't deny it either."

"Look, you hit your head really hard," she'd offered. "It's possible you might not remember things clearly—"

"I know what happened." I'd struggled to keep my words measured and even, but my frustration was growing. I'd pointed out that he'd threatened me with a knife just like before, that he'd only taken metal when plenty of other expensive materials and equipment had been at the garage, but she still wasn't willing to buy it.

"Okay, okay. I never said I don't believe you. But it's not enough to go on," she'd said. "And we're not doing anything until we know for sure. You *definitely* aren't doing anything." I'd opened my mouth to argue the point more, but the look she gave me then shot daggers. I'd dropped the subject.

But I hadn't stopped thinking about it. Mia might not have been worried about another explosion, but just the possibility of it set my nerves on edge. She hadn't been there when it happened. She'd witnessed the devastation, sure, but she hadn't been on the street, trying to herd people away from the scene. She hadn't heard the sound that machine made or felt what it did to the air around it. And she hadn't heard the man who'd been there that day.

I sighed and reached for my phone. Mia had warned me before she'd left that I should limit my screen time, but I didn't care right now. I just needed something to do with my hands while my mind worked over the problem in the background. I clicked open my newsfeed and started scrolling, though my eyes moved past the words on each post without me reading them.

A picture on one post made me stop, however. It was from the holiday lighting event a few hours earlier—or, rather, just before it. The picture showed the buildings still gilded by the sunset, but it focused on two familiar silhouettes on a roof: one in all black, one in purple and white.

It was still a bit weird, seeing myself everywhere without anyone knowing it was *me*. Hearing my name mentioned under people's breaths was one thing, but the pictures and conversations online were a reminder of just how public part of my life was now. Someone was always watching. I sighed and continued scrolling.

The realization struck me a few seconds later. Someone *was* always watching. And they weren't just watching me. I opened the search bar and typed in a few keywords. I had to skim through quite a few results, but I eventually found the kind of post I'd hoped I would.

"Anyone else see the new art installation by the clock tower?" It was dated the same day as the explosion, only a few hours before. That one hadn't received any responses, but just a little further down, someone else had made a similar observation.

"Only at Everett can you watch someone metal sculpting like his life depends on it before your 9 AM," the post read. This one had a few comments, and I clicked on one to expand it.

"I've seen him a few times. People I know were calling him Futurist. No idea who he is." They ended with a shrug emoji.

Futurist? I typed the name into the search bar, hoping it would pop up with something interesting. I was hit with a flood of results, but most were useless. I skimmed past plenty of tech ads and random comments with the word buried in the text, but none of them looked like they were from anywhere even close to Everett. I was about to give up when I spotted an option to filter my results.

My results pool shrank to just one page, including the posts I'd already seen. *Geotagging to the rescue.* The last result was one of the tech ads I'd scrolled past earlier. But in the middle was a post from earlier this afternoon that included an image—grainy, and with no caption except for "#Futur-ist???" I clicked on it and zoomed in, trying to get a sense of what I was looking at. It looked like somewhere downtown, though the shadows made it hard to pinpoint exactly where. Whoever had taken the photo had zoomed in considerably, which didn't help the situation. I rolled my eyes, which sent my head throbbing, and squinted at the screen.

And then I realized what was confusing me. The photo was from an odd angle, making the person in the photo little more than an outline. But as I looked closer, I could see the shape of his head. His torso. His long trench coat. It was taken a few hours before people had started to gather for the holiday lighting, and there was little to identify him beyond his coat, but what were the odds that this wasn't the same man from earlier? More importantly, he looked close enough. And this person had tagged the photo with the same name people had used with the man from the clock tower.

"Oh my god," I whispered. My stomach somersaulted, and I put a hand to my mouth. Did I actually have *proof*?

My gaze had drifted vacantly to the wall as thoughts rushed through my head, but in an instant, I turned back to my screen. I tried clicking on the person's profile, but before I could, my phone buzzed in my hand. A name flashed across the screen. It was Mia. *Perfect.*

I answered. "Hey, we need to talk. I'm still feeling fine—I've been keeping ice on it like you said. But I may have just found someth—"

"It'll have to wait." It was hard to tell through the phone, but it sounded like her voice was shuddering. I could hear her running. "Suit up and meet me outside as fast as you can. We've got an emergency."

She hung up before I had a chance to respond, but with the panic in her voice, I'd already tossed my phone aside. My hands moved faster than my brain; they dug out my suit from where I'd shoved it underneath my bed and swapped my sweatpants for the reinforced leggings faster than normal. I slipped on a pair of shoes and stuffed the rest of my outfit under my arm, then headed out my door and toward the stairs.

Mia's words on the phone had just started to sink in as I paused at the building's side door to tug on the rest of my suit. She hadn't given me anything to go on, no clue of even where we were headed. Part of me was still annoyed with her from earlier. But I couldn't think about that; not now. This was I had signed up for—we worked together, whether I was upset with Mia or not. My gloves were the last to go on. I tightened them on my wrists just as I opened the side door to the building, the brisk night air stinging my eyes. Seconds later, I heard the thrum of a motorbike rounding the corner.

I took a steadying breath. It was time to be a hero.

CHAPTER ELEVEN

Mia's tires squealed against the pavement as she came to a halt in front of me. Without a word, I climbed on behind her, and we tore off into the night.

"I'm sorry. I didn't mean to have you back out doing anything so soon," she shouted above the rush of the wind. "You should be recovering." I couldn't see her face, but guilt laced her words.

"It's fine," I promised. "What's wrong?"

"Not entirely sure," she said. "People have been calling in saying they heard a loud bang and smelled smoke in their apartment. All the same complex."

I wasn't sure why, but my gut twisted with a sick feeling. "First responders?" I asked.

"On their way, but they were across town when the call came in. We're faster."

The streets were mostly empty this time of night, but I wasn't sure we would've obeyed traffic laws any better had there been other cars on the road. Mia zipped through intersections and leaned into each turn without slowing. The streetlights and holiday decorations were colorful smears in my periphery as we blew past, and the wind nipped at my ears until they hurt. Still, I silently urged us on faster.

I smelled it before I saw it. Even from a block away, acrid smoke hung in the air, clinging to my mask and the inside of my nose. The haze in the sky glowed brighter until it snuffed out the stars. Then, as we rounded the corner, the building came into view. I recognized it instantly. It was one of the oldest complexes in town, its facade normally muted compared with the flashy student housing they built now. This one had always been too far from campus for many students to bother renting here—most of this building's tenants were families. I watched now as flames billowed out of its windows, tossing up plumes of ash and smoke. Even in the freezing temperatures, the heat seeped through my clothes.

Mia brought us to a stop right outside the building's entrance. As I climbed off the bike, I looked at the horror looming above us. The fire roared louder than anything else around it, crackling and hissing with each new thing it consumed. But amid the cacophony, I could just make out a whisper of other sounds too—yelps and shouts from the upper floors, pots and pans banging together. A bedsheet fluttered outside one of the windows like a flag. People were still trapped in there.

"We've got to get them out," I shouted, pointing. Mia nodded, already crafting a plan.

"I'll go in first," she said. "The heat won't bother me like it will you. Stick close, okay?" I nodded. We moved toward the building's front entrance. The door already hung ajar, and a faint, orange light shone from somewhere down the main hall as we approached. It didn't deter us. I steeled my nerves as Mia ran through the opening first. I watched her outline vanish behind the smoke, and after I sucked in one last breath, I let the building swallow me as well.

My breath outside hadn't mattered. Once I was through the entryway, the heat pulled the air from my lungs, and my next breath burned in my throat, more smoke than air. I crouched lower to the floor. The air was thick, but after a moment, I finally spotted Mia down the hall, her visor glinting in the firelight. She waved me forward and gestured. She'd found the building's main stairwell. I moved toward her, already sputtering through my mask. The stairway was a tight fit, and it was already engulfed in smoke. But we didn't have a choice. I fought back another cough, then nodded. Wordlessly, we began to climb.

The smoke grew thicker as we ascended, turning the air around us to ink. I could hear Mia coughing behind her helmet as we reached the top floor. The fire was quickly growing worse here; it licked up the walls, sizzling and popping around us. I watched as a welcome mat at the end of the hall caught a trailing spark and erupted into part of the larger monster.

"Is anyone here?" Mia managed to yell, her voice raspy. We strained our ears to hear past the fire. If I listened closely, I could just make out—

"Phase, this way!" I called. I ran to the end of the hall, the one bookended by the blaze. The pounding grew louder, more frantic. That was it; the room on the left, next to the one with the burning welcome mat. I reached for the door handle, but it hissed the moment I brushed against it. I recoiled, crying out.

"Wait, let me." Phase moved in front of me, reaching for the handle herself. The metal steamed as it cooled the instant she touched it. She wrenched the door open, calling out for whoever might still be inside. I turned, scanning the rest of the hall. There was something odd about one of the doors on the other end. I blinked the ash from my eyes, moving closer. A towel poked out haphazardly from underneath the doorjamb. It was sopping wet; someone was still in there.

Phase was still preoccupied with the room down the hall, and I wasn't about to try the handle again on my own. Taking as deep a breath as I could muster, I reeled back, throwing my weight against the door. It slammed open, shaking on its hinges. Smoke poured in around me, and I pressed my face into the crook of my elbow, trying to keep from inhaling it all. In here, I could hear something—a quiet whimpering, like a child crying. But it was so faint. "Where are you?" I yelled, my voice straining. No answer. The whimpering started to fade.

I stumbled forward, scouring the living area for signs of someone. Anyone. The fire was starting to creep its way closer from out in the hall. We were running out of time, and every second counted. I pulled my arm away from my face and readied my hands, then shoved myself back.

I stood in the entryway again, the fire still in the hallway, as it had been five seconds ago. The living room was a bust, so I ran toward the first door I'd spotted on the opposite wall. A bathroom. I peeked behind the shower curtain, stifling a cough that was still trapped in my chest, but no luck. I rewound again.

The second door I tried was a master bedroom, but it was empty. The door on the farthest end of the room was my last hope. I crossed my fingers and tried again. My lungs were screaming. But as I stumbled forward this time, I could just start to make out the whisper of a voice. The door swung open easily, and I stepped into a children's bedroom, the two twin beds both mussed . . . yet empty. I spun on my heels, searching. Just as I started to raise my hands again, the closet door swung open. Two children tumbled out, a boy and a girl, followed by another girl who looked a few years younger than me. The boy clutched a wriggling terrier in his arms.

"I didn't know what to do," said the older girl—the babysitter, I guessed, as she looked nothing like the other kids—as her chin wavered. "I—" She fell into a coughing fit before she could say more, and I placed a hand on her shoulder to help her get below the smoke.

"It's okay. We're going to get you guys out of here," I promised. I led us back out into the hallway, spotting Phase in the haziness. Her helmet had turned gray from the soot. She led her own group of survivors: an elderly couple helping support each other on shaky limbs, each with an arm wrapped around the other's shoulders and a washrag held to their face to protect against the smoke. Our groups met on the stairs, the heat from below already singeing our exposed skin. Without a word, I took the back of the group and watched as Mia paved the way at the front for the rest of us.

The stairs were worse than before. As we descended, Mia kept her hands constantly moving. She held together the oozing plastic on the stair treads and cooled the metal handrails before anyone could touch them. The fire had crawled up one of the outer walls of the stairway and threatened now to close the distance to the other wall, blocking our path. But with little more than a glance, she waved a hand toward one of the pipes stretching up the center of the room. Molten metal began to drip and pool down its sides, and steam hissed out from the hole it made. She reached her other hand out and gave a sharp twist of her wrist, and the steam turned back into liquid, tamping down the blaze and wetting everything enough to keep the fire from spreading while we passed. She was clearing dangers none of the rest of us had even considered. Yet I could tell it was taking its toll. Her pace was starting to slow, and she slumped over to cough and hack every few steps, trying to catch her breath. She might've been immune to the heat, but her powers couldn't do anything about the ash that burned in her lungs. As she paused again, worry for her coiled around my throat. I forced the feeling down with another raspy breath.

As we passed the fourth-floor landing, the little girl—the youngest of everyone by far—let out a sudden wail. Everyone's faces whipped around to meet her. Just then, the ground started to tremble beneath us. I reached out to the wall to steady myself, and my eyes widened. I met Mia's gaze on the landing below. "The building's starting to give!" she shouted.

The man that Mia had helped free clutched at his chest, his terrified cry still muffled by his washcloth. He leaned his tired body against his wife's. She just looked at Mia, pleading.

I caught the babysitter's gaze. One of the fingers on her free hand was held tight in the little girl's fist; the babysitter's other arm was occupied by the puppy the boy had been carrying earlier. "Go," I urged. It seemed to be the permission she'd been waiting for, because the three of them and their puppy began to move at double their pace from earlier. They disappeared around the corner without a second glance. As they did, I moved up beside the elderly woman, taking her husband's arm from around her shoulders and looping it over my own. The man was conscious but weak. I watched his lips shape around words, and though their sound was lost among his wheezing, I could tell he was trying to mouth "thank you." I just nodded, first to him and then to Mia.

We continued on, making it to the third-floor landing. The air was still thick and noxious, but the flames had already eaten away at most of the drywall and insulation on the landing, leaving behind smoldering embers and charred remains of the building's main support structure. At least, that was the case in the stairwell. Intense heat still seared the back of my neck as we put our backs to the third-floor entrance, and I grimaced behind my mask at the thought of what it meant for the hallway and the apartments beyond.

There was a small window on the landing here too—the glass had been blown out from the heat, and I could see swirling tendrils of smoke trailing out of it into the night. It was too small to offer much relief, but still, we all reached our heads up to it as we moved past, hoping for a sip of air.

"Playback," Mia coughed. I turned back. She stood slumped against the railing, her visor pointed toward the window. She raised a hand and pointed. "Is that what I think it is?"

I squinted at what she was referring to, fighting my own lightheadedness. From here, I could just make out the flash of something white in the corner of the window frame, flapping against the heat that filtered out. My stomach dropped. "Is that someone trying to flag for help?" I asked.

"We need to be sure."

I turned to the man I was supporting, my mind racing. But before I even had time to consider my options, a hand rested on the crook of my elbow. "I can take him the rest of the way," his wife said. Her voice was firm, determined, even though I could see her chest shuddering with each breath. I swallowed. I wanted to argue, but I didn't have time. With a nod, I slipped under the man's arm and let her take over.

Mia and I raced side by side back up the stairs, our footsteps thundering out into the hallway. In here, flames crackled and popped around us, no longer one monster but several greedy offshoots that worked to consume what the larger inferno had left in its wake. There was only one apartment with a balcony that would've reached the window in the stairwell, and as we came to a stop in front of it, I noted severe burn marks on the door and handle. Mia reached a hand out to turn it, but nothing happened. She cursed, sounding out of breath. "The heat warped the metal," she said. She rolled her neck, then held her hands up in front of her. "Stand back," she warned. I did as she asked.

For a second, nothing seemed to be happening. Mia's arms wavered with her effort as she focused on the door's hinges. Then, another wave of heat joined the stifling temperatures already in the hallway. I watched the metal on the sides of the door begin to glow and deform, starting from the top. The door creaked and groaned with each hinge that gave way, but Mia didn't let up. She moved her focus to the last piece connecting the door to the wall, her whole body trembling.

As she worked to free the last corner of the door from the wall, a deep groan issued from somewhere above us. I glanced up. Neither of us had realized it, but the top of the door in front of us was nearly flush with the rest of the wall. With each second that passed, the structure warped and bubbled outward even more. A crack issued from the center of the doorframe and climbed up behind the drywall that was still intact. The whole of the building was settling, and all of it seemed to be resting on a single building block.

"Careful," I started to warn.

Mia's hands lowered, and she doubled over in a coughing fit. I couldn't tell if she'd heard me. But the damage was done. In my periphery, I watched as the door buckled outward under the weight. I didn't wait to see the chain reaction it would cause. Too far away to reach her in time, I shoved against time instead, sending us back.

My position didn't move, but everything around me jumped back into position. I flung myself forward. "Mia!" I shouted. My voice broke her concentration, and she looked at me, stifling a cough with the back of her hand. I didn't wait to explain—reaching to the side, I let my palm brace against the apartment door, the zap echoing against my skin, then grabbed Mia's shoulders. I pulled her to where I'd stood before, barely making it out of the way myself before time was up. I felt a gush of hot air burst from behind the door. The wood and metal shrapnel it sent outward whizzed past my back, and I tucked Mia down into a crouch along with me just in time. A second, louder boom shook the ground around us, rattling up into my teeth. A cloud of dust and debris rained down, and both of us collapsed into wheezes and coughs.

I straightened first, turning to see the aftermath. A support beam from the ceiling had fallen in front of us, crushing the floor where Mia had been standing only a few seconds ago. Now, the smoldering wreckage blocked our path into the apartment. We were going to have to climb over it. I grimaced and turned back to Mia.

"We've gotta . . ." she started, but as she stood, she tipped toward me, and I only just managed to catch her.

"Hey, you good?" I asked.

She nodded, a little unsteadily. But I could feel the weight she was leaning on me. Her legs wobbled, and her head drooped.

"No, you're not." I glanced at the room, closed off enough until a moment ago to have avoided most of the smoke. It filtered in now, but I knew a way I could avoid the worst of it. I turned back to Mia. "You can't breathe. You've got to get out."

"Cass, I'm—" But a distant wailing interrupted her argument. The sirens were growing louder, and I felt the fight drain out of Mia's body. She nodded, standing and taking in a cautious breath.

She looked at me one last time, and I nodded. "Go! I'll be right behind you," I called. I waited until she began to move toward the staircase. Then, I faced the support beam once again and began to clamber over it, feeling its charred edges slice and scrape at my fingers.

Once inside the room, I took just a moment to catch my breath. I'd hidden it in front of the others, but the smoke still clawed at my throat and made my lungs tighten, same as Mia. My head was swimming, but I placed my hands on my knees until the feeling eased, then pushed on. Someone was still counting on me.

The layout in here matched that of the apartment I'd been in earlier. I had to turn to the right to find my bearings, but once I did, I recognized the door to the bathroom, the kitchen, the second bedroom. Somehow, most of the apartment was still intact. The rest of the building had faced a vicious heat that came in blinding, billowing waves and swallowed entire rooms and hallways in a flash. But it felt different in here. Flames licked into the room from inside the walls and snaked across the floorboards, leaving a trail of dimly glowing edges traced with a dark charcoal shadow. Smoke wafted up, creating a hazy fog in the room that matched what I'd seen in the air outside. The rest of the apartment had felt the fire's wrath; in here, it crept in quietly, inviting you to let your guard down. My breath hitched. I turned and headed for the master bedroom.

As I rounded the corner, a sense of relief washed over me. My shoulders dropped. The door to the balcony stood ajar, and at its edge, I could make out the outline of a man, standing and waving his arms above his head. Sirens from below drowned out his shouts, but the bedsheet he'd tied to one of the guardrails translated them well enough. I made a beeline for him.

"Sir!" I hollered above the noise. He jumped at my voice. Still in a T-shirt and sweatpants, he looked like he was just younger than my mom. His hair stuck out in odd directions—he must've been asleep when the fire started. His eyes were wide as he turned, and even in the dark, I could see the fear in them. I held out a hand. "Come with me. I can get you out of here."

But the man shook his head forcefully.

I hesitated, furrowing my brow. A second ticked by, and smoke filtered up through the slats of wood he stood on. "What is it?" I finally asked.

"I . . . I think I'd rather wait for the firefighters."

I moved forward a step, and the man pressed himself farther back against the guardrail. I stopped, holding up my palms in submission. "What do you mean?"

"I don't know you," he countered.

I softened. "I'm Play—"

"You're Playback, I know," he finished for me. "But you're just some girl in a suit. Why would I trust you?"

The smoke grew thicker from underneath his feet. I heard gasps from the crowd below, and I glanced down. If it was hard to make out from my angle, it would've been impossible from his, but the orange glow that was growing brighter from the ground below was enough for me to fill in the gaps. My stomach somersaulted. I turned back to the man.

"You have to trust me. Please."

"No!" His knuckles were white on the banister.

He was running out of time. I didn't know how much we had left, but I knew how much more I could give us. I shoved my hands forward, rewinding the conversation. Time for a new tactic.

"Please, you have to come with me," I begged. "That balcony could fall at any moment."

"I can't breathe in there. I can't see through the smoke."

"Come on, please. I'll help you."

"The firemen are here. They'll help." He gestured toward me. "What are you gonna be able to do? You're, like, half my size."

This was taking too long. I pressed my palms out again, then bent over, hacking and coughing at the phlegm in my throat. I reached up and pinched my mask away from my face for a moment, my lungs screaming for air.

"See? You shouldn't even be in here. How are you going to help?"

"I know a safe path out," I croaked.

"Like hell you do," the man said. I could hear a tremble in his voice though. He wasn't mad; he was terrified.

I was starting to feel the same. I shoved myself back again, fighting the nausea that rolled through me. My vision filled with spots for a moment. He was only breathing in a few seconds' worth of smoke each time we replayed this; I'd already spent minutes working in the worst of it, and now I was accumulating more. I needed to be done asking.

"I'm getting you out of here. I'm not abandoning you."

The man glanced down at the ground, then back at me. "You can't. I can't get out of here."

"Yes, you can." I struggled to keep my voice steady, to keep from coughing again. "You have to, and you will."

"I can't. I'm going to die! Oh, God . . ."

"You're not going to die," I promised. But the man wasn't listening to me anymore. He just stared at the ground below, repeating the same "Oh, God" to himself again and again. His lower lip quivered, and I let out a shaky breath. I rewound time to try again.

Each time I pushed against time, I could feel myself growing weaker. I couldn't keep my balance. My limbs and voice shook, and my chest heaved against the fumes. Still, I refused to abandon him here. I would not leave him—not when he was in this much danger. Not when I could save him.

But I couldn't do this for much longer. My vision was starting to blur at the edges, and the collar of my suit strangled me. My mouth gaped like a fish behind my mask. *Air.* I needed air. I needed to breathe.

If I couldn't convince him to come with me, we were both going to die.

I rewound time again, and this time, I ran forward. As I reached the entrance to the balcony, I grasped desperately at the man's arm. Terror ran across his face, and he ducked out of my reach, moving to the other corner of the patio. But as he did, something below jolted. A crack echoed in the night air. It stretched out the seconds that followed, hanging between us. His eyes met mine as he began to tip backward, and he reached a hand toward me.

I lunged forward again, slamming my ribs against the metal bar on the floor. My fingertips brushed against his. But my fist caught only air. The rest of the deck carried him down silently, quickly. His eyes bore into mine the whole way until they disappeared from view forever.

I know I made a sound in my throat, but I couldn't have identified what it was. It never reached my ears. Tears stung my eyes, and I readied myself to rewind things again. But as I let go from the doorframe to try, I felt myself lurching toward the ground as well, and I had to catch myself before I met the same fate. The seconds ticked by in my head, and all I could do was stare at the inferno below while its heat filtered up and burned my horror into reality.

Chapter Twelve

Minutes later, I reached the top of the fire escape next door and clambered out onto the roof, collapsing against the ground. With each ragged breath I forced through my mask, the fabric caved into my mouth. I ripped it away from my face and balled it up in my fist, sucking in lungful after lungful of air before coughing it all back out. It didn't help. Anguish had already dug its claws into my chest, and every movement I made drove them in deeper.

Mia was up here already, her back to me as she looked out across the city. She turned when she heard me come up. "Hey, do you see—oh my god." She was only on the other side of the roof, but she sounded so far away. I heard her footfalls as she ran toward me, but I couldn't bring myself to look. I curled myself into a ball, my eyes squeezed shut, and tried to focus on moving air through my lungs. Nothing else—just breathing. In. Out. I shuddered when I felt a hand on my shoulder, gently prying me apart. "Cassidy?"

Her voice still sounded hoarse. I wondered if mine was the same. I opened my mouth to speak, but any words I found lodged themselves in my throat. I choked on the truth. So I let my tears fall freely instead.

"Are you hurt? What's wrong?" Her voice was frantic, and I could feel her cool hands on my neck, on my hands, searching for an injury. I just shook my head.

"He—" I rasped. "I couldn't—" But the memory reached the surface and spilled down my cheeks before I could put it into words. I turned my eyes to hers, pleading silently for her to understand. Her confusion melted away.

"Oh, Cass . . ." she said, and the sobs racked through my body even harder. She scooped me against her chest, and I nestled there, trembling. I closed my eyes, and I saw the man's face as if he were right in front of me once again. I felt the bruise across my chest where I'd slammed into the floor, and I felt where I'd scorched my fingertips reaching for him.

As she tried to hug the broken pieces of me back together, I found the only words I could manage to say.

"It was my fault," I sobbed.

I wasn't sure how much time passed with us like that. Maybe it was only a few minutes, or maybe it was an hour. When I finally stopped crying, Mia handed me a bottle of water she'd nabbed from one of the first responders. She helped me wash the soot and tear stains from my face and gave me the rest to drink, then steered me to the opposite end of the roof, away from the chaos at the apartment. We sat on the edge there, our feet dangling, and watched the stars move across the sky in silence.

In the wake of it all, as the adrenaline wore off, the night caught up with my body. Even with the gloves' insulation, my hands stung from how many times I'd rewound time. I rubbed at my palm with the pad of my thumb and waited for the feeling to pass. My arms and legs and back all hurt to move, and my stomach ached from how much I'd been coughing. I was fairly certain my throat and lungs had been scorched from the inside by the smoke. And the back of my head throbbed. It took me a moment to remember that I'd hit it earlier this evening. It felt like a lifetime ago.

Even as I took stock of my injuries, the rest of me felt numb. Part of me wanted to cry more, but I was dehydrated, my body depleted. I'd spent the last of my energy on tears earlier, and now every emotion I wanted to feel and every word I wanted to say was trapped inside me. As we sat there, a cool breeze blew past us, tossing my hair where it had come loose from my braid. I reached behind my head and brought it over my shoulder to tame it. It felt stiff and brittle, and I looked down to examine it. The last few inches had been badly singed. I rubbed a few strands between my fingers and watched them crumble into black dust. Normally, I would've cared, but tonight I felt nothing. I turned my attention back to the sky.

"You know," Mia said quietly, "I was a few years older than you when I got my powers. I thought it was the most amazing thing that would ever happen to me. Of course, I didn't have the heart that you do. The first thing you did was go and help people; I just did dumb shit to impress my friends." She laughed sadly, and I finally turned to face her. I watched her gaze fall to her hands in her lap. "My girlfriend was the one who convinced me to try and be more. To become Phase."

She faltered. "I didn't know anything about being a hero though. I didn't try to hide my identity . . . mostly because I didn't think about how dangerous it was. I got in way over my head." Her expression hardened. She flicked at a piece of rubble on her jacket, then looked back out over the city, shaking her head. "I made an enemy, and he decided to get even. And when I went to stop him . . ." She paused, closing her eyes. "We were on a bridge. We were fighting, and a car went over the edge. I had to save them, but my girlfriend had been hurt. I—I had to make an impossible choice. And she died because of it. Because of me." She opened her eyes, and a tear trailed down her cheek. She smudged it away with the back of her hand.

My heart ached, as much for Mia as it did for everything else I'd been through. Her gaze was lost somewhere in the skyline. I wanted to say something. But what was there to say? No combination of words would take away any of the hurt either of us felt. Nothing would make it right. So I didn't try. I just turned my attention back to the city as she had, and I let the sounds below filter up and fill the space between us.

It was a few minutes before she spoke again.

"Cassidy," she said, "none of this is your fault. There isn't always a right choice to make, but if there is, you'd know it better than anybody. And I know you did everything you could to save that man." A lump formed in my throat. I closed my eyes, but she paused, reaching out and touching my hand so I would look at her.

"Being a hero doesn't mean winning every fight. It means doing what you can to help as many people as you can. And when things go wrong, it means getting up and doing it again no matter how much it hurts. Because people need you."

I swallowed hard. I wish I could say her words were exactly what I needed to hear in that moment, that they eased the pain in my chest and the visions of fire and smoke that still played behind my eyelids. But I couldn't. My gaze fell into my lap, and I stared at my upturned palms. Sure, I knew all about choices. Ever since that day when I'd decided to let Mia train me, I'd thought about them. The power they held. But I'd never stopped to consider the weight of their consequences. That man had needed me too. I'd had countless chances to say the right thing, do the right thing. And somehow, I'd still managed to fail him. That weight was going to sit on my shoulders forever.

Then again, it looked like one had already been sitting on Mia's shoulders for a lot longer.

I looked over at her. Her eyes glistened in the light that filtered up from the street down below. She hid it well, but I knew her better. I could see the anguish that brewed just behind her mask of composure. "It never stops hurting, does it?" I asked, the edges of my voice rough. She didn't look at me, just shook her head. I nodded at the answer I'd already known, then asked the other question that had been dancing at the tip of my tongue. "Can I ask what her name was?"

She was silent for a few seconds, and as the question hung in the air, I considered rewinding time. This wasn't my place. But just as I began to raise my hands in front of me, regretting the words that I'd let slip out, she spoke.

"Amelie. Her name was Amelie."

I placed my hands back in my lap, but if she'd noticed, she didn't say anything. Her eyes drifted up to the constellations, and after a moment, mine did as well. Exhaustion wore on me, but I was afraid to leave this roof. I didn't want to face anyone and pretend everything was fine. I didn't want to close my eyes—every time I did, I saw the man's horrified face again, falling, disappearing in the space of a breath. Mia must've known all of it. Neither of us said anything after that, but we stayed there until the pale hues of sunrise outlined the horizon. Only then did we silently help each other to our feet and climb down to head back home.

Chapter Thirteen

A FEW DAYS LATER, I sat with Andrew in the library, papers, books, and a laptop spread in front of me. My head hung in my hands. We'd been at this for only an hour, and already the words were blurring together. I could feel the weight of Andrew's hand on the center of my back, and though I appreciated the gesture, it was doing little to comfort me.

"I don't know how I'm going to get any of this done," I whined, cautioning a glance at the assignment list I'd written out. I was hopelessly behind on readings and had four essays to finish by the end of next week, not including the extra assignment I'd begged for from my sociology professor to try bringing my grade up. All of my classes were suffering, and I'd stretched most of my extensions about as far as they would take me. Forget declaring a major. After Thanksgiving break, I had five more days of lectures before finals would start, and if I couldn't save my grades by then, I was going to lose my scholarships.

Andrew moved his hand from my back, reaching for a textbook lying open across the table. "We could start with this one?

What class is this, economics?" he asked, marking the page with his finger while he studied the cover.

I groaned and uncurled my fingers from my hair, finding my notebook and a pen. I felt like death; I probably looked the part too. Dark circles creased the skin beneath my eyes, and beneath my flannel and jeans, I was still covered in bruises. I hadn't slept since the night of the fire. Every time I turned out the lights and rested my head on the pillow, I was back in that apartment building, suffocating in the smoke, falling with my fingers stretched toward the man on the balcony, never able to reach him. I'd woken up gasping for air more than once, and I wasn't entirely convinced I hadn't been using my powers in my sleep with the way my hands constantly ached. I massaged my fingers now before flipping to a clean page, and Andrew's eyes drifted toward them. His lips set into a thin line.

"Have you talked to her at all since that night?" he asked. I sighed and shook my head.

"It's not her fault. She's got classes too, and a deadline for the newspaper." I shrugged. "It's just . . ."

"You need someone to talk to," he finished. "Someone who gets it." He raised his eyebrows and gave a knowing look.

I frowned, my stomach fluttering. "No, it's not that."

His expression shifted into a softer one. "You know it's okay if it is though, right? I'm not upset that you've got a life outside of me. And with what you just went through . . ."

"I know." I really did, but hearing him say it aloud was some comfort. Still, the thoughts that were weighing on me were quick to drive the feeling away. My forehead creased again. "Have you ever heard of the Futurist?" I asked. Andrew thought for a moment, then shook his head. I nodded, taking a breath. "Well, a few weeks back, when that explosion happened by the clock tower, there was this guy I'd spotted. Then, before . . . that night" —I wasn't sure I could mention the fire right now without crying— "I ran into him again." *Literally*, I added in my head. "I think it was the same guy. The Futurist. I *know* it was," I corrected myself. "But Mia didn't believe me."

"Why not?" Andrew asked, his face setting into a deep frown.

I shrugged, then let a breath out between my teeth. "I don't know. Maybe she just wanted more proof? Which I found, by the way." I sighed. "Something about this whole thing just bothers me, and I don't know why."

Andrew stayed quiet for a moment, working a thought around in his mind. I chewed on my lower lip. I didn't mention the other idea that had crossed my mind—that she was avoiding me after what we'd talked about on the roof. I couldn't blame her if she was. The way she'd spoken about Amelie . . . I could tell it had been a while since she'd mentioned her to anyone.

"You said she's got a newspaper deadline, right?" Andrew asked. I nodded. He snapped his fingers and pointed at me. "I'll bet it's that article on the physics department then. I mean, that's what she was interviewing me about, and they should be getting the new equipment within a week or so."

"I mean, I guess, but she interviewed you weeks ago."

"It really wasn't that long ago, actually. You've just been through a lot since then," he offered. "But either way, from what I've heard from my professors, it's supposed to be a pretty big feature on the program. This equipment is a huge deal."

The way he said it made his eyes flash a little brighter in the warm light of the library. I hadn't seen him this excited since that morning in the coffee shop when he'd told me about his internship. I turned to face him better. "About that—I know you've explained it before, but remind me again what this new tech actually *is*," I told him. Sure, part of me was just looking for a distraction from my own thoughts, but the eager look he wore was adorable and infectious. I would've bottled it if I could.

He grinned and leaned forward in his chair. I couldn't help it; I leaned in too. "Okay, you know what a particle accelerator is, right?"

I laughed. "In theory?"

He nodded. "I mean, it basically does what the name says—it's a tool that lets us study particles as they move at insanely fast speeds, faster than they'd ever normally be able to travel. Most of them are massive. They'll build miles-long buildings to house these things. They also take an insane amount of power. Or they did." He smiled. "One of Everett's alumni figured out how to make a renewable energy source that could keep particles doubling back fast enough that we don't need the massive versions, and he's gifting his prototype to the school."

I cocked an eyebrow, confused. "It's just an energy source? Nothing else?"

He nodded. "That's where the grant comes in. Thanks to research that was started years back by—" he paused, his eyes flicking to mine and growing serious for a moment, "—by your father, the department thinks they can build a mini version of the other particle accelerators. Cassidy, it would be groundbreaking. We'd be able to study *so much*, and instead of an entire campus to house it, we'd need a classroom."

"That's going to be incredible," I said.

Andrew nodded, practically glowing. "I mean, the implications . . . There's radiation therapy, synchrotron light sources, sterilization. I was just reading a paper your dad wrote on what we could do if we could start to experiment with more than just individual particles, and—I've lost you again, haven't I?" I bit my lip, giving an apologetic shrug. He laughed and tried again. "Well, that last one is all hypothetical for now anyway. But let's just say they might give us a little more insight into how Playback's powers actually work." He gave a knowing look.

My gaze drifted away for a moment. I wanted to say something, but a soft "wow" was all I could mutter. It wasn't necessarily for *what* he'd said—I'd known there had to be some scientific explanation for what had happened to me, and there was plenty else he'd listed that I barely understood anyway, try as he might to explain it to me. But it was the *way* he'd said it. His words carried a gravitas that didn't require explanation.

Watching him now, I was reminded that some people didn't need superpowers to change the world. "That's amazing," I said.

I meant it.

Andrew smiled, his cheeks coloring a little. But then he reached out, placing a hand on top of mine. His expression shifted. "I know you're worried. And . . . hurting. But Mia cares for you. I don't think she'd avoid you on purpose, especially not now. Maybe she's just giving you both time to heal."

I sighed. I knew he was right. I turned back to the mess in front of me—to all the things I'd been neglecting every time I'd put on the suit. Maybe what we both needed most was time to just be Mia and Cassidy for a bit.

There was no way to sugarcoat it. Thanksgiving a few days later sucked.

We'd always lived too far away from my grandparents for them to make the trip down, so I was used to having a smaller holiday. Usually, it was just the three of us for dinner. Mom, Dad, and I would spend all morning making our favorite dishes and elbowing one another for more space in the kitchen. We weren't ones for the traditional turkey and stuffing—instead, Dad would make a lasagna entirely from scratch, or Mom would make a spicy gumbo. I always baked focaccia. Then we'd change into PJs and binge Christmas movies late into the night. The busiest our house had ever been was last year. Andrew's family had come over when the weather had turned icy last minute, bringing their assortment of sides and desserts with them to add to the feast. Seven people for dinner might've been an everyday occurrence for some, but it was the closest I'd come to understanding the crowded tables and hectic atmospheres everyone else always described.

But none of that happened this year. Instead, Mom and I sat across from each other at the table, each trying not to look at the empty third seat next to us. We ate quietly. Mom had made a curry recipe she'd learned. I'd still made my focaccia. They both tasted delicious, but neither of us had needed to fight for space at the counter.

"You cut your hair a bit," Mom noted as we ate. She gestured with a piece of bread toward the braid that hung over my shoulder.

I felt the end of it, the ends still crisp from where I'd snipped off the rest of my burned hair. "Oh," I said. "Yeah, it was just a trim. Had some dead ends that were getting unruly."

"I like it," she said. She smiled a little. I tried to return the gesture, then scooped another forkful of rice. We both ate a few more bites before she looked up again. "Listen, I know we usually stay up kind of late with the movie marathon, but I was thinking—if we call it an earlier night tonight, we could get up early tomorrow and go visit Dad at the new care facility." I looked up from my plate to see her already studying my face. Her eyes pleaded in a way her words never would, but I'd already made up my mind anyway.

I nodded. "Absolutely. Let's do it."

It was a short and rather simple trip the next day, but I hadn't realized how much I needed it. One of the nurses gave us a tour of Dad's new facility, and Mom talked with the medical personnel on staff to learn how he was progressing. He was showing promising signs, they said, but they still couldn't make any guarantees. "And with how long he's been unconscious, if he wakes up, he will need extensive therapy before he'll be ready to go home," they reminded her.

"*When* he wakes up," she corrected them. I looked down at my feet. I wished I were always as assured as she was.

I listened politely for a little longer, but after a few minutes, I slipped away and found a seat in my dad's room. I pulled the chair up until it was right next to his bed, then sat down, leaning over to hold his hand in mine. He was gaunt, the skin on his face waxy and sagging slightly in a perpetual frown. His hair was long too, though Mom must've been helping keep him clean-shaven during her regular visits. But looking past all that, he was just Dad, asleep on the couch after a long day at work. The memory brought a smile to my lips while tears dotted the corners of my eyes.

"Hey, Dad," I said quietly. "How're you doing?"

There was no answer, only his steady breathing.

"I've been okay, I guess," I said. "I'm just tired. And school's been a bit stressful. Andrew's been helping, but I always feel bad asking him. I know he's busy with his own stuff already. And even if he did mind, we both know he wouldn't tell me." I felt the tiniest fraction of a smile part my lips at the memory of our study session. "I wish you could hear what he's been working on. He talks about this stuff with the lab the way you used to. He's so excited about everything." I paused to laugh. "Though when he tells you, could you maybe explain it to me? He tried, but I'm still not sure I fully understand it."

It felt good to sit here like this. The words were a release I'd been needing for months without knowing it. More of them settled on the tip of my tongue—things I'd been wanting to share with someone but couldn't. My face grew serious again as I considered whether to say anything at all. But when I opened my mouth, the thoughts tumbled out, and I didn't try to stop them.

"I feel bad that I haven't been there for Mom as much, or for you. I should've called her more often or come home on the weekends. It's just . . . ever since the wreck, things have been different. Things have changed. I feel like I've been living two different lives, and I've been trying to make the right decisions—to make a difference. But I don't know. It's not as clear as I'd thought it would be." I thought about the fire. The fights with Futurist. I stared at our hands, Dad's limp one in my own. "Maybe that was just me being naive." I shook my head, and a tear sneaked past my lashes. I concealed it with a laugh, brushing it away before he could see. "Now's about the time you'd tell me a silly joke or force me into a hug, so I'd forget I was crying."

I stayed silent a beat, watching the rise and fall of his chest. "Everything just feels different now," I continued after a moment had passed. "And I don't know, maybe it's supposed to. But . . . I really wish I could ask you for advice." Admitting it out loud framed the hollowness that I'd felt in my chest since waking up in the hospital. After more than a month, I still wasn't accustomed to it.

As I sat there, I became vaguely aware of a set of footsteps approaching from the hallway. I didn't have to turn around to tell they belonged to my mother. I could sense her behind me, watching us, and I imagined her leaning against the doorframe, arms crossed, smiling the same way she would when Dad told me bedtime stories as a little girl. The memory made me smile too, and I rubbed the back of Dad's hand with my thumb. It was the three of us finally—not in the way we would've ever wished for, but at least we were *together*. I refused to take that for granted anymore. After the past few months, and especially after last week, it was more than enough to be thankful for.

Mom drove me back to campus Sunday afternoon. Once I arrived, I holed myself up in my dorm room for the rest of the day and into the next, only leaving for my classes or to grab food from the dining hall. I was determined to get as much of my classwork done as I could, and by Monday evening, I'd made decent progress. It was enough, at least, to reward myself with a change in scenery, so after I put the finishing touches on my sociology assignment, I packed up my laptop and the latest reading for my history class and headed to the common area down the hall.

I hadn't ever spent much time here since moving to campus. Most of the time, the others living on my floor used the space to socialize or escape annoying roommates. Since I didn't have to worry about roommates, and my social group consisted of two people, neither one living in this building, I hadn't ever really felt the urge. Still, the chairs in here were more comfortable than my desk, and with finals looming, the room did seem much quieter than usual.

Calling it a "room" maybe wasn't the right term. It was an open space with large windows stretched across one wall, though the blinds stayed closed most of the time. Thin, scratchy carpet helped mark off the area, which was decorated with sofas and armchairs in the same vivid blue hues as the Everett logo. The coffee tables in the center, thankfully, were an exception—there, the school had opted for less flashy, white-top furniture. Normally by this time in the evening, the space came with a soundtrack of a sporting event on the TV and several loud conversations happening at once. Tonight, though, a study group had already claimed one of the sofas and was quietly comparing answers on a questionnaire, and another student had fallen asleep on the opposite one. A few other people I recognized from my hall dotted the area. One sat in the windowsill to read, and another stretched out on the ground, her laptop and a coffee cup set up on the coffee table in front of her. An armchair in front of the TV on the far wall sat unclaimed, so

I headed toward it to settle in. The TV was already tuned to a local station, but the volume was low enough it would be easy to ignore.

Once I'd gotten situated, I started on my next assignment, trying to force myself to focus. I'd hit a stride over the past two days in catching up on some of my work, but it would've been a lie to say my mind hadn't been wandering. I'd finally gotten a response back from Mia this morning. Her clipped text wasn't quite the message I'd been hoping for.

JSYK I'm retaking an exam tonight, so probably won't be able to patrol.

Nothing about whether she was upset with me or why she'd gone radio silent after that night on the roof. I still hadn't had a chance to talk with her about the Futurist, which meant I hadn't come any closer to figuring out what had been niggling at the back of my mind since I'd put together that he was my mystery man from the clock tower. Social media hadn't offered any more clues. I'd set up alerts for his name back at the beginning of break, but nothing useful had come across so far.

I tried to push it all out of my mind. I didn't have any reason to worry about Futurist right now beyond the fact that I'd learned something new, and with as swamped as I was, it would be foolish to think Mia wasn't under the same workload. Plus, she had the newspaper to worry about. She was allowed to have a life outside of superhero work as much as I was. I blinked hard, turning my focus back to the book I was supposed to be reading. It didn't last long—a flash from the TV screen drew my gaze back away from the tiny text. The words "BREAKING NEWS" ran across the bottom of the screen in red text, and the anchor from the local station appeared on screen. I couldn't quite tell what he was saying, but a few seconds later, an image of the old apartment building popped up next to him. My stomach lurched. I reached for the remote and flicked on the closed captions.

"... investigation has revealed a small detonation near a power box attached to the unit was the cause of the blaze, which injured dozens and killed one earlier this month. Firefighters deemed the residence a total loss."

An explosion had caused the fire, on the same night the Futurist had attacked two officers and made off with metal tubing. I kicked myself, and guilt riddled my insides. How could I have not realized it sooner?

There was something else the news anchor had said about *where* the blast had taken place. The electrical box on the side of the building . . . Hadn't Mia said the pipes Futurist stole were made of copper? Dread made room in my chest. I had a feeling I now knew what tied the Futurist's attacks together. Pushing the textbook off to the side, I pulled my laptop closer and opened a new tab on my browser. I found the URL for the news station's website and typed it in, pulling up their search bar. As it loaded, I opened another tab to a satellite map of the city.

First, what I knew. Two explosions, at least one that had a direct tie to the Futurist. I knew what had caused the one at the apartment building, so I focused on the clock tower instead.

After some searching, I found it on the map and zoomed in. Sure enough, the solar panels on the roof of the old restaurant were still there. He hadn't set up there because of the clock tower—he'd chosen that spot for the power source.

I flipped over to the other tab and searched for the keyword "explosion" on the news station's website. I only got five hits, and the two most recent were the two I already knew about. I scrolled to the next one. It had happened at a small electrical plant toward the end of October, on the outskirts of Santina County, causing a short that knocked out power to a couple neighborhoods for over a day. The second oldest one had been in Everett again, happening near the computer sciences building. It had been a week or so before I'd come home from the hospital. The explosion had somehow knocked out the internet for the computers throughout campus. The article only offered a vague description, but if I'd had to guess, the blast had happened near the side of the building where they housed their server bank—and the extra power source to run it.

The final article had a publish date from early October. I clicked on it, then made a small sound in the back of my throat. I recognized the car in the image, though I hadn't ever seen the "after" picture until now. The front of it was blackened and twisted, caved in toward the driver and passenger seats. The front wheel axle was busted as well, and one wheel turned at an awkward angle from the other. The car had come to rest in a small ditch, right below an electrical line. Everyone had said it, but I don't think it had sunk in before just how amazing it was that both Dad and I had survived.

Eventually, I pulled my attention from the image to the rest of the article. It was short, with most of the space spent describing the car we'd been driving and our injuries. The last line stood on a paragraph of its own, however, and it held the answer I'd been searching for.

"The cause of the crash is still unknown, though an exploded power transformer may be partly to blame, said SCPD Public Information Officer Barb Davies."

I closed my laptop, my mind racing. Back at the clock tower, my hands and wrists had prickled and stung the same way they had before Mia had given me the gloves, only I hadn't been using my powers. Now I knew why. Futurist had been behind all of it. I closed my eyes, and the memory of that bright flash played behind my eyelids, the dull ache in my limbs an echo of the agonizing pain I'd felt that night. I squeezed my fingers into fists and flexed them outward, then opened my eyes again, a new realization dawning.

I pulled out my phone and tapped out a message to Andrew: *Didn't you say the new tech you guys are getting is an energy source?*

Three dots appeared below my message within a few seconds. *Yeah, why?* he sent back.

My fingers hovered over the screen, about to type out my next question, but the images on the TV screen answered it before I could. A reporter stood outside one of the banquet halls downtown, the people behind her all dressed in flashy attire. "Tonight's event is just starting to get underway, and we've already had a chance to catch up with several notable Everett alumni."

I gathered my things and headed back toward my room, trying my best to act casual. My heartbeat thudded in my ears though, and I swore it threatened to give me away. As I turned and headed down the hallway, I clicked over to Mia's number in my phone. "Please pick up," I muttered. I was praying her exam hadn't started yet. As the line rang, I reached my room, and I shuffled everything awkwardly to the other arm to unlock it. I didn't even wait to turn on the light before kicking the door closed and tossing my things on the bed. Still with the phone to my ear, I reached under the bed and found the familiar bundle of clothes.

"Hello, you've reached Mia Dominguez, reporter for the *Santina Enquirer.*" The professional lilt of Mia's answering machine message played in my ear. A curse slipped out as I hung up. I turned to the suit lying in a heap on my bed, a whiff of smoke still clinging to the fabric. My breath shuddered at the thought of putting it on again, especially without Mia as backup. But I didn't have a choice.

Whatever it was Futurist was building, he needed a power source. And the university was about to give him the biggest one yet.

Chapter Fourteen

B y the time I made it to the banquet hall, the gala was already well underway. Coming up on the brightly lit building, I worked to steady my breathing as I searched for an entrance. As it was, my late arrival probably made it easier to slip inside. With everyone seated on the main level, I found a side entrance and climbed the staircase up into the balcony, clinging to the shadows afforded by the ornate banister and the bright lights below.

The gallery was one of the more lavish sights I'd seen, at least when it came to something associated with the university. Tables filled most of the floor space, each decorated with a separate bouquet and a cream tablecloth. Table markers stretched upward from the center of the bouquets, printed with gold-embossed script that matched the dinnerware in each place setting. Along the walls, sconces bore flowers like those on the table and gave off a warm yellow light to the outskirts of the party, but most of the light came from the chandeliers that hung from the vaulted ceilings above.

Guests occupied almost every available seat, and their outfits were just as opulent as the rest of the space—all trim black suits and shimmering evening gowns that sent rainbows dancing across the room. A few camera crews from local news stations stood along the walls, whispering quietly to one another as they set up their shots. They seemed to be trying hard to blend into the background, but the guests already paid them little mind. Most of their attention was trained on the food and the laughter and conversation that rang out from the others at the event. And mine? My gaze had drifted to the one space not filled with distinguished scientists and professors and their dates. A lone glass display case sat in the center of the room, gallery lights directed to the long metal object inside, a piece about the length of my forearm. To me, it looked like any piece of metal someone might find in a hardware store. But I knew otherwise.

Just then, a hush rippled out from the front of the room. I glanced up, watching as the university president made his way to the podium. He tapped the mic, drawing the rest of the guests' attention. I sighed and leaned back against the wall. I wasn't sure when exactly Futurist would make his move, but I doubted it would be while so many people were around. He'd been operating so far on top of empty parking garages or in alleyways between buildings—I got the sense he wasn't one to make a scene if he didn't have to. The commotion at the end of the event as everyone headed toward their cars would be when he'd make his move. All I had to do was wait. I settled in for a long evening.

"Ladies and gentlemen, distinguished colleagues and alumni, members of the media, thank you for joining me here this evening." He gestured to people in the crowd as he spoke. I scanned the faces below to see if I recognized any of them. Andrew probably would—he would've been itching to meet some of these people and ask them about their work. A smile spread behind my mask. How many years would it be before he was sitting at one of those tables? The way his eyes shone when he spoke of the work he was doing already, even as a freshman, left me little doubt that he'd found his calling.

Dad had been the same way. Sure, the job wasn't always perfect. He'd had his fair share of complaints about university policies that changed to keep shareholders happy or budget cuts to the programs he worked on. His salary had always been lower than Mom and I thought he deserved. But he loved his research—and using it to help others. I hadn't ever found something I was passionate about in that way. I glanced down at my gloved hands. Then again, maybe I had. Maybe Playback was my way of trying to fill his shoes. To find my place in the world, the same way he and Andrew had.

As the speaker droned on, my mind drifted back to my last text conversation with Andrew. I still hadn't explained why I'd needed to know about the tech. Of course, I'd been a bit preoccupied, but I also didn't want him to worry. I pulled out my phone and sent him a quick message to let him know everything was fine. Then, I flipped back to the home screen, studying it for a moment. Still nothing from Mia. My brow furrowed, and

I tilted my head to try to get a better view of the media crews below me. Andrew had said she was writing about the particle accelerator. Maybe she was reporting on the gala after her exam?

My efforts were thwarted by a voice in the stairwell. I slipped out of my seat and into a crouch, then crept behind a beam in the wall a few rows behind me. With careful maneuvering, I tucked myself into the corner. A security guard stepped out onto the balcony a few moments later.

"I'm up top," he mumbled into the radio on the shoulder of his vest. "Everything looks good from here." It crackled in response a few seconds later.

"Great. We'll move everyone into position down there in the next few. We've got about twenty or so minutes before they wrap up and everyone starts heading out."

The guard on the balcony nodded to himself. "Still not moving the case?"

"Nah," said the voice on the other end. "It'll be easier once the crowds are gone."

I grimaced. I guess I wasn't going to have much backup protecting the thing—not that I would've thought a hired security service would've been much help. Futurist had already taken down two cops without batting an eye, and he hadn't been prepared then. The officer lingered a few minutes more at the edge of the balcony, listening to the speakers on stage go through their list of recognitions and special awards for faculty in the department. Watching him from the corner of my vision, I couldn't help but roll my eyes. I wished he would leave already—I was starting to get a cramp in my side standing like this.

"There's another final thanks we'd like to bestow on someone who was not able to be here tonight." The speaker's voice filled the room, waiting for the lingering applause to dissipate. The officer cleared his throat, and I heard him shift his weight on the floorboards. "Charlie Sinclair worked at this university for almost twenty years before his retirement, and without his research, our university would not have been given the wonderful gift you see before you tonight."

The presenter continued with his speech, but his words grew fuzzy, distorted, drowned out by the roar in my ears. *My dad.* I fought to keep my breathing steady and even, not wanting to risk drawing attention. But my grief washed over me again, accompanied this time by a new feeling: anger. He should've been down there. Instead, he was lying in a hospital bed, and my mom was spending every night alone, praying he would wake up. All because of the Futurist.

He won't hurt anyone like that again, I promised myself. Tonight, I would make sure to put a stop to his tyranny once and for all.

As the university president took to the podium to say a last farewell, the officer on the balcony finally moved to take his post down on the main floor. I waited until I could hear his footsteps echoing in the stairwell before I came out of my hiding spot, and I stayed crouched to keep out of sight. The white noise of layered conversations grew as people got up from their seats, wishing one another congratulations and safe trips home. And then, as the minutes ticked away, everyone filtered out to the parking lot, and the sounds followed. Soon, I was the only one left in the room. Silence echoed off the cavernous ceiling. I found the stairs down to the main floor and moved to the back of the room, beneath the balcony I'd just left. In the shadows, I waited.

I heard him before I saw him. His heavy boots trod softly down the hallway, but even with his careful movements, their sound carried. He paused at the edge of the room, casting a glance around the empty banquet hall. His gaze never reached my hiding spot. After a moment, he moved forward again, his dingy trench coat swishing with each step. I used the sound to conceal my own approach.

"It's over, Futurist," I called. He spun on his heels at the sound of my voice, his hands raised to attack. As his eyes met mine, his demeanor shifted.

"You again," he answered. "You are a thorn in my side."

I ignored him, keeping my eyes trained on him while I traced a wide berth between tables toward the case. Rage boiled my insides, and for the first time, I fought against an urge to attack first. He must've sensed the difference; I watched his expression settle deeper into the creases of his face. His lips tightened into a thin line, and his blue eyes hardened to ice. When I lunged, he was ready.

But he wasn't when I rewound.

As the seconds reset, I made the same move as before, but when he threw his punch, I sidestepped, letting the weight behind his swing pull him off-balance. Before he could right himself, I grabbed his arm and hooked a leg behind his knee, pulling it out from under him. The move forced him to the ground but brought me down with him, and we both scrambled to get up. For once, my size was an advantage—although he was bigger, I was faster, and I was on my feet first. I used the extra time to grab one of the tablecloths within reach, sending plates crashing to the ground as I pulled the linen taut in front of me. Futurist let out a huff, his glare darkening. He reached behind his back, this time with both of his hands.

"Two knives now? You weren't threatening enough with just one?" I taunted, though my voice carried little humor. He stomped toward me, and I pivoted to keep one of the tables firmly between us, my back to the display case a few yards away.

"I'm done screwing around," he answered.

"Me too."

He ran forward, and I flung the tablecloth in front of myself just in time. One of the knives pierced the fabric, shredding it down the middle. I twisted the tattered remains around his wrist and spun them over my shoulder, heaving my body weight against it. I felt him jostle against my grip, and something sliced my suit just below my shoulder. Still, I didn't let go. My back was to him now, but I could hear the fabric tear as he sawed at it with his free hand. I yanked on the cloth harder, and he answered with a grunt of pain. A second later, metal clattered.

I couldn't help a dark smirk of satisfaction at the noise. But it didn't last long; the ripping from the fabric grew louder, and I felt the tension going slack in the linen. In desperation, I reached a leg forward and snagged a chair with my foot, then flung it backward, just as the last few fibers gave way against Futurist's remaining blade.

My distraction hadn't been much, but I took the chance to sprint ahead. I just needed to get there before he did. I pushed off a table as I passed it, closing the final few feet between me and the case. As my fingertips pressed against the cool glass, I braced myself against it and spun around.

"You think this is going to end any differently than last time?" he sneered. He knelt down, picking up the weapon that had fallen at his feet.

"I know it will." My answer came before I had a chance to realize what I was saying. I raised my palms, taking on a fighting stance. "Last time, I didn't know who I was fighting."

Something about what I'd said morphed his expression, though I couldn't read it. The knives in his fists lowered by a fraction. He looked away for an instant, then into my eyes.

"I'm sorry about your father."

It took a moment for my brain to untangle the meaning of what he'd said. He knew who I was. The air in my chest grew thick and heavy; it took effort for me to expel it. "Why do you care?" I seethed. I squeezed my fingers into fists to hide them shaking.

"You think I wanted any of this? I didn't mean to cause that car crash. And I certainly didn't mean for *this* to happen." He gestured toward me. "You think I wanted to make any more of you? Jesus, dealing with one 'hero' was enough." His mouth twisted around the word "hero" as if it tasted bitter on his tongue.

"Phase *is* a hero," I countered. "She's saved this city—from people far worse than you."

"Heroes like her destroyed my world!" he shouted back. He scoffed as he collected himself. "Heroes like you," he said, quieter this time, and somehow more sinister.

I wasn't sure how to respond. His words played themselves over in my head, but I must've misheard. My lips had parted in surprise, and when I finally found my voice, I asked, "Your world?"

"Yours too," he said. "I'm from a timeline in the future. Keep that in mind next time you think you're 'saving' people. You superheroes aren't saving anyone. You're the reason the rest of us are fighting every day just to survive."

Inwardly, I scrambled to make sense of everything he was saying. Could I even trust him? The back of my mind warned it all could be a distraction—a way to throw me off my game. Then again, as long as I kept him talking . . .

"How did you get here?" I asked him.

"A time bridge. We were running from some . . . let's just say they're not very friendly people." He wrinkled his nose in his condescension. "I came across a lab with one still intact, and we needed a distraction, so I activated it." He looked away, anger flashing behind his bushy brows. *At himself?* I wondered.

"Time bridges don't work," he continued. "They're all faulty."

"Looks like this one did." I shrugged.

"Yeah? And look what it did to you." He raised his palms in my direction, miming my powers around the blades he held. I swallowed and hoped my mask hid the embarrassment flushing my cheeks. Of course, it hadn't been just any explosion that had given me my abilities. But things still weren't fully adding up. I ignored the jab, pressing him on a different point.

"So you make it to a world that's apparently much nicer than yours. And you decide to start blowing it up?"

"I'm not blowing anything up," he protested. "I told you—time bridges are faulty. They're volatile." His jaw hardened. "They hardly work even in the best of conditions. I thought I could get by using a different power source, but no dice. Nothing you guys make is strong enough to even activate one for a few seconds. Except for that." He pointed behind me.

At the reminder, I adjusted my stance as if to better block the device from his view. "If your timeline is so awful," I asked, "why the hell would you be trying to build a bridge back to it?"

"So I can escape you and the other flashy costume before you destroy anything else?" he sneered. But there was a moment that passed. Another shift in his expression, to something that looked like . . . fear. "My kid. Oslo. I can't leave him there alone."

I shifted my feet and sucked in a breath, the weight of his admission hanging on my shoulders. "You said 'we' before. 'The people we were running from.' You don't mean—"

Footfalls at the room's far entrance interrupted the thought before I could finish, and we both tensed as we turned toward the noise. Mia's familiar silhouette strode through the entrance, her voice ringing clear and commanding even from behind Phase's helmet. "I can't let you do this, Futurist." I watched him raise his fists at her approach, and my adrenaline surged. About ten feet away, she stopped in her tracks, her gaze finally landing on me. "Playback?" She sighed. "I didn't want you dragged into this."

"Dragged into *what*?" I asked, stiffening. But I didn't wait for an answer—there wasn't time for that now. "Phase, wait. Hear him out. This isn't what we thought—"

"I already figured it out," she said, cutting me off. "This whole semester, I've been trying to piece it together, ever since I learned about your powers. I mean, come on—no normal car crash would do *that*." She gestured to me as she spoke. "But then you took that call in the stairwell, and Andrew mentioned their new equipment. The physics department reviving its research in particle acceleration at the same time you learn you can rewind time?" She paused. "I pitched that story to give myself an excuse to poke around the physics building more . . . and then you told me about what happened at the clock tower." She gestured to Futurist, turning to face him as she spoke. "I've been two steps behind him this whole time, but after the fire, when we were up on that roof, I saw him a few blocks away. I went back the next night, and I managed to find where he's been hiding. I've been staking it out since then." Hostility dripped from her voice. "He talks to himself, you know? And in his sleep. He's killed people, Playback, before he even made it to our time. Whatever he told you, he's not the saint he's making himself out to be."

"Congratulations, you've figured me out," the man said, his voice laced with sarcasm as he threw his arms wide. "The name's Vince, by the way, Miss Detective, so you can stop with that whole 'Futurist' crap. And you have no idea the lengths I've had to go to make it this far."

"You're right, I don't. But I know what you're planning now. And it's not going to happen."

"You think you're going to stop me?" he asked.

"I've stopped monsters like you before. You won't be any different."

My eyes flicked from one to the other, my brain trying desperately to follow the leaps in the conversation. "You said the time bridges have been causing the explosions, right? What happens to the ones that work?"

Mia spoke before he could. "None of them do; that's the thing. They all collapse eventually. And the longer they stay open, the worse it gets. With what he's planning, he'd wipe out all of Everett."

I was quiet for a moment, trying to wrap my head around what she was saying. Futurist—Vince—wasn't fazed, however. "I don't have time for this," he muttered. He moved forward and threw his knife in my direction, toward some target just beside my shoulder. Out of instinct, I shoved my hands forward. As the interaction replayed, I followed the knife's trajectory from before, reaching out to grab it by the handle midair, just before the blade could make contact with the glass case and shatter it.

Still holding the knife, I raised an eyebrow at Futurist, then tossed the blade on the floor and kicked it backward underneath one of the far tables. I turned back to Mia. "I hear what you're saying, but come on. He's got a kid. We've got to try."

"No, we don't." Mia squeezed her hand into a fist in frustration, then released it, turning to me. "Look, I'm sorry I didn't tell you sooner. I really am," she said. "But I know what it's like to be forced to make a choice like this, and I didn't want to put you through that."

"What choice?!" Vince exploded. "My kid is out there. Alone. You think I'm the worst person out there? Honey, I may not be a saint, but there are men a thousand times worse than me where I come from. And believe it or not, the ones we were running from weren't after me."

"Actually, I do find that hard to believe," she quipped.

He glowered. His voice lowered again. "If I don't get to him before they do, they *will* kill him."

"And what if he's already dead?" Phase's question put a chill in the air, and I turned to her, horrified. "I know; it's awful to say," she continued, staring at him as she spoke to me. "But he's risking our entire city, *everyone's* lives, for someone who we don't even know he can save. For someone you and I don't even know actually exists."

"Phase—"

"Then I'll kill them," Futurist interrupted. He said it so casually, so coolly, as if he were telling the time. A shiver traced up my spine.

Mia didn't move, just kept her eyes trained on Futurist. "Point made," she said quietly.

"Phase, I—we still can't just strand him here," I said. I wasn't sure whose side I was on, but Mia's option couldn't be the only one. "What if we ask Andrew? Maybe he could help figure out something—"

"We absolutely can leave him here," Mia responded. "You're talking about putting the entire *city* at risk for him and a kid we don't even technically know exists. And even if we could find a safer way to do all this, get him back to his timeline, it would take years to work out the math and build the thing."

"Come on, Phase, please," I begged. "Listen to yourself."

"I *am* listening. Think about who we're talking about here. This man is the reason your dad is in a coma, that two cops spent a week in the hospital. All those people from the apartment that lost everything? That man from the balcony? He did all of that." She sighed. "Look, Playback, I know this is hard. But I let someone like him go a long time ago. It didn't end well." She paused, and I thought I saw the slightest shudder in her chest, as if her breath caught on a memory. "You think he's going to wait around until we can cobble something together that *might* work? No. The second we turn our backs, he's gone. And you'll carry that with you the rest of your life." Mia turned to face him, and her hands twitched ever so slightly. "Believe me." The man said nothing, only glared back at her.

The mention of my father tore open the same old wounds, and for a moment, I felt a flash of the earlier hatred I'd felt toward the man. Now though, the emotion swirled against the concern already in my core; things were spiraling out of control, and I wasn't sure how to stop them. My silence must've been enough for Mia. She set her shoulders. "I'm sorry, Vince. There's no way for us to know your son is in danger. But our city is. We can't risk this."

I looked at Vince's face. His rage was unmistakable as he stared at Phase, and I didn't have to turn back to her to know she wasn't backing down. "I wasn't asking your permission," he said, his voice so low it was almost a whisper.

I had to put a stop to this. I had to protect my friend. I took a careful step toward Mia. In the same instant, the two exploded toward each other. Mia vaulted over a table to close the distance between them, using her forearm to block the swing of Vince's knife. She answered with a blow to his jaw, sending him stumbling back a step. With her free hand, she reached for the knife and tried to wrestle it from his grip, but he was stronger, and he wrenched it back—I heard her small exclamation as he yanked her wrist.

The sound was enough to pull me into the fray. I ran at Vince, waiting until the last second to drop down and slide between his legs. With his arm raised to strike again, I jumped up from behind, clinging to his back as I tried to grab the blade. I reached an arm up and drove my elbow down against the soft spot between his collarbone and his neck. He grunted, slamming himself—and me—against the side of the display case. Glass crunched, and I crumpled to the ground, trying to find my breath.

"Playback, watch it!" Mia barked. I rolled to the side just as a wave of heat crawled up the back of my neck. Where I'd fallen only moments before, a pool of molten glass oozed onto the floor, leaving scorch marks on the hardwood. I scrambled to my feet. Vince stood at the opposite corner of the display case, held at bay only by the liquid glass puddling beside his boot and the device's red-hot glow. I turned to see Mia, her fingers stretched toward the metal gadget. She stared straight at Futurist, a silent challenge. I was all that stood between the two of them.

"You destroy that, I kill you," he said to her.

"You can try," she replied, "but you won't get the chance."

Vince took her bait. He blew past me, reaching his free hand out to grab her arm. He spun her around, forcing her into a chokehold. He pressed her back against him, his knife hovering just below her helmet. "Lucky, you wearing this thing," he said, tapping the knife against her visor.

"Not luck," she rasped. "Experience." Her hands strained against his arm, trying to make space for her to breathe, but she lifted one for just a moment and waved it toward them both. Vince swore viciously—he yanked his hand away and let the knife fall as metal hissed against the handle and nearly seared his knuckles. With him distracted, she slid out of his grasp and ran toward me, still gasping for breath behind her helmet. "He's got no weapons. It's just him now," she said.

"That's all he needs," I said.

"I know." She cracked her neck. "I'm ending this now." She reached a hand toward the case, and my stomach plummeted.

"Mia, please don't do this," I pleaded.

She whipped around to face me. "Whose side are you on?"

"I—"

She huffed, not waiting for me to make up my mind. She turned back to the device, and her breath strained as she focused her efforts on the device's metal structure. In a panic, I turned to face Vince, whose face had gone ashen at the realization of what was happening. He took a glance at the ground beside him and stooped to pick something up. As he straightened, a switch flipped; his pallid face reddened, and he barreled toward the both of us. Something flashed in his hand. The other knife.

Even without the use of my powers, the seconds stretched out before me. The metal in the case turned white under Mia's influence, all her attention focused on it. Vince's face had contorted beyond fury. He was two strides away now, one stride—

In desperation, I threw my hands out, brushing my fingertips against a shirtsleeve. A faint zap ignited within my fingertips; it stung more than usual. But it worked. Beside me, Mia stood suspended in time, arm still outstretched. The heat of the metal behind me faded instantly. I turned toward Vince, my fists raised.

It didn't matter. Without wasting a beat, he'd changed course, singeing his sleeve as he used it to scoop up the device.

"No!" I screamed, sprinting after him. I leaped over an overturned chair, gaining ground as he neared the exit. He spun on his heels, flinging something in my direction. I ducked to the side, narrowly missing his remaining knife, though the point of it still managed to graze my cheek. Yet that distraction was all it took. Before the blade even made contact with my skin, the Futurist had disappeared.

I didn't have time to react; in the same instant, something had thudded against the ground from across the room. I ran back toward Mia as she pulled her helmet off, letting it roll to the side. She clutched a hand at her chest. My mouth went dry. "Mia?"

Using the frame from the melted display case beside her, she pulled herself to her feet. Her eyes met mine, the pain in them unmistakable. "What. The hell. Did you do?" she asked. Each word was a blow to my gut.

"I'm sorry. I'm so sorry. I just wanted . . . I didn't know . . ."

She staggered forward a step, bracing herself against the back of a chair. "He's going to kill everyone."

I sucked in a breath. "We—we don't know that. We can still find him, we can make sure—"

She didn't speak, only shook her head, but I fell silent nonetheless. She waited a second, looking down at the chair. "You made your choice," she whispered. Her body quivered.

When she raised her head again, tears welled in her eyes. "I can't let you interfere anymore."

Mia stood shakily, moving her hands from the back of the chair. She waved them both in front of her, a flippant gesture, and for a split second, I wrinkled my eyebrows in confusion. Then my palms grew warm, sweaty. The sensation multiplied, and before I realized what was happening, every part of my hands screamed. I cried out, my arms shaking as I looked down at them. The grips that had once insulated me from my powers were now a sludge, seeping through the cloth fibers of the glove, melting to my skin. I tried to claw the Velcro loose with my fingers, but I trembled too much to find a grip. Desperate, I moved one hand up to my mouth and tried to find a hold on them with my teeth. The glove loosened, but I couldn't find the strength to peel the fabric away.

Agony traced up my arms, through every part of me, and I sank to the floor. My hands rested limp in my lap. The gloves had cooled and stiffened back already, but every visible patch of skin around them was bright red and angry. I looked up through tears, watching as Mia gathered her helmet. She stumbled away, leaning against the furniture for balance. Without another glance, she slipped around the corner toward the exit, leaving me alone.

Chapter Fifteen

Somehow, I found strength enough to pull myself to my feet. With the banquet hall deserted, I headed back in the direction I'd come—the same way Phase had gone. My breath trembled. *She left me.* I looked toward the exit, through the glass double doors that led to the outside world. To the empty street beyond. Standing on shaky legs, I turned in the other direction.

The restrooms were a few feet farther down the hall, and as I ducked into one of them, I barely thought to check beneath the stalls before I tripped toward the sink. I bumped the faucet handle to the coldest setting with my elbow—even that rippled waves of pain through my fingers. Water poured into the basin, and I sucked in a breath and held it. Then, I eased one of my hands into the stream.

Searing heat radiated deep beneath my skin, even though the marred fabric of my gloves. The temperature of the water made no difference; all I felt as it trickled over my palm was something brushing against my skin and setting it alight once more. I squeezed my eyes shut and stomped my foot, failing to stifle a cry.

How had this happened? I opened my eyes again, meeting the face of the reflection in the mirror in front of me. It no longer looked like my own. Same copper hair, same purple mask. But this person's hair was untamed. Strands of her hair had fallen loose and tangled on the sides of her face. The mask was tinged with blood, and the person behind it looked hollow, her eyes red and glazed over with pain.

How had it all gone so wrong?

I worked my jaw beneath my mask, then glanced down at the sink. My gaze stopped at the faucet, which had gathered condensation along the spout; I couldn't bring myself to look any lower. Gingerly, I felt for the faucet handle again and eased it down with my arm, and the trickling subsided. In its place, I only heard my own labored breathing, echoing off the tile and amplified in the silence. I was completely and utterly alone.

No, not alone. I still had one person.

I made it back to campus without being spotted, though my heart raced as I wove between shadows and ducked behind buildings. I wasn't sure where either Mia or Vince had gone, but I was in no condition to face either of them. Every movement or whisper of air that met my hands sparked new waves of pain. I held them close to my chest as I walked; even in the dark, I was afraid to see the extent of the damage Mia had done.

When I finally reached the familiar gray building, I veered around the corner to the side farthest from the road. I tried my best to recall the hallway that would've been inside, counting the rooms in my head as I passed their windows. The fourth from the end—was that right? I checked the decorations pinned up in the window: an Everett University calendar and three small photos taped at a diagonal. I closed my eyes and breathed out a sigh, then rapped my elbow softly on the glass.

Inside the room, a low shadow moved. After a few seconds, the blinds raised, and the window creaked open. Andrew's face showed through. "Cassidy? Oh my god. What happened?"

"Is Ben here?" I asked quietly. I leaned my head against the side of the windowsill. Exhaustion had set in—it was taking all my energy just to stay on my feet.

Andrew shook his head. "He's out for the night. Frat party."

I nodded, unhooking my mask from one ear with my pinkie. "I need help," I whimpered. He nodded, hurrying to lift the window farther. Once it was high enough, I used my shoulder to prop it up the rest of the way, then climbed into the room.

"Here, sit on my bed," Andrew instructed, moving out of the way. I found a seat on the edge of the mattress, facing him. He latched the window again and then inched closer to me, reaching a hand out to gingerly trace the cut on my cheek. I leaned away.

"Not that." I winced, holding my hands out toward him. Andrew's mouth parted, and a dark expression crossed his features.

"Who?" he asked. "That 'Futurist' guy?"

I shook my head, my throat closing around the truth.

It took him a moment to discern what that meant. "Mia did this?" he asked incredulously. I just nodded. He stayed silent for a moment, turning my hands over in his own as delicately as possible. He ran a finger along the palm of one of the gloves, and I gasped and jerked away. "Sorry!" he muttered, then set my hands back on my lap. He reached out to place his hand on my arm and met my gaze.

"Cassidy . . . we've got to get these off. But I don't know if I can—"

"You have to," I whispered. "Please."

He let out a weighty breath. "They're melted to your skin," he gritted through his teeth. "You need a hospital."

I shook my head. "I can't."

Andrew leaned back in his wheelchair, rubbing his chin with his hand while he stared at my hands. Guilt gnawed at my stomach for what I was asking him to do, but I stayed silent, chewing on my bottom lip. I didn't have another option. Finally, he closed his eyes, heaving a shaky breath. "Okay. Ben's got a first-aid kit somewhere. Let me see if I can find it."

Andrew ended up having to cut the gloves away from my hands. He worked as carefully as he could, but the process was torturous. Each snip of the scissors exposed more of my swollen, raw skin to the air, and he had to move with agonizing slowness as he peeled the fabric away to avoid taking anything else with it. I had to bite the inside of my cheek to keep from yelping, and by the end, I tasted blood.

Somehow, it seemed to hurt Andrew just as much. Every whimper that escaped, every small involuntary jerk flashed a reflection of my pain in his eyes. When he was finally finished, he tossed the last bit of fabric into the corner behind him and dropped the scissors back into the first-aid kit on the corner of the bed, then let his head fall into his hands. I shuddered.

After a moment, he looked back up, then gestured to the cold compress he'd already activated. I reached for it and let it balance on my palms. The cold seeped into my skin and dulled the fire in my nerves. My body relaxed ever so slightly. I turned back to Andrew, watching me with his chin balanced on his clasped hands. His mouth was set in a hard, thin line. "Can you tell me what happened?" he asked.

My gaze wandered toward the ceiling. I explained everything as best I could remember—the connection I'd found between the explosions, sneaking into the gala, Futurist's backstory, why Mia had gone quiet after the fire. What I'd done to her during the fight. "I could've killed her," I whispered. The horror of it all was worse after having sat with it for this long. My gaze dropped to the bed beside me—I still couldn't stomach the thought of looking too closely at my hands. "She says getting him back to his timeline is too risky, and I know it is, but . . . Andrew, I can't just give up on that kid."

"He said he was building a time bridge?" Andrew asked.

"Yeah. Why?"

"Nothing, it's just . . ." He frowned, tapping his fingers on the rim of one of his wheels as he thought. "Thinking about what your dad's research said." His attention snapped back to me. "If that's really what he's building, then Mia might not be too far off. I mean, it would depend on how long it were to stay open, but if you can't shut it down, warping things on a scale like what he's talking about . . ." I waited for him to continue, but he just let the thought trail off.

"You're saying she was right?"

He looked me square in the face. "I never said that," he said softly.

I wet my lips, my attention drifting to somewhere just past his shoulder. "Neither one of them is going to stop," I said. I wasn't really talking to Andrew anymore, just voicing my fears aloud. "They'll kill each other, and maybe everyone in Everett with them."

"What are you going to do?" he asked, his words careful.

My answer was honest, yet it terrified me all the same. "I don't know."

A few moments passed between us in silence. To fill the void, Andrew reached over and felt the cold pack with the back of his hand. I bit back a grimace. "I'm going to go get some water," he said. "That's already getting warm again." He grabbed a metal water bottle off his desk, and with a promise that he'd be right back, he left the room.

As the door shut behind him, I looked at the pile of fabric Andrew had left in the corner, the purple and white cloth that had once been my gloves. A few weeks ago, I'd thought they were a ticket into this life that I'd wanted. Or maybe they were just a life raft from the one I'd already been living. After that wreck, as Cassidy, I'd felt like I was drowning, but when Mia had gifted me those gloves and made me into Playback, she'd made me feel strong enough to stay afloat. Now, the fabric was unrecognizable, warped into odd shapes from the melted plastic that seeped into the fibers and glued them together, darkened and singed from the heat that had been given off. They were gone, and Mia was too.

And I wasn't sure I could be strong anymore.

I looked down at the cold pack still draped over my palms. The condensation on the plastic bag clung to my damaged skin, hiding the worst of the burns. Ever so slowly, I began to peel my hands away, sucking air in through my teeth with each area I freed. Using my fingertips—which had escaped mostly un-scathed—I placed the pack back on the bed beside me. Then, for the first time that night, I examined my wounds. My hands could've been made of wax for the sheen they'd taken on. They were puffy and splotched, a map of grisly pink and red hues just beneath each of my first knuckles and along the fleshier parts of my palm. Blisters were already forming near my thumbs. The burn marks had imprinted the gloves' padding on my skin; I could trace the zig-zag pattern with my eyes. I tried stretching my fingers by the tiniest fraction, but even that rekindled the fire in my nerves. After a moment, I let them go limp in my lap once more. Tears finally prickled behind my eyelids, hot and angry. *Mia did this.*

I could sit here and run everything over in my head a thousand times to try to find the best outcome, but the truth was she'd made her decision back in that gala. We all had. Futurist had always been willing to kill to make his choice, and even before I'd frozen her, Mia had been ready to die to defend hers. Whatever happened from here on out, when everything was finished, I would have to be able to live with the one I made.

The door to the room clicked back open. Andrew came back around the side of the bed, the filled thermos and an empty bowl balanced on his lap. I met his eyes. "You said the bridge gets more dangerous the longer it's open?"

Andrew's jaw stiffened, but he nodded. "Once he connects it with his timeline, it's going to get increasingly unstable. You'll have maybe a couple of minutes before it'll collapse."

"Any idea how I can shut it down?"

Andrew pursed his lips. "Like I said, your dad's work was all theoretical. But no power source, no power, right?" He looked down. "It'd still be messy, but maybe it would contain it some."

"'Maybe' will have to do." My attempt at confidence did little to hide my nerves. "Then I'm going to need something to wrap my hands. Something that can't melt."

Mia wanted to save the city. Futurist wanted to save his son. To save everyone, I was going to have to stop them both.

Andrew secured the last of the white cotton bandages to my arms, and I turned them over, admiring his handiwork. He'd kept the wrappings thin enough I could still use my hands, though I could tell he didn't trust it was enough. He'd insisted I take a painkiller, and he'd slathered my palms with burn cream beforehand, but even after that, he wore a dissatisfied frown. I wiggled my fingers as a test. The medicine helped a little for now. The feeling wasn't pleasant, but it wasn't anything I couldn't push past.

He raised his eyebrows. "Only one more thing to check?" He posed it as a question. I nodded grimly. Without the insulation in my gloves, I was guessing this was going to be the worst part. Rolling my shoulders back, I raised my hands, took in a breath, and rewound time.

My palms sizzled with an electrical current, different from the searing pain of the burns. The sensation lingered in my fingertips a few moments longer, fading into a prickle somewhere deep in the bones. But it wasn't unbearable the way I remembered. It was something familiar, grounding me. It was there for just an instant, then left, and for the first time, I welcomed the whisper of the other timeline that was left on my skin.

Andrew asked his question again.

"I just checked," I said. "It'll work."

He pushed his glasses up on his nose. His chest shuddered just slightly. "All right then." He reached a hand out and placed it on my knee, looking as if he wanted to say more. Instead, he leaned forward, and his lips crushed against mine. The kiss took me by surprise, but I didn't shy away. I leaned into him, returning the gesture, feeling both of our heartbeats fluttering in my chest. I could taste our anxiety on my tongue. I was heading into a war, and we both knew it. His hand cupped the back of my neck and pulled me closer to him, and for a moment, I wondered if I could stretch this feeling out into infinity. But then he pulled away, resting his head against my shoulder. It felt like fighting against gravity. "Please be careful," he whispered.

I nodded. "I will," I promised him.

He let go and handed me a crumpled piece of purple fabric. My mask. I slipped it on, then slid off the bed, stepping around Andrew's wheelchair and the remnants of my gloves. Without a sound, I climbed through his window once more, back into the night.

The frigid air soaked through my clothes as I crossed campus; it was an unexpected jolt of energy that I needed before I faced what was ahead. While he'd worked on my hands, Andrew had told me that the device on display at the gala had been there partly for show. Only one place in town had the tools needed to actually get the energy source working, and that was the device's new home. It loomed ahead of me now, a few blocks away: the bright, stately dome of the physics building.

My breath pushed clouds of steam ahead of me, and my heart pounded. As I reached the edge of the path up to the building's entrance, my senses perked. Part of me secretly hoped to hear the distant purr of Phase's motorbike or feel an electric charge in the air as I got closer, some hint as to what I was about to walk into. Instead, all I met with was the sound of my own footsteps and the faint glow emanating from the windows on the building's main floor.

In a way, it was as good a hint as any. I reached for the door handle and headed in.

Chapter Sixteen

M Y FEET ECHOED ON the hard linoleum as I stepped inside. A large atrium spanned several yards in front of me, an open room that took on the shape of spokes on a wheel as it split off into hallways and lecture halls at the far end. The plastered walls of the main floor and the second-floor balconies above carved a wide circle, turning the entryway into a continuous tunnel up to the dome's spire. Along the walls were curved wooden benches engraved with the names of old professors and canvas banners that boasted the school's accomplishments over the years. And in the center of it all, directly ahead of me, stood one of Futurist's machines. The metal archway was still empty for now, but its shiny surface already cast a faint white-blue glow throughout the space. A large light was focused on the workspace, but the machine's creator was nowhere to be seen.

My gut did somersaults as I scanned the room, eyes wide. Except for the light beside the archway, the atrium was only illuminated by the stars shining through the skylights. As far as I could tell, I was alone. *This is too easy,* I thought to myself. I didn't want to trust it. I took a few cautious steps, then stopped. Vince stepped out from the shadows at the back of the room.

"I've got to be honest," he said. "You weren't the one I was expecting to come." He sounded vaguely hurt, though it was hard to tell whether it was an act.

"Phase *is* coming, you know."

He shrugged. "Let her. I'll be ready."

My hands still stung underneath layers of burn cream and bandages. Part of me doubted he would be. "I want to help you, I do. But I can't let you do *this*." I gestured to the machine between us. "I can't put my city at risk. Just trust me. I promise I'll find a way to get you home."

"Look, I really don't give a shit what happens in your time-line." He knelt down at the base of the archway and twirled something in his hand—a wrench, it looked like. "I wasted too much time already on machines that don't work. I'm not wasting any more."

"But what if we could find a way to do it safely? We could save our city, and we could send you back to the moment you went missing in the first place, right?"

He shook his head with a dark laugh. "You sure you're Sinclair's daughter?" I swallowed the embarrassment that rose up at his comment. "I can't control them like that. Too unstable, and it gets worse the farther out you go. Besides," he mumbled, "I'm not betting his life on a bunch of damn kids."

I bit back a retort, then paused, thinking. There was something about the way he said that last part . . . *I can't control them.*

I turned back, testing the theory that was brewing in the back of my mind. "It's not the first one you've made, is it?" I asked. "Not just here, I mean. You made all of the time bridges. It's how you know how to build them, and how you know they're faulty."

He was silent, but even in the dark, I watched his eyes narrow. The wrench stilled in his hand.

"It's why you apologized about my dad," I finished.

"I used Sinclair's research to figure it out. Particle acceleration, but on a massive scale," he said. "When I got stranded, I thought he might've been able to help me. Then I heard what'd happened to him after the wreck. I realized I was on my own."

He watched me carefully from the corner of his eye, but I didn't react. I'd just needed him to confirm my suspicions; emotions would have to wait. I took a step closer. "I want to help you," I tried again. "Just give me a little time—"

"You? You want me to give *you* time?" He scoffed, the irony of the request not lost on him. "No. I'm done waiting. I'm done playing it safe. I'm done trying to be civil." His voice was unnervingly quiet, even as he rose to his full height. He loomed over me, the wrench still held tight in his fist. But I didn't flinch. "I'm going back. Tonight. I'm going to get Oslo. And I'm not afraid to kill anyone who gets in the way of that."

I set my jaw. "I wasn't really giving you a choice," I said. I raised my fists, gritting my teeth against the pain in my hands, and took a fighting stance. In the final instant of calm, I breathed deeply. And when his body shifted forward, I charged ahead.

We clashed together in front of the archway, his arm raised in a swing. I dipped to the side, reaching up to block my face at the last second. The wrench connected just above my wrist, and I hissed in pain. But as he pulled away, I twisted my arm around, letting my fingers brush the metal. The zap from my powers felt stronger than I was used to, but I welcomed it; it assured me that my plan had worked. He yanked his arm away, and the wrench slipped from his hand. Another shock against my fingers, and it fell into mine. I tossed it aside.

The loss of his weapon didn't deter him. He made a grab for my hair, tangling his fingers in my braid. He pulled my head backward with a jerk, but I righted myself and jammed a knee between his legs. His grip fell away, and I used the moment that he was distracted to leap and plant a kick square in his chest.

Futurist stumbled backward a few steps, but he regained his footing almost too quickly. My mind raced ahead, but I waited to see what move he would make next. And when he shifted forward, I rewound everything. He grabbed for my hair. I batted his hand away, answering the move with the same two I had used before. This time, however, I dropped to the ground and slid toward the wall behind him. The shadows swallowed me whole.

I gathered myself into a crouch. It wasn't much of a secret where I was, but I hoped it would buy me a little time. I groped around for something, anything I could use. I stopped when my hand wrapped around something metal. *The device*. I could tell just by the feel of it—I didn't even have to see it to know I was right. I picked it up and hid it behind my back as I stood.

Just as I turned back to the room, a hand wrapped around my throat in the darkness. My heart stuttered. "Vince," I wheezed. I could barely make out his outline in front of me, but my free hand clawed for his face anyway. "I'm not your enemy." His fingers squeezed tighter, and the shadows in my vision began to fill with stars. I fought to keep my panic under control. I tried to twist in his grasp and bring my elbow down against his arm, but this was a battle of pure strength, and he would win every time. I let the device fall from my hand and clatter against the floor. My palms struck Futurist's chest as I rewound time, and the burns flared as I found myself crouched once more, gasping and sputtering for air.

There was no more hoping I was well hidden; if Futurist had spent any time guessing where I was the first time I'd lived these seconds, he had no doubts now with the noise I'd made. I pulled myself to my feet and felt for the device with my boot. I kicked it somewhere down the hall behind me, then spun frantically, trying to find my bearings. I bumped against something solid in my confusion. Vince. He wrapped a forearm around my throat and yanked me backward. He backed us against the wall, leaving me with little purchase on the floor to work against him. "Anyone who gets in my way . . ." Vince whispered through gritted teeth. "That includes you." My hands groped at his sleeve, trying to make space for air in my lungs. My feet kicked outward, an involuntary response. The toe of my boot caught on a bench just beside us, then slipped off. My mouth gaped open, and my eyes were wide. Come on. Stay calm, some part of me urged. *You can do this.*

I swung my leg, catching the bench a second time. I kicked against it and gained some leverage. I landed a kick off the wall with my other leg to follow through and twisted farther out of his grip. Finally, I made a wild grab at one of the hanging canvases behind us as I fell back down, and it made a satisfying rip as it came loose. The heavy tarp draped itself over his head. I tumbled the rest of the way to the ground and rolled a few feet away, just behind Vince's metal structure.

My breath came in wheezes and coughs. I took the single moment I could spare to fill my lungs, then rose back to my feet. As Futurist untangled himself from the poster, I raised my fists once more. But a movement in our peripheries drew our attention away from each other. I turned slowly. There, through the archway, I watched as a figure moved toward Vince. Mia's hands were at her sides, fingers twitching in anticipation. Even with her helmet, I could feel the fire that burned behind her eyes. Part of my heart swelled with something akin to relief—she was okay. But the feeling didn't linger. Leaving Futurist behind, I stepped through the archway and directly in front of her.

Neither of us said anything. We didn't need to. The anger that rolled off her already tore into my heart as her attention turned toward me, but there was something else there too, in the way she adjusted her footing, the slightest hesitation as she raised her hands. Pain. Not from what I'd done to her, but because of what I was doing now. The choice I was making. I heaved a sigh, my lungs still burning from my encounter with Futurist moments ago. I raised my palms.

Mia closed the distance between us in two steps, leaping up at the last second to plant a kick against my chest. Her attention shifted past me to the archway, but I batted her leg away, drawing her focus again as I swung at her exposed ribs. She faltered, but only barely. She spun back around, and her movements became a flurry of kicks and jabs, almost faster than I could keep up with. I answered them when I could, sending a knee to her stomach, a punch to her kidneys. Her fist slammed against my jaw in one moment, splitting my lip open beneath my mask; I responded by hooking my leg around her knee, pulling it out from under her.

She found her footing again easily, rolling backward until she was in a crouch. She met my gaze. "I'm sorry," she said. I could hear the sting of my betrayal in her voice. "I know you think what you're doing is right."

"You can't punish his kid for what he's done, Phase."

"No. *You* don't get to decide one life is worth more than everyone else's."

I glared at her and opened my mouth to respond, but all that came out was a huff of frustration as metal clanged behind us. We both spun around to see Vince tinkering with something on the archway; realizing he now had an audience, he dropped what was in his hand and stood, his gaze resting on the two of us.

At his movement, the two of us started forward—but Mia had something else in mind first. Before I'd taken two steps, she reached her hand out and clasped one of mine, digging her fingernails into the bandages on my palms. I screamed, and instinct forced me to the ground, out of her reach. I cradled my hand to my chest and watched her run forward, and though I found my footing again only a fraction of a second later, it wasn't fast enough. By the time I reached the two of them, the Futurist had an arm wrapped around Mia's throat, pinning her against his chest as she struggled to breathe. With his free hand, he pried her helmet off, revealing the terror in her eyes, then started to curl his fingers around her shoulders and cup his other hand around her jaw.

"No!" I yelled. I grabbed his wrist and threw my weight against it, pulling it away from Mia's throat. In the next instant, he yanked his hand from my grasp, slamming it into my stomach instead. My insides clenched around the air in my lungs, and I doubled over, struggling for a breath. Seconds ticked by, and I watched from my periphery as Mia stumbled toward the archway, hands raised.

I finally heaved a gasp of air into my chest, and I shoved myself back in time. The motion sent me stumbling backward a step, and I whipped my head around, trying to reorient myself. A few steps away, I spotted Mia, still sputtering from the pressure on her airways. I grabbed her arm and hauled her backward, toward the center of the room. This time, I could see the emotions in her eyes—the rage, and the hurt.

"Please," I tried. "I don't want anyone to get hurt."

"Then stop this, and we can make sure they don't."

I swallowed, then shook my head.

Her lip curled. "Then I guess I'll have to stop you." She raised her fist. And just like she'd taught me to in all those weeks of training, I blocked it before it connected.

As we volleyed, each swing became all of my strength against all of hers. Every skill she'd taught me, every lesson we'd had together—they all flashed through my mind as we fought, and Mia left me little room for error. My palms sizzled with more electricity than pain. The smell of smoke and melting plastic told me I wasn't the only one using my powers anymore. As another punch came toward my ear, I blocked and danced out of the way, barely avoiding the water fountain that burst from the wall in my direction and the puddle of ice it left in its wake.

"Phase—"

We were near the building's front entrance again, on the far end of the room from where Futurist had been. I didn't want to risk a glance now to see how close Vince's machine was to being finished, but as long as I could keep Mia distracted, keep Vince from getting ahold of her again . . .

I took another step back toward the wall as Mia marched forward, and I threw a palm out and connected with Mia's nose. I felt it crunch, watched her stumble backward a step and use the back of her hand to wipe away the trail of blood that formed. There was a small fan half-stowed near the front door; she stooped to pick up its electric cord as she passed, yanking it free from the wall. "Please, just stop!" I tried again. She ignored me. She pulled the cord taut between her hands, then swung a fist toward my face. Out of instinct, I threw my hands up to protect myself.

Her movements were deft, assured. She coiled the cord tightly around my forearms at the same time I realized my mistake, then yanked me forward as she looped the other end through the arm of a bench beside us. In the next moment, warmth fanned out toward my fingertips, and the smell of singed wood filtered into the air. I hazarded a scared glance. A mass of plastic and wire strands had molded to my forearms and around the bench. *No. Please, no.*

Panic crept back into my chest. I twisted around as much as I could, until I could just see the edge of the time bridge in my periphery. It glowed slightly brighter now than before, casting a cool hue over the scene. Its high-pitched hum rang in my ears, like that of fluorescent lights just flicked on. It wasn't just my powers that were causing the lightning bolts stinging in my palms anymore.

Futurist stood just off to the side, bathed in blue light. He held something metal in his hand, and he stared at something just outside my field of vision. Phase.

"No," she murmured.

With a dark look, he turned back toward his machine and clicked the device in his hands—the archway's main power source—fully into place.

A blast surged from behind me. I pitched forward, and my shins knocked against the edge of the bench. Energy crackled through my limbs. My eyes widened, and I gasped. The space around me buzzed against my skin, the timeline twisting and distorting around itself without the help of my hands. The time bridge was working—it must've been. Which meant if Andrew was right, we had minutes.

I turned toward my restraints, my heart in my throat. Behind me, I could hear the other two staggering to their feet. I tugged against the bench, rubbed my mask down onto my chin to bite at the wires, tried to move my arms enough to trigger my powers. Nothing worked. Grunts and shouts echoed around the cavernous room, and Phase screamed—I couldn't tell whether it was out of anger or pain. I raised a leg and tried to snap the melted cord off with my foot, but it only made the ties dig into my arms more. I shouted a curse, kicking at the arm of the bench.

The bench shifted.

My mouth went dry. An idea was forming—not a perfect one, but it was the only option I saw. I crouched down, twisting until my fingers could just touch the bench. I froze it in place, then stood back up. I raised my leg just like before and slammed my foot against the armrest. It didn't budge. I kicked again, and a third time, driving as much force as I could muster into the action. The cord seemed to constrict around my arms with each hit, but I didn't slow down, storing as much momentum in the seat as I could. When I slammed my final kick against the beam, time caught up with it. It splintered apart, and I fell back-ward against the ground.

I didn't waste any time. Rolling over back onto my feet, I twisted toward the others, my forearms still roped together. Across the room, Vince stood awkwardly, favoring one leg as he tried to guard the side of the archway. Mia stood across from him, sporting a deep gash above her eyebrow. Blood trickled down the side of her face as she glared at him. Neither of them seemed to notice I was free. I ran toward them.

"I'm not letting you do this," Mia growled. With a yell, she brought her knee up to the soft spot between Futurist's legs, then reached an arm out toward the time bridge. He caught her wrist in midair, spinning her around until her face pressed against the side of the archway. Her face con-torted in pain as he twisted her arm up behind her back.

Bile burned in the back of my throat. My hands were still bound, but I grabbed at Vince's sleeve as best I could to pull him off of her. He elbowed me away with a growl. Still, it was enough. As his grip slackened on Mia's arm, she slammed her head back against his and wormed her way free. He toppled backward.

My attention turned back to Mia. With Vince distracted, she reached her arm out behind her, pointing her fingers toward the base of the archway. I lunged forward, but even before I brushed against her, I watched the muscles in her hand flex. In the same instant, another sound filtered into the room, almost imperceptible at first. The voice came again, distant and distorted, calling out Vince's name. No, not calling. *Screaming.*

"Oslo!" Vince shouted.

It was too late. The side of the archway began to soften and collapse on itself, turning into a sludge of molten metal. The archway shuddered, Oslo's voice crackled, and a sudden shockwave blasted all of us backward. The building wobbled violently, shattering the glass windows in the dome. They rained down on top of us—death by a thousand cuts—but my arms were bound too tightly to cover my head. I ducked as best I could while the shaking worsened still. After another second, the tremors knocked me onto my side. My eyes were squeezed shut, but I could feel the cuts and slices that had slashed into my neck, could hear pieces of drywall and ceiling tile crumbling against the floor and on top of me. Eventually, the world settled, and I uncurled my body slowly and opened my eyes. Glass crunched underneath me. Dirt and debris fell to the ground as I struggled to my feet and tried to find my bearings, but a cloud of dust still hung thick in the air around me. I coughed and squinted toward where the others had been, but all I could see was the white light from the archway, still shining bright enough to illuminate the room.

"Playback!" Mia's voice came from across the room, sounding strained. I climbed over the rubble until I could make out the shape of her on the floor. Her face was twisted into a grimace, and she reached for her leg, pinned underneath a piece of the wall that had collapsed. My arms still tied, I reached down and helped leverage it off of her, the two of us panting with the effort.

"Where is he?" I asked her as she got to her feet. She favored her ankle a little as she stood. I repeated the question, but she just stood there, her eyes wide. Distant.

I spun around, spotting an odd shape not too far away among the rubble—the toe of Futurist's boot. Yet before I even took a step, I froze. Pins and needles prickled along my spine, and every hair on my body stood on end. An electric current danced a warning across my fingertips. "Phase!" I warned. I turned toward the archway, just in time to watch as the world splintered apart.

Before I had even registered what was happening, the second blast rippled out across the room. I lost sight of Mia and Vince as my body was wrenched back into the air. I lost sight entirely; in that moment, my vision filled with white, and the air around me crackled, blocking out any other sounds. The event stretched out into infinity before me. Only when a hunk of metal slammed into my shoulder did I come back to reality. The twisted remnant of the archway pierced my suit, and my mouth gaped. My eyes widened. I was weightless. Falling.

Just before I came back to earth, I gathered all the strength I could muster, and I shoved my hands forward.

I stood amid shards of glass and bits of drywall, my feet planted firmly on the ground. My shoulder throbbed underneath my jacket, and my arms nearly buckled taking on the weight of the wall again. Mia scrabbled out from underneath in the same instant, getting clear just as my grip slipped.

My ears still rang from the explosion before as the wall crashed back to the ground, but the rest of the room was settled, the tremors in the building gone. A few feet away, but through a mess of dust and debris, the archway, listing dangerously to one side, hummed with life, bright light emanating from its center.

A breath shuddered in my chest, and I shifted my weight forward, ready to run. At the same time, I began to count. *Five seconds.*

CHAPTER SEVENTEEN

F IVE SECONDS TO SAVE everyone. I locked my sights on the archway, running forward as the rubble beneath me shifted. I heard Mia's voice, but I forced myself to ignore it, picking my way over the ruins to the center of the room.

Four seconds.

Her groan as she struggled to her feet reached my ears. I prayed she understood why I'd left her. I stumbled over a broken section of linoleum and wrenched my injured shoulder trying to catch my balance. A cry escaped my lips, but I kept going.

Three seconds.

"Your hands!" Mia yelled from across the room. Without slowing, I raised my bound wrists above my head and felt a biting cold spread against my skin. I yanked my arms apart, and the brittle mass of wires finally cracked and fell away.

Two seconds.

Each step that brought me closer to the archway ramped up the voltage beneath my skin by another level. The electricity hummed in the air and deep within my bones, as if I were already using my powers. The time bridge vibrated against the floor—I could feel it through the soles of my shoes. Time was warping beyond what the machine could handle, but maybe I could help contain it.

One second.

As I pressed my palms against the side of the archway, every nerve in my body lit on fire. I'd used my powers countless times, but I'd felt this kind of stinging, icy heat only once before. I squeezed my eyes shut, seeing spots behind my eyelids while I tried to freeze the archway in this moment. But this time, it felt different. Instead of a small shock against my fingertips, I'd plugged my hands into a power socket. I wasn't pushing myself through time anymore; it was pushing against me.

I gritted my teeth, whimpering. I had no idea how long I'd already been standing here, but it must've been longer than five seconds. My hands throbbed as I worked to restrain the archway's energy. *If I could keep it frozen for long enough . . .* Another moment passed, and I could just start to make out Mia's voice from across the room. I forced myself to open my eyes.

"Cass?" she asked, her voice an octave higher than usual.

"I'm—I'm okay," I managed. "I think."

"Before? Did you hear . . . ?" She never finished the question, but I nodded, knowing who she was asking about. If I listened past the groaning and buzzing of the archway now, I could still make out the young voice that filtered through from the other side. "Check on Vince," I told her. "I couldn't get to him last time."

I didn't turn, but after a few seconds, I could hear rubble shifting while she did as I asked. I let out a small breath to steady myself, then closed my eyes and tried to keep from passing out. Mia's panicked voice came from across the room. "He's barely breathing." My eyes flew open. I turned toward her, as if I thought she might have been joking. But she knelt beside him, her expression grave. Her three-word diagnosis hung in the air between us. My arms quivered from trying to hold the archway together, and my heart sank.

"Mia. I don't think I can hold this much longer." Amazingly, my voice was steady. Inside, I felt like the time bridge—on the precipice, ready to fracture. "I don't know what to do. Maybe if you can take Vince and get yourselves far enough away . . ."

She stayed where she was. "You know that wouldn't work," she said, her voice quiet. Yes, I knew. But the thought of the alternative ached into my core. Everyone I cared about, everyone I'd tried to save tonight—they would all be gone the moment my fingers lifted from the archway. All because of me.

"If we destroy the power source, maybe it will break the connection with the other timeline before it explodes. We could keep the blast contained to in here . . ." She glanced around the room, the plan obviously not setting well with her.

My mouth went dry. "We can't—" I had to pause to catch my breath. "We can't. What about Oslo? Vince did all of this so he could protect him."

Mia wet her lips and looked at Vince, then down at her feet. "I didn't think he was telling the truth," she admitted, barely loud enough for me to hear. Finally, she met my gaze. "What if I go through first?"

"Mia—"

"I can do it." She stood. "This is my fault. All of it." Her gaze settled just next to me—on my hands. "I should help make it right."

Tears welled behind my eyes. I could hear them in her voice too. "Let me go," I said, my voice breaking. "We've no idea what's out there. Remember what Vince said, about the people they were running from? What if—what if you can't get back?"

She shook her head, her mouth turning up in a sad smile. "All the more reason. You've got family here. You've got Andrew. Besides, who else is gonna keep this thing from falling apart?" She hesitated, then laughed to herself and shook her head. "More impossible choices."

My gut twisted. "Help as many people as we can, right?" I asked. It was the same thing she'd said to me the night of the fire, when we'd sat together on the roof. She nodded and echoed the words back to me. I watched as she took a steadying breath, then made her way to the front of the archway. She stopped in front of it, staring into the light at its center. Neither of us had any idea what she was walking into beyond the hellscape Vince had described. And though we wouldn't say it, I knew we were both wondering if she'd ever be able to walk out of it.

"Mia," I said. She looked at me, and for the first time since I'd known her, I saw fear in her eyes. "I don't always get to know the right choice," I told her, "but this time, I do."

She nodded, taking in a breath. She pulled her shoulders back, straightened her spine. Even without the helmet, as she stood there, she looked every part the hero I'd always looked up to. She turned back to me, and she smiled. This time, the expression was genuine. "I'll find him," she promised. She turned and stepped through the archway.

A ripple moved through the bridge and into my hands as she crossed into the next timeline. The energy waned for just a moment, then returned full force, and I knew she was gone. I turned my attention to the device just below where my palms rested. There was no time to grieve; I still needed to save Everett. With as much force as I could muster, I raised a foot and began kicking at the long hunk of metal, trying to dislodge it. It didn't budge. I paused, panting, then tried again. Still nothing changed, except that my head was starting to spin.

I needed more force, but the bridge's buzzing had amped up even more than before. My strength was starting to leave. My arms and hands throbbed—except somehow for my palms, which had started to go numb, even to the burns. Maybe if I could pry the thing off? I scanned the room as best I could, then growled a curse. Even if I could've found something to try and wedge it apart, there was no way I would've been able to get to it amid all the rubble.

No, it was going to have to be me. I turned back and tried to kick the thing again, but my foot slipped, and I nearly lost my contact with the archway. My stomach clenched. *Too close.* I allowed myself a beat to focus on the buzz of the archway against my fingertips. They ached, but the pain was proof the machine was still suspended in the same moment.

And maybe that was the answer.

I stared at the device. How was it Andrew had described it to me that day in the library? It created power by doubling back energy. So if everything inside of it stopped moving . . .

"No power source, no power," I repeated. My heart beat a staccato inside my chest as I pulled my hands away from the archway and pressed them against the device instead. Against my tired limbs, the metal somehow felt both warm and ice cold. But the flutter of static beneath my fingerprints was unmistakable. The machine's hum faded; its light dimmed considerably. It began to groan, and I sprinted toward Vince.

I leapt over the larger bits of debris, skidding to a stop just beside him. His lower half was still pinned beneath chunks of drywall and ceiling tile. I wasn't sure how safe it would be to move him, and even then, I wasn't sure I had time. I fell onto my knees and grabbed an overturned bench that had been thrown in the blast. I tipped it up against me and prayed it would be enough to save us both.

An awful grinding sound pierced my eardrums, and I scrunched my face against the noise and hunched myself farther over Vince to protect him as much as I could. As if in answer, the archway's whine raised in pitch. And then, just as quickly, it shifted to an eruption too loud for my ears to manage. Cotton suddenly clouded my eardrums, silencing the fireball that bellowed a few yards away. The air around me went still, then became a vice. It slammed against me from every side. Pressure squeezed inside my head, behind my eyes. The ground shook, and where the archway had been behind me, I heard wreckage crash against the linoleum. The bench I'd used as a shield felt suddenly too heavy to hold. My legs and arms trembled—I couldn't tell whether fear or exhaustion made them shake—but somehow, I held it. Dust rose up, coating my eyelids and slipping underneath my mask, then drifted back down. And almost as soon as it had started, it was all over.

I forced myself to wait an extra second in the stillness. I had to know for sure that it was finished. But it was all I could spare. My body had nothing left to give—every inch of me ached under the weight pressing down on top of us. A shout built up in my throat as I gathered my strength, and muscles stretched and strained in my back as I wriggled from underneath it. After an agonizing moment, the bench tipped to the side and landed with a thud. A chunk of brick and plaster slid to the ground too, the size of a small car. My skin grew clammy at the sight.

I turned back to Vince. Even beneath the dust, his skin had gone gray. Dirt clung to his beard and eyelids. He gave a feeble cough, and his chest shuddered with the effort. I collapsed onto the ground next to him, searching for his hand beneath the rubble. "Vince?" I said. My voice came from somewhere far away. It was distant, mumbled. I tried his name again, but if he heard me, he made no move to show it.

Without the archway, the room had been plunged into relative darkness once more, except for the pools of moonlight that streamed in through the hole in the ceiling. Still, it took a moment to recognize the flashing lights that glinted off the broken glass nearby. I squinted toward the building's entrance. Campus police cars lined the drive outside. Somewhere in the distance, a fire truck wailed.

Get up. Some voice in the back of my head repeated the words. I had to help Vince. I had to move. I let go of his hand and tried to stand. But I couldn't anymore. I took a step, and my legs buckled beneath me.

I landed on one of my knees and winced. Carefully, I tucked my legs to the side and sat down, but my arms quivered even just supporting my own weight. After everything that had happened, I was spent. My hands didn't quite sting anymore, but my fingertips prickled strangely. My shoulder throbbed—I glanced down and saw the crimson that had soaked through the fabric of my suit. My mouth felt stuffed with cotton, and something sticky ran down from one of my ears, tracking through the dirt on my jaw.

The voices and shouts from outside were coming closer, but my brain was too fuzzy to make out what anyone said. Deep down, part of me knew I should leave before they found me here. But the cool air was starting to feel good on my skin, and my head weighed so heavy on my shoulders. I eased myself onto the ground on my back. Above me, only the framework of the dome remained intact. The ceiling filled with dozens of stars in its absence, and their twinkling put me at peace in a way I couldn't explain. My thoughts muddled. A pair of footsteps sounded behind me, but they barely registered in my ears. The last of my fight—what little remained—was leeching from my bones into the floor. At last, I closed my eyes and let the night carry me away.

CHAPTER EIGHTEEN

S OME TIME LATER, THE world started to come back into focus, a few details at a time. A strange chemical smell burned slightly in my nose. I blinked away the light that stung my eyes and took note of the small room. The strange bed. My mattress was propped up slightly, just enough for me to look around. My gaze landed on a familiar face beside me, and my heart warmed.

"Hey," I managed.

Andrew looked up, startled. When he saw me, his head dropped into his hands. "Cassidy," he said, his voice a mixture of exhaustion and relief. He looked back up at me, then reached forward. "Here, let me," he said. The too-soft pillow had started to slide, and without thinking, I'd reached to fix it. Every muscle and joint protested the idea. I winced as he reached behind me and moved it up beneath my head. My hair spilled loose over the sides, and he smoothed it before he sat back. "You mom's on her way," he said. "I think she was asleep when they called her. She sounded really stressed on the phone. But she told them I had permission to stay with you."

"What did they tell her?" As I asked, I twisted toward him to try and hear better. One of my ears kept up a dull ache, and it made everything sound like I was underwater.

"You got caught in a freak explosion—probably some gas leak that no one picked up on." He sighed. "I told her I'd forgotten my textbook in the lab, and you'd offered to go get it for me. That's why you were across campus so late at night."

I frowned. "What about my . . . ?" I trailed off, but after a moment, he filled in the word *suit* on his own. He shrugged.

"I honestly have no idea. No one's mentioned anything about it."

His answer probably should've worried me, but I had too many other thoughts clamoring for attention at the moment. I closed my eyes. "Vince? Did he . . . ?"

Andrew looked down at his hands and shook his head. "He was dead by the time they got you both to the hospital."

I bit my lip and turned to face ahead. Andrew just stayed silent. A few minutes passed before we spoke again. I raised one of my arms in front of my face, examining the comically large bundle of fresh gauze that encased my hand. Andrew reached for it and held my wrapped arm between his hands. He studied it, never quite meeting my eyes. "What really happened?" he asked, his voice low.

In hushed tones, I walked back through the fight as best as I could remember it, including how Vince had used Dad's research to build the time bridge in the first place.

"That's why he'd stayed around campus instead of finding somewhere with a better power source," Andrew guessed.

"He said he couldn't control things as well if too much time passed," I remembered. "If he'd left Everett, he might not have found something in time to make the machine."

"I mean, I'm sure some of it was that too. But he was also probably hoping to find your dad and have him fix the problems in the bridge's design. And then, when he couldn't . . ."

I nodded, considering. "My appearance probably freaked him out too. Two superheroes when he's from a world that people like us destroyed? I mean, think about how many more risks he took after that." It couldn't have been a coincidence the explosion by the clock tower happened the day after Playback's first fight. "He never wanted to hurt anyone. He was just desperate."

Andrew adjusted his glasses, nodded. "And . . . Mia?"

Tears welled in my eyes again, and I looked across at him. Telling Andrew about the explosions was like reliving them all over again. I trod through my memories as if they were part of the rubble that had been left behind—carefully picking them apart, always worried they could crush me at any moment. Mia had made the same decision I'd been ready to make, but the knowledge didn't make it hurt any less. When I finished, Andrew's gaze rested heavy on the mattress. He didn't seem to be staring at anything in particular, just processing what I'd told him.

"She did it for you," he finally said. It was nothing more than a statement of fact, one that we'd both already known. I nodded.

In that moment, something caught in my throat and kept me from saying more, but if I was being honest, I was grateful that the words wouldn't come. They kept me from asking Andrew the one question I had left: *Would I ever see her again?*

I already knew he wouldn't be able to answer, and hearing that response likely would've hurt more than anything else I'd lived through tonight.

The next afternoon, I stood in front of the bathroom mirror in my hospital room, eyes trailing along my reflection. The bruises on my skin had darkened since yesterday, tracing ugly patterns of purple and green along my ribs, my arms, my stomach. Some of them I recognized, like the rope marks on my forearms, but most of them I couldn't even remember getting. I leaned in to study the faint marks on my throat, courtesy of Vince. Luckily, my hair and sweater would work to cover those. There were the bandages too—the butterfly strips on the slice on my cheek, the massive bandage on my shoulder to protect my stitches, and the gauze on my hands still wrapped thick enough to be mistaken for oven mitts.

But even beyond the injuries, *I* looked different. My figure was more muscular than it had been a few months ago, and I stood a little straighter, my head held a little higher. My eyes had become more guarded than I'd realized—still bright and hopeful, but wiser too. It was still hard to reconcile the face that owned them with the girl who'd admired superheroes through news articles on her phone and acted on instinct to save those kids on the crosswalk.

With a sigh, I finished getting dressed and fumbled my hair into a messy braid. Even though I was banged up, my injuries were all superficial enough to let me out of the hospital. Well, for the most part—the doctor who'd seen me that morning had warned my hands would probably need surgery to heal properly. *If* they would heal properly. I pursed my lips at my reflection, then flicked the light off and headed back into the room.

Once they'd realized I was awake, everyone from the doctors to Everett PD to my mom had kept up a steady stream of questions at my bedside—most of which I had no way of answering. At least I thought my version of events had sounded somewhat believable. I'd gone to the physics building to pick up a textbook Andrew had forgotten, like he'd said. As I was leaving, I'd gotten caught during the first explosion, then had tried to help another man I'd seen in there get free before the second explosion went off. The doctors had asked about the dirty bandages I'd had on my hands already, and I'd explained how I'd burned them on the radiator in my dorm earlier that day. "I lost my balance and grabbed it when I fell," I'd said. "It was really stupid." It certainly wasn't my best excuse, and the doctor seemed a little skeptical. Still, if she doubted me, she never said anything more on the subject, except to admonish me for not going to urgent care.

In all the rounds of questions, I only faltered once, during one police officer's especially relentless play-by-play. "Do you know a Mia Dominguez?" he had asked me without any warning. It had taken me a moment to place his face, but I recognized him—he'd been the officer who'd sneered at Phase and I outside the grocery store. "She's not been heard from since yesterday evening, and we have reason to believe she might've been in the building around the same time you were."

I'd stilled for a moment, working to keep my emotions at bay. "Her name sounds a little familiar," I told him. "But I never saw anyone else."

"She wasn't there with you last night?" he pressed.

"Like I said, as far as I know, it was just me and that other guy."

The officer opened his mouth to ask something else, but my mom had shooed him off then. "That's more than enough questions for one day," she said. Even a foot shorter than him and in her hushed voice, she made sure he knew he was out-ranked. "She needs to rest."

As it turned out, the internet had come closer to figuring out the truth. Just as soon as news of the explosion had spread on social media, rumors of Phase and Playback being the cause had started circulating online. Someone had claimed they'd seen the two fighting in the middle of the main courtyard on campus, and while most people doubted that story, another had caught a blurry photo of Phase's motorcycle heading in the same di-rection as the physics building. It wasn't much, but it had been enough to stir everyone in Everett into a frenzy, which meant it was enough to spike my anxiety until Andrew finally stepped in and told me to turn my phone off.

At the thought, I touched my phone where it now rested in the back pocket of my jeans. I gave the room another cursory glance as I did so, making sure I'd grabbed everything. I'd only been here one night, but there was still the odd collection of items I needed to be sure and take with me when I went. Small creature comforts that Mom had brought me from home, like the throw blanket from the back of the couch. Toiletries. The bag of clothes I'd been wearing when I got here—it contained just a tank top and my leggings, evidently, but they'd cut them both off in the ambulance, so I doubted I'd be wearing either of them again. Looking around the empty room now, my eyes fell on a black duffel bag on the armchair in the corner. Mom must've left it in here while she visited the nurses up front. I moved to pick it up, and then I noticed the note laid on top.

Cassidy,

Sorry it took me so long to return this to you, but I had to find a time when no one would see me. When I found you last night, you were unconscious, so I slipped this off and hid it in my bag. I didn't want any of the other EMTs to figure out who you were. I hope that's okay—I wasn't sure what else to do.

Don't worry. Your secret is safe with me.

Simon Choi

I chewed on my lip as I eased the zipper apart. A glimpse of purple fabric peeked out at me. Relief flooded my chest. It was still dusty and covered in dirt and blood from the fight, but it was undoubtedly my suit.

I had no idea who Simon was, but when everything calmed down again, I was going to have to track him down and thank him. For now, I slipped his note into the bag and closed it again, swinging it over my good shoulder.

I sat on my bed in my dorm room a few days later when a soft rap sounded on my door. I opened it to see Andrew waiting on the other side. "You ready?" he asked, his expression solemn. I nodded.

The two of us made the trek to the campus courtyard in relative silence, just watching the sidewalk disappear beneath our feet. The streetlamps and the faint glow that lingered on the skyline lit our path; the early winter sun had already dipped below the horizon a while ago. In its absence, the day's icy air grew sharper, biting at my ears and the tip of my nose and turning our breath to mist. Normally, I would've probably wished for another layer. But tonight, I hardly paid the cold any mind.

As we neared the courtyard, we joined silently with a few other groups heading in the same direction. Their numbers only continued to grow as we got closer. When we finally reached the edge of the path that led down to the lawn, I paused. The path was on a slight downhill, and looking at it now, there was no mistaking the crowd of hundreds who had already gathered there. An odd sensation crawled up the back of my throat. Vaguely, I was aware of Andrew going ahead a few paces and exchanging hushed words with someone standing there. But I couldn't bring myself to tear my eyes away from the scene below. Only when I felt his hand brush against my arm did the two of us continue on.

We found an open space on the edge of the lawn, toward the back of the crowd. It was easier on Andrew's wheelchair, but it also afforded us a little extra privacy. As we settled in, I hugged my arms close to my chest, losing myself in the low murmur that filled the air. Andrew's low voice broke through my trance. "Cassidy," he said. I glanced down at his outstretched hand, then quietly took the candle he'd offered. He held up his own, then pulled a lighter out from his pocket and ignited both. Their golden halos joined the soft, warm gleam that was starting to spread through the sea of people in front of us.

A few minutes passed, and then someone climbed the podium ladder at the front of the crowd, drawing everyone's attention. "Thank you all for coming tonight," the woman said. She looked like another Everett student, though likely a few years above Andrew and me. She waited until the murmur had died down to continue. "Thank you for helping us honor the life of Mia Dominguez."

I fought back a shiver, though not from the cold.

"I had the joy of working with Mia at the *Enquirer*, but I've actually known her since we were freshmen. We were in the same Journalism 100 lecture, and of course, most of you probably know that making it through that class already bonded us for life." A few knowing chuckles rippled throughout the crowd. The speaker gave a sad sort of smile, then grew serious again. "Mia was the most determined, dedicated, enthusiastic journalist I've ever known. She knew that the work we did helped people, and she wanted to help as many as she could." The woman paused. "She gave her life doing exactly that," she said, her voice faltering.

She continued on, telling stories about how smart Mia had been, how kind. As she spoke, I tuned her out, but a weight settled in my chest, dark and heavy. Of course, in the days since the explosions, no one had found Mia's body. But a note she'd left for her editor in the newsroom that night, coupled with the story she'd been writing on the lab, led the campus police back to the physics building. After a day or two of searching, they'd drawn the conclusion that she must've been caught somewhere under the rubble. The faculty had organized a vigil, declared they would dedicate the new building in her honor. The journalism school had labeled her a hero.

I wasn't quite sure how to feel about all of it. There was the heartbreak that she was gone, yes, but also the pain that lingered every time I looked at my hands or thought about Vince. The pride at Mia's sacrifice for a man she hated and a child she'd never met, and the anger that smoldered in my chest—at her, that she had put me in this position, but also at myself. The more I thought about that night, the more I wondered if none of it had to have happened this way. If I'd just kept them talking in that gala or tried to catch up with Vince when he escaped with the device, if I'd relived everything and made a different set of choices, would it have changed anything? Maybe Vince would've made it home, and Mia would still be here.

Or maybe I'd still have been in this courtyard, watching wax bead down the side of a candle and harboring the unique ache that came with keeping all of those emotions a secret.

After a little more than an hour, the crowd of students dissipated. The light they'd created extinguished, leaving behind the smell of smoke and a night sky that was both darker and colder than when we'd arrived. Andrew and I returned our candles to the person he'd talked with before, then walked back toward his dorm room. He paused just outside the building's front entrance. "Are you okay?" he asked quietly.

I looked up at the stars. Thought about how to answer. "I will be," I finally decided, then met his gaze again. "Eventually."

He nodded; I could tell he was working another thought around in his mind. I waited. He'd share it if he was ready.

"I've been going back through your dad's research," he said slowly, "trying to fill in the gaps and figure out exactly what Futurist did. See if maybe I could find a way to bring them home. The thing is, the time bridge can control *when* you come out, somewhat. But I don't know if it can control *where*."

"But we heard Oslo's voice that night," I remembered. "He was shouting Vince's name, and Vince was yelling back."

He shrugged. "Maybe he figured out a way to focus that part of the connection? But even then, that was before the bridge started to fail. You said you were barely keeping it together by the time Mia went through. With it being that unstable . . ." He looked down at his lap, playing with the fingers on one of his gloves. "Look, maybe Vince rigged it so she would've come through right where he and Oslo got separated. And even if she didn't, she's smart. She'll figure something out. But when it comes to us tracking her down again?" He sighed, and his gaze wandered to somewhere across the street. After a moment, he focused his attention back on me, though I could tell he didn't quite want to meet my eyes. "I'm really sorry, Cassidy. And I promise, I'm not giving up on this. I just figured you would want to know."

I nodded and mumbled something I hoped sounded like a thank you. I *was* grateful, even if I couldn't find the energy to say as much. He seemed to understand. He reached forward and guided me down to his level to give me a soft kiss goodnight, then headed inside. I watched him go for a moment, waiting until he disappeared into the lobby before I turned back toward my own dorm. My feet felt sluggish as I made my way back into campus, my energy sapped. In the silence of the late hour, Andrew's words echoed in my mind.

As I headed back into the night, a gust of wind picked up and tickled the back of my neck. My hair stood on end. No, it wasn't the same as the energy that had crept up my spine when I'd stood near the time bridge, but it didn't matter; the icy breath on my back unearthed the memory all the same. Mia had been so ready that night to take Vince's place, even when I'd seen the fear behind her eyes. Maybe she'd done it for me or to make up for what had happened to Vince, but maybe the woman at the vigil earlier had the better explanation. Mia had always been determined, whether she was wearing a mask or not. She would find Oslo—of that I was certain.

And if Mia wouldn't give up, then neither would I. One last lesson to learn from her.

The wind came again, and I shrugged deeper into my coat and ducked my head at the bitter cold, which soaked through my skin for the first time that night. I picked up my pace back toward home, whispering a new promise to myself: "I'll see her again."

Chapter Nineteen

For once, Andrew was already waiting for me when I arrived at the café Monday morning. He smiled at me as I crossed the room, dodging the long line for to-go orders that wove between the tables and almost reached the cushioned sitting area. The place seemed only a little busier than usual for this time of day, with a handful of students occupying the smaller tables to thumb through flashcards or skim their notebooks one last time.

As I reached our table, I slipped my backpack off and sat down. Wordlessly, Andrew slid one of the paper cups, steam escaping from the top, toward me. "Well?" he asked.

"Apparently it's too late to switch to pass/fail for any of the classes, but because of 'numerous extenuating circumstances,' my professors have all agreed to let me take an incomplete grade." I used air quotes around my advisor's formal wording.

"Numerous extenuating circumstances," he repeated with a chuckle. "As in the faculty wants to do anything to keep you happy, so you don't sue?"

"Pretty much." Knowing the things I did about the true cause of the explosion at the physics building, I wasn't too keen on taking legal action against the school, but my mom had already been sure to make everyone aware she wasn't ruling out the option. Then again, if it kept me from getting kicked out, I figured I could play along a little.

"So an 'incomplete.' That's not a suspension, so that's good, right?" he asked.

I nodded. "Basically, she said if I can complete the overdue work by the end of next semester, then I can still get credit for it. It sets me back a semester, but I'm still enrolled, which means at least some of my scholarships stay."

He beamed, turning his cheeks pink. "I'm so happy it worked out."

"Me too," I replied, taking a sip of my drink. Taking advantage of the lull in conversation, I glanced around at the tables around us. "You think this is what finals week is usually like?"

Andrew raised an eyebrow. "Considering you don't have any exams and mine all got canceled on account of the building blowing up, I'm going to take a guess and say no."

I gave another half laugh. "Fair enough."

"Then again, I don't know if either of us gets to use the term 'usual' for much of anything anymore," he continued. After a moment, the corner of his mouth tilted up in a half smile, and I returned the gesture.

"I guess it's something we're both going to have to get used to," I commented.

He was right. Nothing looked the same as it had when we'd first stepped foot on campus back in August, and nothing probably would again—not for a long time, in any case. *At least we get to go through it together*, I thought.

Our conversation floated along lazily over the next half hour from one topic to the next, until our coffees were drained and the crowd at the front of the shop had waned, then started to pick back up with the next round of morning customers. Andrew checked the time on his phone. "I should probably get going," he mused. "I need to finish up a paper for my English class, and I told my internship supervisor I'd meet with him this afternoon before I left for break." He paused, looking back up at me. "Want to come with?"

"That's okay." I told him, smiling softly. "Actually, I think I'm going to take a walk."

I entered back out in the crisp morning air with a lightness in my step that was hard to explain. If I was honest with myself, I wasn't even sure why I'd opted not to go with Andrew, or where I was headed. Something about the final trek across campus simply felt right, and I didn't have the desire to question it. So I started forward, letting my feet carry me along the familiar streets as my breath danced in front of me. My worries seemed to ease with each step I took.

The first day of finals week was a cold and dreary one. Clouds blanketed Everett from above, threatening to powder the ground with white. The temperature had settled just low enough to make snowflakes a possibility; it had been dropping steadily all weekend, keeping most everyone cooped up inside but tempting them with ideas for the cozy three weeks of vacation just around the corner. Even I had to admit I'd been daydreaming about sleeping late and curling up to watch movies under a thick blanket. A chance to simply exist, and a chance to maybe put some space between myself and everything that had happened.

As I rounded the corner, I turned into a breeze. The sudden bluster ruffled the fabric of my coat and tugged at the wisps of hair that had fallen from my braid, and in answer, I shoved my hands deeper into my pockets. Or, rather, I tried. The thick wads of gauze that still wrapped around my palms kept me from fitting much past my fingertips into the folds of fabric. I tugged at my lower lip with my teeth. Over the past few days, I'd noticed a strange sensation against my skin when the wrappings rubbed against it, and I felt it again now. It wasn't painful; in fact, it was difficult for me to tell if I felt much at all. Not for the first time, the words "nerve damage" came to mind.

They'd mentioned the term that night in the hospital, when the doctors had listed off my injuries and talked me through the prognosis. I knew it was a possibility, but my stomach twisted at the thought of what else it could mean. I hadn't used my powers since that night with the time bridge. The night after I'd left the hospital, when I'd told Andrew about my suit and Simon's mysterious note, he had convinced me to wait. "Give your body time to heal," he'd urged, and I'd relented. Now though, I was almost too scared to try it. I'd only had my powers for two and a half months, but I already wasn't sure who I would be if I lost them.

I continued deeper into campus, listening to the wind that moved past my ears and scattered the few dried leaves still on the ground. Normally, the sidewalk in this corner of the university would've been bustling with students by now, but today, everything still seemed asleep. The small fountain that normally bubbled outside the student center had already been drained for the winter months, and almost everyone who was out and about this early walked with purpose. No one dawdled in the cold or in getting to their destinations, so the streets remained quiet and mostly empty. I was the exception, it seemed, taking in the sights and sounds around Everett without paying any of them much mind. Until I realized where I had ended up.

My footsteps slowed, then stopped altogether. I stared up the hill in front of me, the concrete steps that had once paved the way to the university's proudest landmark. Now, they led to little more than a pile of rubble. Construction vehicles parked along the edges of what remained, already starting to clear it away. To start over.

Another breeze blew through, this time rustling something at my feet and knocking it against my shoe. I lowered my gaze to the bundle of mums that had tipped over. They weren't there alone; all along the pavement in front of me, piles of photos, flowers, cards, and candles stretched out in a line. Even without looking, I knew who they remembered. My throat went dry at the memories that started to resurface. I knelt and righted the flowers that had fallen, propping the bouquet in place with a stone, then moved down the line.

Absentmindedly, I wondered if people would think I was strange for doing this, especially since I wasn't supposed to have known Mia all that well. Was it rude for people to look at the items other people left behind at a memorial? I wasn't sure, but I quickly decided it didn't matter. No one else was around to see me. I stopped a few feet away and crouched down to read a newspaper clipping pinned in place by a tall glass candle, the flame long since burned out. The article was from the front page of that weekend's *Enquirer*. I recognized the headline— "A LEGACY LEFT BEHIND: Mia Dominguez remembered for bright, inquisitive spirit." I skimmed the article, reading the life story the newspaper staff had penned and wondering about all the details I'd never even known. Mia had a twin brother, Rafael. She'd grown up near the mountains and loved to ski. She'd wanted to move to a city and become a freelance journalist covering underprivileged populations when she graduated.

As I reached the end of the story, I scanned the rest of the page, though my mind went on autopilot. I'd thought I'd known more than everyone else just because I knew Mia's secret identity. Maybe I'd been wrong. I turned my attention to some of the other gifts and mementos that had been left behind. A little bit farther down, as the sidewalk began to curve with the next street, a small stuffed dog leaned against a note someone had left. I moved the puppy's paw out of the way to read the message, then reeled back slightly.

"We're sorry they failed you," it read.

My mouth firmed into a thin line, but my insides ached like I'd been punched. Whoever had written it meant Phase and Playback. I knew they did. The rumors about the two of us fighting that night had only grown, and the "coincidence" that it happened the same night as the explosion had been too much for some people to accept. It just so happened that, in this case, they were mostly right.

I'd thought it through that night in the hospital, when I'd first read people's posts about us online. There was no way for any of them to know the full story—not unless I told them, and that would mean giving up my secret identity, and probably Mia's too. Even then, some people still wouldn't trust us. But staring at those words now, I realized the knowledge didn't hurt, at least not quite like I'd thought it would. No one had to know the truth of what happened that night for it to mean something. No one had to know the futures I'd lived or the choices I made for them to be right. *I* knew. I reached forward and nudged the toy on top of the note, covering the words again, then turned back toward home. The heaviness of that night dissipated with each step I took.

Because I wouldn't have changed any of it, I realized. And that's what mattered most.

EPILOGUE

A FEW WEEKS LATER, I sat in the chair nearest the fireplace, bathed in the warm glow it cast about the room. In the corner, by the window, lights twinkled on the Christmas tree, dancing across the hodgepodge of ornaments—some glass balls, some plastic statues of snowmen or reindeer, and a few popsicle-stick crafts Andrew and his brother, Samuel, had made in elementary school that, despite their protests every year, their mom simply refused to get rid of. It was the evening of Christmas Day, and I hadn't stopped smiling for hours.

"Thank you again for dinner," I said, turning to Andrew's mom near the head of the table. Andrew had parked his wheelchair beside me, and the rest of his family completed the circle around the table in his dining room. Mrs. Simmons softened.

"You're always welcome," she said. "I wish your mom could've made it here too."

I nodded. "She said she wanted to stay with my dad this afternoon," I explained. Rather than spending the morning by ourselves, we'd visited the care facility early that morning, exchanging our gifts for each other at Dad's bedside. Mom had set up a tiny tabletop tree in his window for the nurses to admire—"and him, when he wakes up." She'd added that last part as an afterthought when she'd told me about it. It sounded more like a reminder to herself than anyone else, but I hadn't said anything. I knew how she felt. Still, somehow, amid all the tears and laughs, the bittersweet morning had been almost perfect—or as close to it as we managed these days. And for once, I hadn't shuddered at the thought that Dad might be aware of what was happening around him while he slept.

As I spoke, Andrew's hand moved to rest on my knee beneath the table. Mrs. Simmons smiled. "I can't blame her," she said.

As she spoke, Andrew's dad entered back into the dining room, carrying a pot of coffee in one hand and balancing a set of mugs in the other. "The pie isn't quite cool yet, but I figured we could go ahead and pour this," he said.

Samuel's lanky frame straightened in his seat, and his eyebrows raised. "Can I have some?"

His family laughed. "Sure, you can have some too," his mom said. "Go get a mug." She nodded toward the kitchen, and Samuel darted off. Beside me, Andrew shot his parents a questioning look. Mrs. Simmons just shrugged. "What? It's Christmas."

As his dad set everything down at the head of the table, Andrew undid the brakes on his chair and moved to help pour the coffee, letting his dad distribute the full mugs. He set one in front of me, and I thanked him, reaching for the cup.

Both Andrew and Mrs. Simmons started. "Doug, is that cool enough for her?" Andrew's mom asked, looking at her husband.

He felt the sides of the mug with his fingertips for a moment. "Feels okay," he said.

I felt my cheeks color a little, and not from the steam. "Thank you," I muttered, then reached for the coffee again. I clasped both hands around the mug, letting my fingers curl around its shape, and brought it to my face to blow on it. The steaming liquid warmed my face and threatened to burn my tongue if I took a sip. But against my palms, there was nothing. No feeling of warmth or smooth ceramic against my skin, no sensation except for the slightest tingling along the edges of my palm. The damage was extensive, carrying through several layers of tissue and deep into the muscle. Without the bandages, the scars were hard for anyone to miss.

The moment passed without any more acknowledgement, and soon, the pie made its appearance, as did Samuel with a comically large mug. Dessert faded slowly into the rest of the evening, and as the conversation lulled and Andrew's parents got up from the table, Samuel looked to his older brother. "Do you think I can play my game a little more before bed?"

He chuckled. "Probably, but check with Mom first."

The eleven-year-old grinned. "Cool," he said, pushing against the table to scoot his chair back. As he did, I watched the tablecloth shift beneath his place setting. His mug—still mostly full—tipped precariously toward his lap.

I raised my eyebrows, watching the chain of events in slow motion, then raised my palms.

It was quiet except for the sound of Samuel's fork scraping against his mostly empty plate. I frowned a little, trying to reorient myself in the moment.

"Do you think I can play my game a little more before bed?"

Andrew looked up at his brother and chuckled, and I relaxed, finally recognizing when I was. I waited for Samuel's reply, then caught his attention.

"Ah-ah!" He looked up at the rebuke. "Watch your coffee cup there," I warned. He grinned sheepishly, moving it farther back on the table before he got up.

"Thanks," he said, then ran to the other room. Once he was gone, Andrew turned to me with a knowing look. I just shrugged and smiled. It had only been a few days since I'd mustered the courage to test my powers again, and even there, it seemed, I was having to adjust to a new reality. For one, I felt nothing—no ache in my palms, no sizzle of electricity in my fingertips. Whatever nerves had been fried in my hands meant it no longer mattered whether I wore anything to dull the sensation. That had been the easier change to accept.

The extra ten seconds I seemed to be able to relive . . . *that* was taking a little more getting used to.

After a moment passed, Andrew's expression shifted into a smile as well. "Show-off." He reached for my hand beneath the table, pulling it away from where I rubbed my scars absent-mindedly with my thumb. He nodded toward the other room. "While they're busy, you should follow me," he said in a low voice. I furrowed my brow, but he just tipped his head toward the door and headed silently toward the living room. I followed, confused.

Andrew led me through the living room and down the hall into his bedroom, flipping on the light switch. "Close the door," he instructed. My heart fluttered a little, and I did as he asked. I turned back around. His suitcase of clothes from the dorm still lay open on the floor, and he maneuvered his chair awkwardly around it, searching for something near his dresser. Finally, he paused, then sat up, grinning dubiously.

"What is it?" I asked.

"I've got a gift for you," he said. He leaned down, then pulled out a large, flat box, wrapped in silvery paper and tied with a red bow. He handed it to me. "Merry Christmas."

I opened my mouth to say something teasing, then changed my mind. I untied the bow and set the ribbon aside, then tore carefully through the paper. Inside was a plain brown gift box. I balanced it on the corner of Andrew's desk and eased the top off to reveal its contents. My smile faded, and my eyes widened.

"How?" I finally asked.

"When you were packing up to go home." I could hear the grin still in his voice, but I couldn't tear my eyes away from the familiar purple fabric. "I saw the duffel bag with your things and snuck it into my backpack," he admitted.

"You fixed it," I whispered.

"As best I could." I turned to him then, the shock and awe still written on my face. His expression grew serious. "I want you to be safe. But . . . I also know how much being Playback means to you," he explained. "This city needs a superhero, and it should be you."

I smiled, my eyes misting, and nodded, hoping he understood my gratitude. He smiled back.

"Do you want to try it on?" he asked.

A few minutes later, I stood in front of the mirror on Andrew's dresser, examining my reflection. Andrew watched from a few feet behind me, scratching the back of his head. "Some of the fabric was too torn up, so I kind of had to improvise," he said, the words starting to trip over one another. "Your shoulder was—"

"It's perfect," I said. I looked again at the thin white pads that now covered my shoulders, the extra row of gold stitching that reinforced the zigzagging design across my chest. He'd made a new set of leggings too, reinforced with a thicker, tougher fabric, just like I'd had before. I picked up one of the two cloth rolls that the box had also produced, unrolling it. "For your hands," he said sheepishly. "Even if you don't need anything anymore, it's probably better to hide the scars. And . . . I figured you wouldn't want gloves." I swallowed at the memory, nodding. I recognized these from when Mia and I used to train. They were hand wraps, like the kind boxers used to protect their knuckles. I twisted them around my palms, securing them at my wrist. I turned back to him, then moved in to give him a kiss. "Thank you," I whispered. He cupped my face in one of his hands, pulling me closer. Only after a moment did he move away ever so slightly, his breath still dancing on my lips.

"Glad you did that now." He smirked. He held up the last piece of my costume in our periphery. "You can't forget this."

I took the fabric dangling over his fingers and turned back to the mirror. With a smile, I slipped the mask onto my face once again.

PLAYBACK'S STORY WILL CONTINUE

Acknowledgments

Playback's story could not have come to life without the help of so many people, and I could not be more grateful for their guidance and encouragement.

First and foremost, to the Treehouse of Writers, thank you for writing alongside me for the past year and a half as this story took shape—but also for the six and a half years of storytelling, glitter, and dragons that came before that, and for the many years of (always slightly chaotic) creative joy that I know will follow.

To Robyn Sarty especially, thank you for being my unfailing, unwavering cheerleader and mentor through this whole process. Cassidy couldn't have become a hero without Phase, and neither of them could've been brought to life without your guidance, patience, and reassurance.

To Chelle Honiker, Alice Briggs, and the rest of the *Indie Author Magazine* staff, you've all given me invaluable insight into this corner of the publishing world and answered questions I didn't even know to ask. Thank you for your never-ending patience as I navigated it all for the first time and for the inspiration I've gained through working alongside so many successful authors in a community that has been supportive from day one.

To my non-writer friends who've heard far too much about this book, often with far too little context, I hope some of my ramblings make a little more sense now! Thank you for understanding my random stretches of silence as I've raced toward the finish line these past few weeks. And I hope you can forgive me—as much as I may try, I know it'll probably happen with the next book too.

Matthew, Daniel, and Jessica, you've been my brainstorming buddies, genre experts, deadline defenders, and kind yet brutally honest story critics. Thank you for knowing when I need to write, when I need to stop writing, and some days, for knowing my characters seemingly better than I do. And an extra thanks for not rolling your eyes every time I skipped out on things because of The Book. (Reader: It was a lot.)

To Mom and Dad—I have too much to thank you for to put into words here. Thank you for all the books and notebooks that fed me when I was growing up. For your encouragement from the first time I put a pencil to paper and with each new story I started. For shouting about Playback to anyone who will listen. For teaching me how to make a difference. For being as close to real-life superheroes as I can imagine.

And finally, thank you, dear reader. Playback's story is far from finished, but it couldn't have started without you.

NICOLE A. SCHROEDER is a storyteller at heart. Her love of words has stood fast through heaps of notebooks; countless sleepless nights spent reading as a child; hours perfecting sentences in various newsrooms in her home state of Missouri; three months surrounding herself with books as a publishing intern in London, England; and weekends sacrificed to penning her own works in the midst of it all. If she's not at her writing desk, you'll likely find her in the saddle or spending time with her family: her parents, her two younger brothers, and her younger sister, all of whom have been her best friends and biggest supporters since she first learned to hold a pencil.

To keep up with all her literary adventures, visit LostLibraryPress.com, or sign up for her newsletter at subscribepage.io/LLP-Playback.